Forbidden at the Fazenda

M.J. Marleigh

Gilded Opulence
BOOKS

Peak into the tender and haunting tastes of love longed for and love lost expressed through poetry....

I would love to gift you this poetry collection and share upcoming stories with you at:
mjmarleighauthor.com

Cover Design by Rob at I Love My Cover Designs
Edited by Jake Waller
Proofread by Kendra Gaither of Kendra's Editing and Book Services

First publication: March, 2021
Second publication: January, 2025

ISBN: 979-8-9854896-1-3 (ebook)
ISBN: 979-8-9854896-2-0 (paperback)

www.mjmarleighauthor.com

A Word of Caution

We are grateful to have you as a reader.
This story contains themes that may be
sensitive for some.

For more details, please scan QR code:

Contents

Chapter One

Evangeline "Ivy" Chandonette's stomach sank as she took a small bouquet of pink peonies in her hand. Attached was an engraved calling card that read simply:

Allyn Marsden,
Marsden Hall

That evening, he was to escort her to a ball—without a chaperone.

Her first season, now underway, had been exhilarating, brimming with the allure of fresh encounters and the heady thrill of dances with eligible young men. She usually delighted in the prospect of a ball—the ritual of slipping into an elegant gown, the careful arrangement of her hair—each step an invitation to new faces, lively conversations, and the promise of attention. However, tonight, that anticipation faltered.

As she sighed, her eyes lingered on the vibrant peonies. They should have stirred something within her, a spark of excitement, but the thought of Allyn's cold, reserved presence dulled any such feeling, leaving her chest heavy and unmoved.

The thought of enduring time alone with him made her long for the carefree delight she once felt. Though the dance card, a cherished tradition of pairing partners for the evening, promised separate interludes with other potential suitors, the prospect of having him as her escort now seemed more like an obligation than a pleasure.

As she lightly traced the folds of the flower petals, releasing their soft fragrance, she thought back on her encounter with Allyn two weeks prior. Reluctantly, Ivy had conceded to her father, Lord Elsmere's, wishes and agreed to a garden promenade with Allyn. Aware of her father's dealings with Lord Marsden, Allyn's father, she had regarded the stroll as a polite gesture. More than that, her duty was to entertain advances from those with whom her family had acquaintance.

While she had assured herself the brief encounter would be uneventful with her mother and sister nearby, she longed for its end.

"I couldn't help but notice you were among Monsieur Pierre's pupils last spring," Allyn remarked, his voice carrying genuine curiosity. "I often rode past when his class set up easels just outside the village. Will you continue with painting now that your other studies are complete?"

"Yes," Ivy replied, idly turning a sprig of lavender in her fingers. "Monsieur Pierre believes I possess great potential as an artist. He advises me to employ a more daring array of watercolors to depict the world around me. One might say he is quite fixated on capturing the very soul of landscapes."

"Indeed," Allyn said nonchalantly. "I seem to recall hearing something or other about the rise of Impressionism in France and across the continent. Artists like Monsieur Pierre and his disciples argue that painting surpasses photography in capturing nature's subtleties. Both are gaining recognition in London, but neither interests me."

"Truly?" Ivy inquired, pausing to admire the vibrant daffodils lining the garden path. "Well, then, what *are* your areas of interests and studies?"

"Property acquisitions and the mastery of land," he asserted with confidence. "The knowledge I gained from my father and his associates during our travels surpasses any lessons learned in a lecture hall."

Picking an assortment of blush-tinged hyacinths, Ivy considered his response. "But aren't you already the master of your estate?"

"Father managed to preserve our home, but the rest of the estate was sold off long ago. One might well ask, what use is a country house without land or tenants?"

Ivy was puzzled but continued strolling down the gravel garden path, her flowers in hand.

"I apologize," Allyn said. "I often forget that matters of land and business aren't passions shared by everyone, least of all by a young lady such as yourself."

Ivy glanced briefly at the horizon, her mind already elsewhere. "Perhaps I'm still too young to concern myself with such matters," she murmured, her voice distant as her steps quickened.

"Lady Ivy, would you do me the honor of accompanying me to the ball Lord Windom is hosting in a fortnight? I've already discussed my request with your father, and he agrees it would be a delightful occasion for you."

Ivy paused, feeling Allyn's presence closing in behind her. "Did he?" she queried, her lips forming a thin line. She glanced over her shoulder at her mother and sister, who still followed closely behind, and recognized the limits of her influence.

Meeting Allyn's piercing stare, Ivy felt a flicker of tension tighten in her chest, but she quickly masked it with the same composed expression all young debutantes were taught to wear.

"Yes, of course," she replied, her voice steady, though a subtle chill lingered beneath the words.

"Marvelous! I believe you'll find my dancing quite impressive." He flashed the same smile that had caused her disquiet as a girl.

"Well, I don't want to keep you any longer. Let me thank your mother, and I'll be off." He sounded almost giddy for one with such a stony disposition, Ivy thought.

"Alright," said Ivy in her most cordial tone.

Allyn gave a bow, then turned to meet Ivy's mother a few steps behind. "Lady Elsmere, I want to thank you and your husband for allowing me to pay a call on your daughter today."

"Yes, it has been a nice walk. So glad you could share it with us on such a lovely day," Lady Elsmere replied with a smile.

"I'll be escorting your daughter to Lord Windom's upcoming ball. I do hope my father and I will see you there." Allyn bowed to all three ladies before taking his leave. She returned the nod and watched him head out past the garden walls.

Once he was out of sight, Ivy turned to her mother. "Why do you and Father insist I spend time with him? You've seen Marsden Hall for yourselves and know the local opinion of his family."

"It was your father's suggestion. He and several of his closest peers have investments with Lord Marsden's firm, which is managed in partnership with his trusted solicitor," her mother said thoughtfully. She paused, drawing in a deliberate breath, her gaze flickering to the ground momentarily. "I admit, it is rather strange for a lord to involve himself in such ventures." She straightened as if to emphasize her point. "But the Marsdens, once on the brink of ruin, now occupy a position of notable respect. Their prospects have improved considerably."

Her mother's words echoed in Ivy's mind until the soft chime of the clock broke her thoughts. As the sound faded, Gwen, her lady's maid, appeared in the doorway.

"Milady, it's nearly time. Shall I assist you with your gown?"

Ivy blinked, and as her fingers loosened their hold on the peonies, she watched several petals fall to the floor, mingling with the crumpled edges of Allyn's card. The memory of the garden promenade quickly slipped away, replaced by the reality of the evening that awaited.

Ivy sat at her dressing table, the blush-toned gown—crafted by one of London's finest dressmakers—draping gracefully around her. The fabric settled with an elegant weight, though her mind wandered as she slipped on her satin evening gloves, her fingers moving almost instinctively.

"The pearls were an excellent choice for tonight, Milady," her maid, Gwen, remarked. Her warm Yorkshire accent, soothing in its familiarity, calmed Ivy's nerves.

As Gwen fastened the necklace with care, Ivy offered a faint smile. "Yes, very fine. Thank you," she murmured.

"Now, let us not forget the final touch," Gwen said, lifting a pearl-encrusted comb from a small velvet box.

A gift from her father, it shimmered in the lamplight as Gwen gently secured it atop Ivy's coiffed curls.

"There we are," Gwen commented, stepping back to admire her work. "That comb complements the auburn of your hair beautifully, Milady. Quite the sight, if I do say so myself."

Ivy glanced at her reflection but offered no response.

"Pardon my saying so, but you don't seem yourself this evening. Will you be alright to meet this gentleman?"

Ivy stood, brushing her hands over her skirt, exhaling sharply, her eyes narrowing as she lifted her chin slightly. "Oh, it's nothing, except...this ball was meant to be a pleasant farewell to the season, but instead, it's become another opportunity for my father to push me toward Allyn Marsden." She paused, her brow furrowing as she looked down at her hands. "He's hardly what I would call a dream suitor."

"I understand your father's wishes, Milady, but as my mother always says, the heart's a funny thing—it has a way of leading us down paths we never expect, sometimes even to happiness."

Ivy turned to the mirror, her fingers grazing the pearls at her neck. "That is a lovely sentiment," she said, exhaling softly.

"But beneath all the glitter and formality of the season, I can't escape the fact that my path is one of duty. If only someone else might capture my heart—someone who could show my father there are better choices for me.

Gwen adjusted the delicate folds of Ivy's skirt. "Then let's make the most of it, Milady. Tonight may hold the promise of something far beyond duty."

Ivy straightened her posture, a quiet resolve settling over her. "Perhaps," she replied. Taking a deep breath, she reached for the door handle, and with Gwen's reassuring words echoing in her mind, she felt ready to face the night ahead. "Let us go."

The open carriage ride with Allyn did little to alleviate Ivy's tension. She shifted in her seat, feeling his eyes studying every inch of her, though he averted them when she glanced in his direction. She was relieved to visit the dressing room when they arrived at Lord Windom's country home. Her friend, Fiona, and other recently presented debutants were there to greet her. Their girlish excitement helped to put her at ease.

Ivy powdered her nose and mentally steeled herself for the evening ahead. *You'll be surrounded by friends the entire evening,* she reminded herself. *Nothing can ruin this affair!*

As Ivy departed the dressing room, she spotted Allyn among the other young men, his slight age difference setting him apart. His features, marked by an unusual lightness to his eyes and hair—not quite albino but unnervingly pale—seemed to wash out beneath the brilliance of the chandeliers, giving him a ghostly quality that lingered in her view.

Though his appearance unsettled her, she worked to maintain composure. After all, he was her escort for the evening, and once the ball ended, they would part as friends—no more than that.

She met him at the far end of the hall, where he stood with an air of aloofness amidst the other young men. As they made their entrance into the ballroom, a tidal wave of voices, murmurs, and laughter washed over them. The rustle of ballgowns and petticoats swelled, filling the room to its lofty rafters.

Ivy noticed the stout hostess, Lady Windom, standing proudly with her three daughters as they welcomed guests. Diminutive in stature yet grand in presence, her laughter rose above the chatter, resonating through the heights of the mansion's elaborate crystal chandeliers.

"Ivy, you look absolutely lovely, my dear! I'm delighted you could both join us. Here's your dance card; I'm certain it will fill up in no time," Lady Windom exclaimed with a hearty chuckle, her daughter passing Ivy the card.

"Enjoy yourselves tonight," Lady Windom added warmly, her smile radiant.

Ivy gave a gracious curtsy and expressed her gratitude. She admired the card's scalloped edges before delicately slipping her hand through its ivory cord.

Once they had moved past the ladies, Allyn adjusted his cufflinks and muttered, "I fail to see the point of dance cards and this incessant alternating of partners. It hardly allows the escort and lady to become better acquainted. Wouldn't you agree?"

A few young men passed, offering nods of acknowledgment to Ivy. She masked the flutter of flattery by directing her attention back to Allyn. "I see no harm in a little tradition. See here, I shall reserve the finest waltz of the evening for you." Ivy reached for the tiny pencil tethered to the card, her hand steady as she inscribed his name in the allotted space, the simple act lending her a brief sense of control. As she finished, a voice broke through the hum of the ball.

"Good evening, Lady Ivy," greeted a portly young man.

"Hello, Mr. Donovan. Mr. Marsden, you remember Arthur Donovan, don't you?" Ivy inquired.

Allyn nodded, though he appeared visibly displeased. Arthur returned the gesture with a nod of his own.

"Lady Ivy, would you do me the honor of a dance this evening? You are undoubtedly the finest polka partner in London," Arthur exclaimed, his grin broadening with delight.

"Then the polka it shall be," Ivy replied, a soft laugh escaping.

The young man eagerly inscribed his name on the card. With a courteous bow, he swiftly departed.

"Arthur?" Allyn's voice dripped with clear distaste for the red-cheeked young man. He waved his hand dismissively before adding, "Surely, you won't waste your time with that pudgy fellow."

The announcement of the first quadrille cut through the awkward tension, and as was customary, Ivy allowed Allyn the first dance. She recognized a few familiar faces as they moved among the sets of couples—their presence offering a brief respite from the unease of Allyn's escort.

As the night wore on, more young men approached to claim a spot on her dance card, and Allyn's visible disdain for the ritual remained clear. She tried to ignore his haunting glare while on the dance floor. Occasionally, she found herself so caught up in the twirls and promenades that she briefly forgot about him altogether. Yet his face would inevitably reappear among the guests, reigniting her unease. The unsettling feelings grew, though she resisted giving in to them.

Still, she danced the polka with Arthur, a spirited Cotillion with Alfred, and a lively Lancers Quadrille with Henry as her partner, where the movements of the other couples intertwined with theirs.

Yet, Henry's lingering attention made Ivy feel as though they were the only pair on the dance floor, his focus hinting at desires that reached beyond the fleeting steps of the dance.

Henry Barrington had always ignored Ivy for older girls before going away to Oxford. Now he could not keep his eyes off her. She couldn't deny a certain pleasure in his unexpected attention, a warmth rising to her cheeks just as Allyn approached. With a nod to Allyn, Henry remained near Ivy, his presence evident as Allyn stepped boldly in front of her.

"It's our dance," Henry declared, reaching for Ivy's hand. Allyn reluctantly moved aside, his glare locked on Henry as he swept Ivy onto the dance floor. Ivy glanced back to catch Allyn's bitter expression. Just then, Lady Windom arrived and graciously invited Allyn to dance with her daughter.

He declined the offer and instead chose to find a seat and a fresh glass of champagne.

Henry interrupted, drawing her focus back to the dance floor.

"I didn't expect to see you here tonight, at least not with Allyn. He's a few years older."

The smooth timbre of his voice stirred something within her.

"My father insisted."

"Ah, yes, that explains it," Henry remarked with a smile. "You've matured in many ways, Ivy."

"Oh? How so?" Her skin tingled at the gentle touch of his fingertips where the silk bodice met her back.

"What I mean is, perhaps we could become reacquainted." His grin widened.

"Of course, Father wouldn't mind if you paid a call," she replied, trying to conceal her enthusiasm.

"What I meant was, perhaps tonight?" he pressed eagerly.

"Oh, tonight?"

"Yes. Do you have any dances available after intermission?"

"I have another waltz open. Why do you ask?" Ivy enquired, her curiosity growing.

"Pencil me in," Henry insisted, his voice lowering conspiratorially. "After that dance, I'll pretend to escort you to the dressing room, but instead, we'll find someplace more private. There's something important I want to ask you." His eyes sparkled with a mix of excitement and mystery.

"Mr. Barrington, you know very well I couldn't go off alone with you," she said, her voice firm, though a quiet uncertainty stirred beneath her words.

"I'm Henry to you, Ivy. You trust me, don't you? Besides, wouldn't you like a break from him, even for a few minutes?" he asked, his tone softening as he leaned closer.

Ivy glanced over to see Allyn, his eyes fixed intently on her, a constant reminder of his watchful presence.

"Alright, I'll meet you there," Ivy agreed, her voice calm though her heart raced with excitement. Her cheeks warmed under his intense gaze, and she averted her eyes in a flirtatious manner. She tried to mask her eagerness, though her smile undoubtedly betrayed her. As they twirled around the dance floor, Ivy felt as if she were floating.

Henry's eyes widened with excitement as the music quickened, and they continued their dance in perfect harmony.

Ivy, caught in the moment's thrill, remained oblivious to Allyn as she stepped off the dance floor. She was still lost in the aftereffects of the dance when he intercepted her, his presence a sudden reminder of her other reality.

"I thought you might be thirsty," he said, offering her a small glass of lemonade.

"I am, thank you. This dance was quite lively," Ivy replied, catching her breath.

Allyn's nostrils flared as Henry slowly came up behind Ivy. Sensing his temper rising, she quickly began to speak. "Allyn, you remember Mr. Henry Barrington," Ivy said, striving to keep her tone light.

"Yes, indeed. He hails from quite an affluent family, much of their recent wealth acquired from what used to be Marsden land," Allyn replied, his lips pursed in disapproval.

Henry's smile didn't waver as he shot back, "And yet here you are with the daughter of a lord who owns more of your ancestors' land than anyone."

"Does that bother you in some way?" Allyn remarked with a sardonic grin.

"Now, now, let's put all that behind us, Allyn. After all, one might argue my family did yours a favor, especially considering your grandfather's unfortunate losses in the Poyais scheme of 1820," Henry quipped with a knowing chuckle.

Allyn's eyes clouded with a brooding intensity, and a flush crept up his cheeks, betraying his simmering resentment.

"My family's history, sir, is not a topic for discussion," Allyn retorted with a scowl.

"Indeed, let us confine our conversation to matters more suited to the occasion," Henry replied smoothly. "I couldn't help but notice you have yet to engage any of these delightful young ladies for a dance. It would be rather remiss of us to overlook such an opportunity at a ball, wouldn't you agree?" He gestured elegantly toward several young women nearby.

Allyn's jaw tightened, his demeanor becoming more composed as he appeared to consider his response carefully.

"Perhaps we could take a moment for some fresh air before making our way to the supper-room for refreshments," Ivy interjected, attempting to dispel the tension.

Allyn nodded curtly, fixed and unyielding, as they passed Henry.

"Excuse us, Mr. Barrington," Ivy said politely.

Henry bowed with a slight grin, observing them depart the ballroom.

Allyn escorted Ivy through the hall and out onto a veranda adorned with hanging Chinese lanterns that cast a warm glow on the stone walls and illuminated the path leading toward the gardens. The air was fragrant with the scent of blooming roses as couples strolled along the garden paths, passing by a marble bench where two young ladies engaged in deep conversation. Ivy found solace in the realization that they were not entirely alone.

"Such insolence!" Allyn snapped. "And worst of all, you seemed quite taken by him." His face remained a deep crimson, though his eyes had returned to their pale blue hue.

"I wouldn't say that precisely, though he did amuse me," Ivy replied lightly.

"Ivy, I shall not mince words. I've harbored a desire to call upon you for some time, but propriety due to your age restrained me. Now, however, I intend to speak with your father regarding my intentions," he said, a trace of desperation in his voice.

"Intentions?" Ivy echoed, struggling to keep her voice steady, worried that her tone might betray her perturbed emotions. Allyn took her hand in his, and Ivy looked at him in disbelief before quickly glancing around to see if others were watching.

"What I mean is—I want to marry you," he confessed, his voice earnest and unwavering.

Ivy was momentarily speechless, her mind racing to find the right words. It dawned on her that she had not taken a breath in what felt like ages. Inhaling deeply, she hoped to mask the agitation that threatened to overwhelm her. As she exhaled slowly, Ivy summoned the poise befitting a lady of her stature. Taking a sip of lemonade, the sweetness of the liquid refreshed her parched throat and steadied her thoughts.

A proposal had been the last thing Ivy expected that evening, especially from Allyn Marsden of all people! She knew she had to be straightforward with him, to ensure he did not harbor false hopes about her feelings for him.

"No, Allyn, I cannot," she murmured, gently pulling away.

Laughter and voices drifted from the couples returning from the rose garden.

"It will be intermission soon, and we ought to return inside. My mother will expect us to join her and my father for refreshments," Ivy said softly, watching as the group passed by. She noticed that the two ladies who had occupied the bench had also departed. Now, Ivy and Allyn found themselves alone in the quiet of the garden.

As Ivy turned to leave, Allyn took her arm, pulling her closer to him.

"Please, tell me you'll at least consider my proposal," he implored. After a brief pause, his eyes widened with urgency. "I must depart the country by the week's end."

"I don't understand. Where are you going?" she asked.

"My father conducts business abroad and insists that we oversee matters there. Yet, I would willingly remain to nurture our relationship. I'd have the opportunity to restore the ancestral home to its former splendor. Consider it, Ivy. It could be our home, if only you would accept," he urged.

Drawing nearer to Ivy, he continued, "Take your time to ponder my proposal, but I do anticipate a response." His voice lowered to a whisper. "Beloved Ivy, my affection for you spans a lifetime."

She shivered as he removed a glove and gently brushed her face. Instinctively, Ivy took a step back.

"I've poured out my heart to you just now, Ivy. I am yours if you'll have me," he declared, moving closer still. "You must share my sentiments," he insisted, leaning in to kiss her. The glass slipped from Ivy's hand as she held him at bay.

"How could I possibly? We've scarcely known one another long enough to consider—marriage!" Ivy snapped, her voice trembling with a hint of restrained emotion. Her chin lifted slightly, a reflexive gesture of poise even as her words betrayed her inner turmoil.

"I believe it's time we returned indoors before things become improper," she added, her heart pounding beneath her chest.

Without waiting for a reply, Ivy turned abruptly, her skirts swishing around her ankles as she strode back toward the house. The cool night air seemed to cling to her skin, but she refused to look back, her resolve carrying her through the doorway and into the flickering lamplight within, leaving Allyn motionless on the veranda.

A wave of relief washed over Ivy as she rejoined the guests streaming into the open supper room. Her eyes swept the crowd, hoping to spot her parents, but instead, she found Lord Marsden engaged in conversation with Lord and Lady Windom near the entrance. They glanced her way before bidding him farewell. Lady Windom beckoned Ivy over to her.

Taking Ivy's hand, Lady Windom said, "My dear girl, Lord Marsden mentioned that his son spoke to you about their circumstances?"

"Circumstances?" Ivy replied, feigning innocence with a smile.

"Yes, they received urgent news via telegram at Marsden Hall. They will depart tomorrow morning to attend to a pressing business matter abroad. It must be of considerable importance for them to leave such a delightful affair," Lady Windom remarked, a hint of disappointment in her voice.

"I share your sentiments, your ladyship," Ivy replied, carefully maintaining the expected decorum.

"But now you'll be without an escort," Lady Windom observed, her expression troubled.

"May I offer to escort her for the remainder of the evening?" Henry interjected politely, catching Ivy's eye with a warm smile.

"If Lady Ivy accepts, then I do not see any problem," said Lady Windom, looking quite pleased.

"I accept," Ivy said, her joy barely contained.

"Excellent, then it's settled. Now, do go and enjoy some refreshments. I've arranged for a more continental buffet this evening, allowing guests to mingle freely," Lady Windom announced proudly.

Henry gallantly escorted Ivy to the supper room, where they helped themselves to a delightful array of fruits and dainty sandwiches.

"It seems you'll require another escort for your journey home," he remarked, his eyes lighting up with satisfaction.

"I'll be departing with my parents, thank you," she replied, mirroring his pleased expression.

They sat together in the supper room, savoring each bite, Ivy relishing every shared moment away from Allyn.

She found herself enjoying the way Henry's eyes followed her movements as she enjoyed her meal. He watched intently as she nibbled on a slice of cake, plucked a cherry from its stem, and paused briefly before washing down the treat with a sip of lemonade.

"My apologies for indulging so heartily. I find myself quite famished after all the dancing tonight," Ivy remarked with a smile.

"There are still several dances ahead," Henry remarked, placing his plate on the table. "But there's a brief respite before the next one. I have something to discuss with you, away from the bustle of this room," he added earnestly. "Come with me." With a gentle yet confident touch, he clasped her hand and led her down an adjacent hallway.

They wandered onto a secluded veranda tucked away on the opposite side of the house, cocooned by verdant foliage. The air was filled with the perfume of blooming flowers, their fragrance mingling delicately in the evening breeze. The soft chirping of crickets serenaded them, creating a soothing symphony that provided a peaceful respite after Ivy's exhilarating evening at the ball.

Henry settled onto a wrought iron bench and gestured for her to join him.

"Henry Barrington! I was convinced we'd be caught," Ivy exclaimed, her laughter threatening to spill over. Gathering her gown, Ivy sank onto the bench beside him, her pulse still racing. "But how on earth did you know this tranquil spot existed?"

"I'm an Oxford man, you see? We're privy to all sorts of secrets," he said with a playful grin. Ivy stole a glance at his face, feeling a flutter of excitement in her chest. She had never been alone with a young man before, let alone one so striking.

"So, Henry, what was it you wanted to discuss with me?" Ivy inquired, her curiosity stirred by his assured manner and the allure of intimate stillness on the veranda.

"I must say, Ivy, you look absolutely radiant tonight. When I first saw you earlier, I could hardly believe it was really you."

Ivy felt a blush creeping up her cheeks. Despite the impropriety of the moment, the allure of being alone with such a captivating young man outweighed any concern for social consequences.

"Was I truly such an awkward girl back then?" she said releasing a soft giggle.

"I can scarcely recall. All I see now is the enchanting woman before me."

"Did you intend to ask me something?" Ivy continued, her pulse quickening with anticipation. The night had been full of inquiries, but Henry's was the only one she wished to hear. "Though I fear I've already entertained my share of questions for one evening," she added with a sigh.

"How so?" Henry asked, his curiosity sharpening

"Allyn proposed to me tonight," she replied, a light laugh escaping her.

"Well, now I've heard everything," Henry chuckled, his face animated with a look of disbelief. "What on earth did you say to him?"

"I told him we're practically strangers, and I couldn't possibly accept his proposal."

"So, you made no commitment to him?" Henry asked, his eyes searching hers with a look of intrigue.

"No, not in the slightest," Ivy affirmed with a faint smile, glancing down at her dance card. She lightly traced its elegant, embossed design with her fingertip.

"Ah, quite the astute young lady," Henry remarked, his voice now a velvety undertone filled with admiration.

"Are there any more questions for me?" she said meeting his gaze.

"No more talking," he murmured. His breath was warm against her cheek as he leaned in, drawing her into a tender kiss. The world around them faded as the soft evening breeze carried the faint scent of roses from the garden beyond.

Ivy surrendered to his charms, yielding willingly as Henry's lips met hers with a tenderness she had never known. The sensation of their kiss was exquisite, a revelation that defied propriety and embraced pure delight. His touch enveloped her in warmth, and she couldn't resist the allure of his scent—a heady blend of rum and spices that filled her senses. In that moment, she felt like the heroines she had read about, experiencing the rapture of love, everything she had dreamed of, and more—absolute perfection.

Suddenly, the slippery sensation of his tongue entering her mouth made Ivy recoil, pushing him away with all her strength.

"Henry, no—"

"What is wrong? I thought you were interested. Your eyes tell me you want this." Gripping Ivy's face firmly between his hands he leaned in again.

A surge of propriety, rooted deeply by her upbringing, flooded Ivy's senses. It was as if every lesson she had ever learned about restraint screamed at her to pull away.

"Please, Henry, stop," she gasped, her voice trembling, as the effort of the struggle left her breathless.

"Come now, Ivy," Henry murmured, his tone patronizing. "This is how adults behave. Do not be so naive."

Ivy felt her palm strike Henry's cheek, then sprang from the bench. Her heart raced as she sought refuge against the wall, arms folded tightly over her heaving chest.

Henry tended to his cheek briefly, then to his pride. "So, this is it? Perhaps I should have gone to a real party tonight where any one of the young ladies would be mine."

"I...I did not expect this," Ivy stammered, slightly winded and disoriented by the unexpected incident. A chill swept over her as the evening breeze wafted through the veranda, a cold harsh reminder of the reality crashing in.

The fantasy she was immersed in moments ago had dissolved entirely, leaving her painfully aware of what had almost transpired.

"I should have anticipated your prudishness," Henry scoffed dismissively as he rose to his feet. "Most girls, such as yourself, are presented into society and think smiles and flirts are where it ends. But, my dear, we men crave more and won't be satisfied with empty teasing!" he snapped while adjusting his jacket.

"What do you mean?" she asked, anger rising in her chest.

"What I mean is—" Henry paused to collect himself and then approached Ivy. "It's a shame to think all that beauty will go to waste," he lamented for a moment before heading toward the doorway.

"I'll go in first to avoid raising any suspicions. That would surely cause more of a scandal than what's happened out here tonight."

His icy remark hung in the air as he retreated back indoors.

Ivy felt the urge to lash out, but her anger was more directed at herself for having been lured away from the decorum designed to prevent such occurrences. She had envisioned a gradual courtship where she and Henry would slowly get reacquainted, but that wasn't the case. All he had in mind was to take her virginity.

She was unserved but knew she had to return to the ball to avoid arousing suspicion. Disapproving murmurs would only add to the humiliation she had already endured that night. Ivy might have wounded his pride, but what about her own? She felt a wave of relief as he disappeared around the corner, slipping past a large potted palm where the corridor met the grand hallway.

As Ivy moved to follow him back to the ballroom, she caught sight of a large mirror in the empty corridor to her left. Its gilded beauty offered a momentary distraction from the unsettling encounter. In truth, the mere thought of crossing paths with Henry again filled her with an overwhelming sense of dread. Far worse, however, was the prospect of facing her father, whose stern expression and quiet disapproval she feared above all else.

A glance in the mirror revealed a girl still reeling from the night's events.

In the dim light, her usual rosy complexion appeared pallid, her lips ashen and dry. She pinched her cheeks lightly, coaxing a subtle flush back into her skin, then reached for the small pot of lip paint tucked inside her beaded wrist bag.

The shade was the faintest pink, chosen to avoid drawing too much attention to her lips. Using a little finger, she dabbed a thin layer onto her mouth.

After securing a few loose curls with the pearl-encrusted comb atop her coiffure, she felt ready to face society again.

Ivy was about to leave the corridor when a pair of strong hands seized her waist, pulling her firmly against him. Before she could react, a cold hand clamped over her mouth, stifling her gasp.

"You had better not fight me!" a man whispered, his breath hot on Ivy's ear. "You are mine—I will have you!"

Ivy scarcely had time to think before being tugged into a room. The dimly lit corridor vanished into darkness as the door slammed shut with a resounding echo. With no choice but to follow his lead, she did not struggle. The figure dragged Ivy to a sofa, then pushed himself over her.

He pinned both of her arms above her head then began furiously kissing her. His wet bites and kisses did not relent as he made his way down to her breasts. Her eyes darted frantically through the murky shadows, searching for a face, while her mind raced with uncertainty.

Who could he be—Henry?

Not half an hour earlier, his lips had been like satin against hers, and now Ivy feared he would devour her. She struggled to get her hands free, but the harder she fought, the tighter his snare became.

He spread her legs apart with his knees, then lifted her gown and petticoats with his free hand. Once more, Ivy tried to fight her way free, but he came back like a rabid beast with every effort. Her loose curls clung to her tear-streaked face, making each breath feel stifled. She let out a cry when his fingers ripped inside of her.

"Now, no one will have you!" the figure sneered, now clutching Ivy's face with both hands.

As Ivy's arms dropped to her sides, she swept the damp strands of hair away from her face, only to discover a cold metal object tangled within her locks. It was her comb!

Ivy wasn't certain if she had voiced this realization aloud or merely pondered it silently in her mind.

She only knew that she could not yield to him. Untangling the comb from her hair, Ivy began swinging it at the figure. He emitted a fleeting, guttural groan before relinquishing his grip on her, allowing Ivy to scramble away from beneath him in the darkness. Desperately searching, Ivy finally located the exit. Her eyes caught sight of a staircase across the shadowy corridor. With quickened steps, she dashed toward it, finding solace in the narrow crevice beneath its landing.

Closing her eyes, she took a few deep breaths, attempting to collect her thoughts and regain composure. She flinched as the sting in her private area grew more intense. What would her parents say if they saw her this way? Society would shun them for having a daughter who brought disgrace onto their family. As for Ivy—she would be ruined for going off with a young man alone and putting herself in harm's way. Although she did not partake in any actual sexual relations, she would still be considered a defiled woman now that she had been violated. Marriage would be out of the question. Ivy was young, yet society's rules were ingrained in her identity as a member of the so-called *weaker sex.*

But what she feared most was her father's loss of admiration for her. She shuddered and stifled a whimper that welled up in her chest. She couldn't bring herself to speak a word about her experience. Despite the intensifying stinging between her legs, she stood up straight.

She trembled at the thought of the attacker possibly waiting for her beyond the temporary refuge. Yet, she understood that the longer she hesitated, the greater the chance her parents would search for her.

Ivy prepared herself for the looming threat, strengthening her resolve. If trouble arose, she would have no option but to unleash a piercing scream, shattering the surrounding silence and alerting anyone in the corridor. Moments later, she emerged swiftly from beneath the staircase and proceeded down the main hall toward the ladies' dressing room.

Concealing herself behind a towering potted palm, she ensured her presence remained unseen by any passing guests. Shortly afterward, a group of ladies emerged from the dressing room, leaving the hall cloaked in silence once more.

Once they were out of sight, Ivy clutched the folds of her gown and hurried toward the dressing room door. No sounds stirred within, so she slipped inside and gently closed the door behind her, exhaling deeply. There was no respite to be found; she had to keep moving. Ivy caught sight of herself in the dressing table mirror and was startled by her disheveled appearance. Her hair was a tangle of tousled strands, escaping their elegant arrangement, while her gown bore creases from her hurried movements. She also noticed a few drops of blood on her face and chest.

His blood! she thought, the moment's urgency pressing upon her. With the ball nearing its end, her parents would soon question her whereabouts.

She briskly scrubbed off the droplets with a towel dipped in cool water from a porcelain basin. Once the spots had disappeared, she instinctively reached for her comb, only to realize it was still in the possession of her attacker. Panic surged through Ivy as she contemplated how to restore her appearance—and promptly!

Quickly sifting through the table drawers, her fingers glided over starched linens before closing around a cool, smooth brush handle. She pulled it free, her attention shifting to the box of hair accessories nestled beside it. None, of course, could compare to the comb she had lost. A pang of regret tightened in Ivy's chest, but she exhaled, banishing the thought. There was no time for such distractions now—she had to appear presentable.

Coaxing curls atop her head, Ivy pinned them into a semi-decent pompadour that elegantly framed her face. She then secured the lower cascade of her tresses at the nape of her neck with a ribbon, the soft fabric complementing the shimmer of her gown.

As the sound of approaching footsteps echoed nearer, she hastily smoothed the fabric of her dress and gently pinched her cheeks once more, imparting a rosy glow to her complexion just as the door creaked open.

As a group of women entered, Ivy gave a slight curtsy and quietly slipped out of the room. Almost immediately, the ballroom doors swung open, releasing a wave of voices and laughter that spilled into the hallway. Ivy found herself nearly swept aside by the crowd of guests, each eager not to overstay their welcome.

Fiona approached her with a curious smile. "There you are, Ivy! I been looking for you," she said her tone light and eager.

"I went for a walk in the rose garden—needed some fresh air away from the crowded ballroom," Ivy replied, keeping her tone even. Fiona's eyes swept over her, lingering on the faint creases in her gown, and loosened curls framing Ivy's face.

"Is Henry not with you? He seems to have disappeared as well." Fiona's voice cut through the ambient murmurs of the other guests. Her brow knitted as she studied Ivy more closely. "Are you feeling well?"

"I'm quite alright. The night air did me good," Ivy assured her, though wariness tugged at the edges of her composure. "If you'll excuse me, Fiona, I must find Mother and Father."

"Do get some rest, dear. Let us arrange for tea soon," Fiona added, giving Ivy's hand a gentle squeeze before turning away.

Ivy spotted her parents bidding farewell to Lady Windom near the ballroom entrance; Henry was nowhere in sight.

"Ah, Ivy! There you are," called her father, Lord Elsmere, a note of relief in his voice.

"Where have you been? I didn't see you during intermission," her mother added, her eyes reflecting subtle concern though she maintained a poised smile under Lady Windom's watchful gaze.

"I suddenly felt fatigued, so Mr. Barrington kindly escorted me outside for some fresh air before we dined in the supper room. We sat out the last few dances," Ivy explained, her tone carefully composed, ensuring not a single word wavered.

Her mother's brow furrowed slightly. "And your comb? I could have sworn you wore it this evening."

"Oh, yes." Ivy gave a nervous laugh. "I'm afraid it may have come undone between the quadrille and the polka," she added.

"I shall keep an eye out for it and ensure its return," Lady Windom interjected, offering Ivy's mother a composed nod of assurance. "We were sorry to see Mr. Marsden depart so abruptly, though we are ever so grateful that Mr. Barrington could step into his place."

"Oh, yes. It was a most pleasant evening," Ivy replied, her smile carefully measured. Each word felt like a dagger to her very being, but the polite reassurance seemed to appease Lady Windom, ever conscious of maintaining her flawless reputation as a hostess.

"He seems to have slipped away," Lady Elsmere remarked, with mild surprise.

"We've already said our goodbyes," Ivy said, hoping to steer the conversation away from further scrutiny.

If Ivy's mother harbored any suspicions of impropriety involving the young man or Ivy herself, she certainly concealed them adeptly. The Chandonettes warmly thanked Lord and Lady Windom for the splendid evening before departing. Ivy followed behind, the night's events already etched into her memory.

Chapter Two

1880, 4 years later

Lord Marsden returned to England that fall, and his frequent visits to her father at Chetwynd Manor raised Ivy's suspicions. Upon his subsequent visit, Ivy chose to linger near the library entrance, her instincts whispering that something was amiss.

With the door slightly ajar, she cautiously peered into the softly illuminated room, where her father engaged in earnest conversation beside Lord Marsden at the crackling fireplace. The dancing flames cast ever-shifting shadows on his furrowed brow, drawing attention to the profound lines of worry etched into his weathered face.

"Gentlemen, thank you for coming. My solicitor has informed me that, due to several unfortunate and ill-fated investments, I find myself in a most precarious financial situation. The funds required to maintain my estate are no longer sufficient, and I fear I shall be compelled to sell if no viable solution can be found."

Ivy's breath steadied as her father's words reached her ears. Her heart swelled with sympathy and concern, realizing for the first time that such adversity could touch her father and threaten their cherished home.

The gravity of his message permeated the room, blending with the crackle of the fire as he turned to his companions, as if searching their faces for a solution to alleviate his predicament.

From the shadows, a figure spoke, barely visible except for his long hands resting on the mahogany table.

"That is indeed regrettable, Lord Elsmere," he began, his baritone voice softened with a forced gentleness.

"Our firm specializes in highly lucrative ventures abroad, yielding triple returns, as many of your esteemed neighbors can attest," he continued, his fingers intertwining with calculated precision. "If you had entrusted us from the outset, Lord Elsmere, you would have reaped similarly considerable benefits." He gave a brief pause to let his words settle, then added, "However, if you are willing, there may yet be an opportunity to improve your situation. Indeed, I see no reason why our firm could not assist in your hour of need," his tone exuding a disquieting self-assurance.

"Mr. Travers—" Lord Elsmere started, a note of hesitation in his voice. "It pains me to confess that my inheritance has been exhausted. The failing mines were my final recourse," he declared, his tone laden with resignation. "Our home and the land it sits upon constitute the only collateral I can offer your firm, and even that I cannot sustain," he continued, his voice controlled yet shadowed with an undercurrent of despair. As he extended his hands in reluctant surrender, the dire nature of his predicament seemed to hang palpably in the air.

The room fell into a profound silence, punctuated solely by the crackling of the fire. Lord Elsmere poured himself a drink and observed silently as Lord Marsden finally spoke.

"I understand the gravity of your situation, Gareth, believe me. Allow me to share a chapter from my own past that may illuminate a path forward," Lord Marsden replied, pacing the room in deep contemplation.

"As you may know, the forced sale of our estate in the eighteen-thirties dealt a grievous blow to my own family legacy," he remarked somberly.

"A regrettable chapter, indeed, yet, your endeavors overseas were met with admiration, Alistair," Lord Elsmere concurred, lifting his glass in acknowledgment.

"It is true that after extensive efforts on distant shores, I succeeded in reclaiming a significant portion of our estate," he declared triumphantly. "However, there remains a considerable amount of land under your ownership."

Lord Marsden stood beside Lord Elsmere, his hand gently resting on his shoulder.

"Gareth, amidst our past ruins lies an opportunity—one that could benefit us both. Let's come to an understanding, shall we? Not just about finances, but for our families' futures," he said, his tone measured yet earnest, a flicker of cunning in his eyes. "I understand your eldest daughter remains unwed?"

"Yes, our Evangeline—she goes by her middle name, Ivy," Lord Elsmere said.

Ivy felt her heart begin to drum with uneasy intensity at the unwelcome mention of her name, a ripple of tension threading through her body.

"She has withdrawn considerably from society as of late," he paused momentarily then continued. "But she's always known her own mind, so perhaps that's proven challenging for potential suitors." His voice reflected both pride and concern as he poured more brandy into Lord Marsden's glass.

"Yes, yes, I see," Lord Marsden mused, his brow furrowing in contemplation before he continued with careful deliberation.

"As a father in your esteemed position, Gareth, you surely grasp the delicate balance required in matters of your daughter's marital prospects. Unfortunately, society's patience is wearing thin," he cautioned, his tone carrying the weight of persuasion.

Lord Elsmere appeared to absorb his words, reaching for a drink, the amber liquid swirling gently in his glass.

"Now, hear me out, Gareth. Despite our family's substantial fortune and the ongoing renovations of our country estate, you're well aware of my marriage beneath my station to my beloved late wife," Lord Marsden reminisced, lifting his glass in a silent toast toward the heavens.

"It's because of that, and the losses our family endured, that many doors were closed to Allyn. I've had to take the lead on matters concerning his life. Now, I'm counting on him to uphold our family legacy. To ensure that, he must marry within his rightful station. And this is where you come in, Gareth," he said, pointing his glass in Lord Elsmere's direction, his words striking a chord with him.

"Your lineage traces back to the Norman settlers who flourished into one of this region's most esteemed families. Yet, your family's legacy now stands at a precipice," Lord Marsden intoned solemnly.

"Alistair, are you proposing a union between my Ivy and your son Allyn?" Lord Elsmere inquired, his expression a blend of concern and contemplation.

"Precisely, but there's more to it. In exchange, I propose you return the Marsden land, rightfully belonging to my late father, thus restoring our family's honor, and I'll see to it that your own estate remains intact," Lord Marsden continued, his look deliberate as he laid out his terms, his voice steady and resolute.

Lord Elsmere's eyes widened in realization as he absorbed the profound implications of Lord Marsden's proposal.

'No, this simply cannot be,' Ivy thought, her heart sinking as she silently observed the scene before her.

Ivy struggled to process Lord Marsden's words as they echoed loudly, jolting her from her thoughts.

"The Marsden estate would be secure," his voice resonated, piercing through her shock. "Your daughter would lack for nothing, and both our legacies would endure. My partners are prepared to extend any necessary loans for our ventures in South America, Lord Elsmere. The returns are expected to be substantial and will only grow with time," he assured, each word landing heavily on Ivy as she tried to grasp the implications.

Lord Elsmere carefully placed his drink on the polished mahogany table, his fingers lingering momentarily on the crystal glass. From across the room, Ivy observed the lines of worry etched across her father's usually composed visage.

"I must say, Alistair, your offer is exceedingly generous," Lord Elsmere began, his voice edged with a hint of reservation. "Yet, my collateral is sparse—a mere handful of foreign stocks. Our ancestral estate, without the Marsden lands, would be a mere shadow of its former glory."

Mr. Travers leaned forward, his commanding presence fully on display to Ivy. A pronounced brow and slicked-back hair accentuated his formidable countenance, casting a shadow over the discussion.

"Ah, but you underestimate the value of your family's name, Lord Elsmere," he interjected with deliberate poise, as if savoring each word. The faint undertone of guile in his voice, which Ivy couldn't quite decipher, prompted her to question both his motives and the enigma of his identity.

"Your home and property offer ample collateral," he stated, tapping his fingers together.

"His scrutiny of Lord Elsmere lingered with an intensity that hinted at a deeper interest in their exchange."

Ivy observed in silence, her unease deepening as Mr. Travers' words weighed heavily upon her. The room seemed to darken around her father and Mr. Travers, their negotiation taking on an ominous tone that sent a shiver down her spine.

"Gareth, permit me the honor of assisting you in a venture that promises prosperity for us both," Lord Marsden said, resting his arm once more on Lord Elsmere's shoulder. "Restoring my family legacy has been my life's passion. When my time comes, all I've built will pass to my son and his heir—our heir, should you allow it. Consider it," Lord Marsden proposed, his voice carrying a tone of deliberate warmth.

After a breathless pause, Ivy discerned her father's voice cutting through the tense stillness.

"When shall I arrange a meeting? They'll need to get reacquainted," Lord Elsmere uttered wearily.

Upon hearing her father's subdued tone, Ivy quietly withdrew from the door, exhaling softly as she fought to contain her tears, the gravity of their conversation settling deeply within her.

That evening, Ivy's father summoned her from the stream beyond the gardens, where she had played as a child—a haven of tranquility she often retreated to for painting.

Entering Lord Elsmere's study, Ivy found him deeply immersed in contemplation, his attention fixed on the expanse beyond the large window. A peculiar hush settled over the room as she stepped inside.

"You wanted to see me, Father?" Ivy inquired softly.

"Yes, come and sit, my dear." He gestured toward a plush crimson armchair near the fireplace.

Lord Elsmere crossed the room with deliberate steps, settling against the mantle where his arms came to rest. The crackling fire offered the sole interruption to the uneasy silence that hung heavily between them.

"My dear, there are crucial matters I must discuss with you," he began, turning to face his daughter. Ivy felt her fingers tighten around the armrests as though she might tumble into an unknown abyss.

"There's no easy way to say this, so I'll come right out with it. I've given you ample time to meet or reacquaint yourself with young men at your leisure. Yet, for reasons beyond my understanding, you've chosen to forego this opportunity and close the door to finding a suitable match," he said, his tone a mix of frustration and concern.

Ivy turned her head, focusing on the flickering fire, unable to meet her father's eyes.

"My dear, I won't pry into why you've chosen to retreat from society, but as your father, I must ensure your well-being," he said, his voice unwavering with paternal duty.

"It's time you considered your future and the responsibility you hold to this family."

He directed his attention to the massive oil painting above the mantle. An ancestor sat proudly on horseback, the grand Chandonette estate looming in the background.

Anxiety surged within Ivy like an unstoppable tide, each passing moment tightening the knot of uncertainty in her chest. The gravity of his impending request loomed over her like a darkening storm on the horizon, yet she desperately clung to a fragile hope that it would not materialize.

"I've agreed to a courtship between you and Lord Marsden's son. And once you've gotten better acquainted, we'll arrange for you to be married," he said, briefly glancing in Ivy's direction.

"Arrange?" Ivy uttered with disbelief and disgust. "Father, you must have known I have no desire to marry anyone, least of all Allyn Marsden!" Her voice rose, each word sharp and resolute, as she fought to hold back the tears threatening to spill.

"Ivy, be sensible. At your age, a young woman cannot delay in securing a proper suitor. This young man is interested and wishes to build a life with you," he implored with an underlying frustration in his tone.

"Father, is this arrangement solely for my comfort, or is there another reason?" Her eyes bore into him, an unspoken demand for his honesty. When he offered no reply, Ivy rose to her feet, her posture tense as she turned to face him.

"You place this burden upon me, yet you treat me like a child. Father, do not shield the truth from me! I heard your plans for me in the library." Determination surged within Ivy as she spoke.

Lord Elsmere appeared genuinely startled by her revelation. "My dear, please forgive me. I wouldn't ask this of you if I believed there were better options. But I've made mistakes that will impact our lives. For that, I am deeply ashamed," he murmured, his eyes lowering in remorse.

Ivy's shoulders tensed slightly, conveying her inner turmoil, yet she maintained her silence, granting Lord Elsmere the floor to continue speaking.

"I will not burden you with details, but in truth, I have failed you all, Ivy," he confessed, his voice thick with emotion, his chin trembling as he struggled to hold back tears.

"You do have a choice," he continued solemnly "But I urge you to consider the consequences for your mother, your sister, for all of us, should you refuse this arrangement. They stand to lose everything, Ivy. Our family home and prestige will vanish unless Lord Marsden secures our estate.

Ivy turned away, closing her eyes, the weight of his words pressing heavily upon her chest.

"Father, you mustn't ask this of me—there must be another way," she murmured, a whimper caught in her throat.

"I'm sorry, my dear," he insisted softly, his fingers tenderly brushing through her hair. "With that assurance, I can find solace, knowing I've secured not just our family's legacy but also the future of my grandchildren," he said softly, his words a gentle plea to bridge the emotional distance. To make this possible, I'll need your help. Please—do this for the sake of our family."

It pained Ivy deeply to see her father so shattered that she felt ashamed to demand anything in anger.

He opened his arms to her, his eyes gleaming with a rare softness.

For a moment, Ivy hesitated, then went to him and fell into her father's embrace.

Ivy encountered Allyn amidst the resplendent gardens of Marsden Hall. The once decaying overgrowth had been meticulously tamed, replaced by topiaries and manicured shrubs of various shapes. A vibrant tapestry of foliage in shades of green, gold, and crimson adorned the grounds, creating a lush contrast against the mansion beyond. The edifice, with its crumbling façade, loomed ominously over the garden, its shadows gathered within the ruins' darker recesses, lending it a cadaverous semblance that whispered of its former splendor and lingering desolation.

"It's quite imposing, isn't it?" Allyn remarked, his voice filled with awe.

Ivy studied the weathered structure, a sense of foreboding stirring within her. "It certainly is quite mysterious," she replied.

"The renovations shall be complete within a year's time, and our manor house will surpass its former glory. It will be the perfect place to raise a family someday," he proclaimed, casting a meaningful glance at Ivy. "May we sit for a moment? There is something I wish to discuss with you."

"Yes, of course," she sighed, the hint of impatience rising in her chest.

After a brief pause, she settled onto the white marble bench beside the garden path, Allyn taking his place beside her.

"Our fathers have set their minds on our marriage," he began, his voice carrying a blend of resolve and propriety. Shifting slightly on the marble bench, he traced its delicate patterns with a thoughtful finger.

"But I won't proceed without your consent," he continued earnestly, meeting her eyes with a hint of urgency. When Ivy did not respond, he added nervously, "God knows what you must think of me after the abrupt parting at the ball years ago." A tense laugh escaped him. "I regret not having parted as friends."

"Well, that was quite a long time ago, Allyn," Ivy said, striving to suppress any hint of apprehension.

"While in South America, you were often in my thoughts," Allyn remarked smoothly. "What I mean to say is—perhaps there, as my wife, you'll find the life you desire."

Ivy observed her vigilant chaperones, Lady Elsmere and her sister, Evelyn, strolling leisurely toward a cluster of trimmed shrubs at the garden's edge

"Will you be my wife, Ivy?"

A wave of numbness swept over Ivy as her father's words echoed in her mind: *"I urge you to consider the consequences for your mother, your sister, for all of us, should you refuse this arrangement. They stand to lose everything, Ivy. Our family home and prestige will vanish unless Lord Marsden secures our estate."*

She observed Evelyn, who was merrily gathering a handful of marigolds. Though she was nearly a young woman, her countenance still radiated a tender glow of innocence and tranquility—one that Ivy could not bring herself to disrupt.

"Yes, Allyn," she uttered hesitantly, forcing the words past the tightness in her throat, reluctance pressing against her will. "I will marry you."

Chapter Three

It was a solemn day in December when Ivy made her vows to Allyn Marsden. A shroud of gray mist enveloped the morning, casting a ghostly pallor over the grounds surrounding the chapel. Within that dim sanctuary, Lord Elsmere tenderly kissed Ivy's forehead, a bittersweet farewell as he entrusted her to Allyn. Ivy found a small measure of solace in the knowledge that Allyn had resolved they would not share a marital bed until they were comfortably settled at their fazenda in Brazil.

He departed for his voyage immediately after the ceremony, while Ivy stayed behind to spend one last holiday season in her family's home, savoring the fleeting moments of togetherness.

When the day came to bid farewell, there was an exchange of smiles, tears, and warm embraces. Evelyn shed the most tears of all. "Ivy, must you go?" Her voice trembled, wide eyes glistening with unshed sorrow as she clutched Ivy's hand tightly, as if her grip could somehow defy the inevitable.

"I must, dear sister," Ivy replied softly, gently drying Evelyn's cheeks. "But I promise to write often," she added reassuringly.

Before climbing into the carriage, Ivy took one last, lingering look at her family gathered outside the only place she had ever called home. As the carriage drew away, her focus rested upon the frost-laden shrubbery surrounding Chetwynd Manor—the once lush boxwood and holly now shrouded in icy despair. Like them, a coldness had settled into her heart, a pervasive chill seeping into her very soul.

The carriage ride to the train station only deepened this chill. The brisk wind lashed against the window, biting at her cheeks, and whipping Ivy's thoughts into a tempest of uncertainty. Each rattling jolt reminded her of the growing distance between her and the warmth of home, propelling her toward a life she did not yet understand.

Gwen, her devoted lady's maid, sat quietly by her side, attempting to fill the space with nervous chatter. Yet, Ivy barely heard her; the rhythmic clatter of the carriage wheels drowned out Gwen's attempts to infuse a spark of light into the somber atmosphere.

Instead, Ivy took in the landscape blurring by, each familiar tree and stone fading into memory as the vast unknown loomed ahead like a silent specter. The pastoral scenes she once cherished now appeared as mere shadows of themselves. It was a journey fraught with hope and heartache, compelling Ivy to grapple with the conflicting emotions that churned violently within her, each jolt of the carriage a reminder of the uncertain yet necessary path ahead.

Once in Liverpool, the ocean liner loomed ever larger as they approached the bustling docks, its towering silhouette a harbinger of the unknown. Ivy's heart clenched with a rising dread, an ominous whisper of what lay beyond this voyage.

As they boarded the grand vessel, Ivy couldn't help but feel dwarfed by its immense size and the vast expanse of ocean it promised to traverse. Their journey to Brazil had begun. The days at sea were marked by Gwen's relentless seasickness, her pallor a constant reminder of the voyage's trials. Ivy found herself constantly at her maid's side, administering comfort and care, leaving little room for her own melancholy to surface.

Despite her preoccupations, Ivy's thoughts often drifted to the family she had left behind. She yearned for her mother's tender guidance, her sister's reassuring presence. Yet, these feelings were muted, dulled by the growing numbness that had enveloped her heart since she had accepted Allyn's proposal. It was as if she were being swallowed up in a shroud of indifference, her emotions submerged in a sea of detachment, rendering the world around her distant and muted.

Each night, the ocean's vastness stretched out endlessly, a reflection of the uncertainty that lay ahead. Ivy stood on the deck, staring into the dark, churning waters, feeling as though she were drifting further from herself with each passing wave. The reality of her impending life in Brazil with Allyn loomed like the ship's prow, cutting through the fog of her emotions, leaving her to wonder if she would ever find solid ground again.

Most days, Ivy distracted herself with leisurely strolls around the deck, taking in the endless horizon. On the coldest days, she found solace by the fireplace, her journal her only companion as she poured her thoughts into poetry. Yet, she couldn't help but regret leaving her paints and brushes behind. Her mother had insisted that the only things of value to her now were in her bridal trousseau—trunks filled with new gowns, hats, and other matching accessories, not to mention a variety of nightgowns, petticoats, and handkerchiefs to start her new life on the right note.

All costumes and props for a play with no visible end in sight, Ivy thought.

Other ladies traveling alone wasted no time in attaching themselves to her for tea or dining. One day, while exploring the ship's second-class promenade, she met two ministers' wives. They were on a mission to help their husbands spread the gospel to the natives and kindly gifted Ivy a book on the Portuguese language along with a Bible. Though she was deeply grateful for their generosity, Ivy found it difficult to sit down and read, her mind too restless with thoughts of what lay ahead.

The only solace Ivy found during those long, interminable days at sea was the piano music that drifted from the dining room. Each note seemed to momentarily lift the weight from her heart, offering a fleeting escape from her thoughts. Yet, she knew this limbo was ephemeral; soon it would end, ushering in what she was certain would be a waking nightmare.

When they finally docked in Rio de Janeiro, Ivy felt a twinge of fear pierce through her. She pushed it aside, steeling herself for the next chapter of her life. Gathering her wits and belongings, she stepped onto foreign soil with as much grace as she could muster.

"There you are, Ivy darling. You look absolutely—" Allyn's voice faltered as he paused, his gaze sweeping over her with an intensity that momentarily took him aback. His eyes widened, clearly captivated by the sight of Ivy, who stood before him with an air of fragile determination.

"You remember my most trusted business associate, Mr. Travers," Allyn said, a hint of pride in his voice. "He attended our wedding and has been exemplary in managing all matters concerning the family estate."

"Lady Marsden," Mr. Travers greeted, offering a deep bow that made his large eyes and protruding features seem even more pronounced. Ivy felt a surge of unease at his unsettling demeanor, yet she managed a cordial nod in return.

"We've secured some rooms at a nearby hotel, and your luggage will be sent there shortly," Allyn continued as they stepped into the carriage, the plush interior enveloping them in a false sense of comfort. "I must prepare for a business dinner tonight, and I expect you to accompany me," he added, his tone leaving little room for objection. Ivy felt a mix of apprehension and resolve as the carriage began to roll forward, the city unfolding before them like a grand yet daunting panorama.

Ivy felt Mr. Travers's watchful presence as they rode toward the hotel, but she chose to divert her attention to the breathtaking view outside the carriage. She peered out in wonder at the magnificent scenery unfolding before her. The lush green hills and dark mountains, once mere silhouettes from the ship, now stood in all their resplendent glory. Equally captivating were the local vendors lining the roadside, selling vibrant fruits that seemed to burst with color. The vendors' skin tones ranged from warm tan to deep ochre, and they wore some of the most striking fabrics Ivy had ever seen.

Upon their arrival at the Hotel Pharoux, Ivy's eyes were drawn to the row of hansom cabs waiting nearby, their drivers standing by with an air of indifference. She turned back for one last look at the Harbor of Rio de Janeiro, where the majestic ship that had borne them across the vast expanse of the sea lay anchored. A poignant wave of longing surged within her, a bittersweet ache that tugged at her heartstrings. The thought of the ship setting sail once more made home feel like a distant, elusive dream, an ever-fading memory slipping further into the recesses of her mind.

A burgundy taffeta gown hung gracefully in the large armoire of Ivy's suite, awaiting her arrival. She slipped it on with little help from Gwen, who still appeared somewhat fragile. The gown's off-the-shoulder sleeves framed Ivy's shoulders, while the train, adorned with teal embellishments, cascaded elegantly from the bustle. It was undeniably elaborate and somewhat revealing for her taste.

I'll look like a peacock prancing around in this, she mused silently.

Fully dressed and seated at the dressing table, Ivy watched as Gwen adorned her with a matching string of beads. The final touch was a feathered headpiece resting delicately upon her coiffure of softly swept-back curls, pinned in place, making Ivy feel more like a decorative piece than her true self.

Gwen beamed as she gently arranged a handful of Ivy's curls over her bare shoulder. "Oh, milady, you look like a doll," she declared, though her eyes held a hollow glimmer.

Ivy smiled warmly and patted Gwen's hand, offering a small gesture of comfort. Just then, a knock echoed at the door—it was Allyn. "Are you ready, my dear?" he inquired, pushing the door open. His gaze swept over Ivy, and he paused, clearly taken by the sight of her. "You look... ravishing, my dear. Shall we go?" He extended his hand to her with an elegant gesture.

With a gentle squeeze, she took his hand, and together they stepped out of the room, ready to face the evening ahead.

Downstairs, a maître d' greeted them with a gracious nod, leading them into the dining room. Ivy's breath caught at the sight before her. The dimly lit space was adorned with candles on every table and lanterns illuminating each post, casting a warm glow over the elegantly set scene. The murmur of conversation mingled with the gentle clinking of silverware against china, creating an atmosphere both lively and intimate.

Mr. Travers was already seated when the maître d' guided them to their places. As their dinner guests arrived, Ivy learned that they, too, hailed from Britain, representing their company abroad. The younger gentleman among them seemed quite enchanted by her, engaging Ivy in amiable conversation that flowed effortlessly, covering topics from their delightful seafood dinner to the oppressive humidity of the country's climate.

To alleviate the discomfort of Allyn's piercing focus, Ivy took a sip of wine, hoping its lush flavor would quiet her nerves.

As the evening wore on, the men settled into their cigars and brandy, engaged in spirited discussions about how to elevate Brazil through railroads and other ambitious projects. It seemed to Ivy, however, that Allyn, perhaps eager to diminish the young men's growing admiration for her, called for a toast.

"To my lovely wife, the Lady Allyn Marsden of the Aramina estate—may you long reign by my side," he declared with a flourish.

"Hear, hear!" the men chorused, raising their glasses and gulping down their brandy. Ivy, feeling the weight of the moment, followed suit with another glass of wine. How could she possibly embrace this role?

The room's laughter and the thick haze of smoke swirled around her, leaving Ivy feeling lightheaded. She had reached her limit for the evening. Turning to Allyn, she sought to excuse herself. "My dear, may I be excused?"

"Are you quite alright?" he asked, concern etched across his brow.

"It's been a long day, and I need to rest. It's been nice meeting you, gentlemen. Please, excuse me," she said, leaving the table.

Allyn followed, reaching for her hand.

"Here is your key. He'll see that you get there safely," he said, motioning to the porter by the door.

"I'll come to say goodnight in an hour," he added before lightly kissing her on the cheek. Once the porter led Ivy to the stairwell, she paused, turning to him with a firm resolve. "I can find my way upstairs just fine, thank you," she insisted, her voice steady.

The porter looked somewhat bemused by her insistence. "Pardon me, senhora, but your husband has specifically requested that I escort you upstairs," he replied politely.

Ivy felt a surge of confidence. "Could I step outside from here? I need a bit of fresh air," she said, her tone leaving no room for argument.

The porter hesitated, his brow furrowing in uncertainty as he gestured toward the door at the end of the corridor. "Through there, Senhora, but—"

"Just a moment," Ivy interrupted, swiftly retrieving a few coins from her silk evening bag. "Here you go. Please, tell no one," she added with a conspiratorial smile.

The young man's face brightened instantly. "*Tenha uma boa noite*—have a nice evening, Senhora," he replied, gratitude illuminating his face before he slipped into the lobby.

However, the warmth of his smile was fleeting. The numbness that had settled in Ivy's soul was now giving way to an unsettling panic, a sensation that both confused and frightened her.

Following a short corridor, she was drawn to the soothing sound of splashing water emanating from the grand three-tiered fountain at the heart of a lush courtyard. Rushing toward it, the taffeta of her gown rustled softly with each step, the delicate sound mingling with the click of her heels on the smooth stones beneath them. Settling onto the outer edge of the fountain, she inhaled the cool night air, finding solace in its refreshing touch.

After a few moments, she found her composure and began to survey the dimly lit corners. In one shadowy recess, she discovered a wall adorned with a wrought iron gate. Through its ornate bars, the city lights flickered like distant stars, while beyond them stretched the inky expanse of the sea, its waves seemingly beckoning her to freedom. A torrent of thoughts flooded her mind as she examined the gate. What if, somehow, she could escape her current plight?

Leave now! urged a voice from within, echoing in her mind as she paced restlessly near the fountain.

If she ran, perhaps she could make it back to the docks before the ship returned to England. There were bound to be hansom cabs nearby! Her purse had but a few coins, but she could bargain with the ship's captain. As a daughter of an earl, she could promise him an ample reward. She'd go into hiding and never set foot near Chetwynd Manor again.

That alone would break her heart and infuriate her father. Yet, the prospect of surrendering her entire life to Allyn was an unbearable torment.

Perhaps if Allyn believed she'd been kidnapped, he'd relieve her family of any obligations. But whatever the outcome, she would have to run—now!

Ivy dashed to the gate, her heart pounding with desperation. She knew that if it were locked, scaling its imposing height would be her only option. The distant clatter of passing carriages and the briny scent of the sea heightened her urgency. She pressed against the bars, but the padlocked door held firm against her efforts.

Gathering her gown, she draped the flowing taffeta and petticoats over her forearm, their fabric shimmering in the dim light. Ivy grasped the wrought iron bars as she ascended the bottom rail, unleashing a metallic clank that echoed through the courtyard, tolling like a distant bell. Vines rustled around her as she positioned her right foot into the shallow recess of the gate's intricate scrollwork. The tight space pinched her toes painfully as Ivy struggled to adjust her foot, only to find it hopelessly wedged within the unforgiving iron design.

Her heart raced uncontrollably, the weight of time pressing down as she anticipated Allyn's approach. With one final tug, her foot slipped free, leaving her delicate silk slipper ensnared in the crevice.

"Curse this wretched thing," Ivy muttered, frustration tightening her chest.

Bending as gracefully as her gown's bodice permitted, she struggled to free her slipper when a smooth, cultured voice intruded upon her efforts.

"Pardon me, Miss. You appear quite distressed. May I offer my assistance?"

Ivy turned to find a gentleman emerging from the shadows. The gas lamps cast a gentle, flickering glow across the courtyard, accentuating the deep emerald of his eyes and the sun-kissed tone of his skin, while his dark hair, artfully swept back, flowed longer than customary for a gentleman.

"I am quite well, sir," she replied, striving to conceal her vexation. "The dining room was rather oppressive, so I sought a breath of fresh air."

"Is that so?" He raised an eyebrow, his expression a mix of curiosity and polite skepticism.

For a fleeting moment, Ivy stood frozen, the weight of the day's events crashing over her. From her arrival in this foreign land to the reluctant role she was expected to play as a wife to the chaos of her failed escape—it all swirled in her mind like a whirlwind. Standing before this mysterious stranger, she could not help but wonder how much he had seen and knew. A tightness gripped her stomach, but she fought to hold her composure, returning his regard with as much calm and poise as she could muster. Stiffening and drawing her shoulders back, Ivy steeled herself, ready to mask any trace of unease with polite gratitude. She had to find a way to discreetly return to her room, where she might regain her bearings and contemplate her next move.

"Indeed, I have quite recovered now, thank you," Ivy replied, keeping her voice steady despite the subtle tremor in her fingers as she smoothed her gown.

"Incidentally," remarked the stranger, his tone tinged with amusement, "I too sought refuge from the stifling confines of the dining room, lured by the promise of fresh air." His emerald eyes, deep and discerning, appeared to delve into her very thoughts, enveloping her in an intensity that both intrigued her and made her pulse quicken.

"It's getting late, and I really must be going," Ivy said, her voice steady as she adjusted the silk shawl that clung to her damp shoulders in the humid evening air. She offered a polite smile, her expression carefully controlled as she subtly shifted, eager to escape the stranger's unwavering attention.

"And what of this?" His voice conveyed amusement as he gestured toward the gleaming burgundy object within the decorative metalwork.

This detail brought an unwelcome flush to Ivy's cheeks, recalling her brief mishap. Feeling the mask of composure slipping, she forced herself to remain still, resisting the urge to glance away and betray the tumult simmering beneath her practiced calm.

"Oh! Yes, my slipper caught as I leaned in for a better glance at the harbor. The sea looks so tranquil under the moonlit sky," Ivy said, her words quick as she tried to gloss over her misstep.

"Well, then, allow me to assist," he said, his tone marked by a blend of strength and refinement. With deliberate, measured movements, he rattled the gate lightly, freeing the slipper until it fell softly to the ground. "There you are, as promised. You may resume your path." His gaze remained, betraying an almost imperceptible curiosity, as though he were unraveling the mystery of her presence.

"You don't strike me as the sort of young lady who would be wandering out alone at night. Nor should you," he remarked, his tone carrying a trace of superiority.

His eyes briefly rested on the ring she wore, and Ivy sensed the shift in his demeanor before he spoke with respectful deference. "It appears you have misplaced your husband, Senhora. May I escort you inside? Perhaps he is there."

"I am quite capable of finding my way and need neither a husband nor a stranger to guide me." She gathered her gown and edged around him with a sharp movement, irritation simmering beneath the surface.

Upon returning to her room, Ivy experienced a fleeting sense of relief, though the familiar surroundings provided only a temporary reprieve. Shadows danced along the walls, and each creak of the floorboards intensified her anxiety, as if the very space conspired to unveil her failed escape.

Inevitably, her thoughts drifted back to the elusive stranger, his presence lingering in her mind and haunting her with the precariousness of her situation and the uncertainty that lay ahead like a darkened path.

Chapter Four

vy had scarcely risen from her bed when a gentle knock at the door announced the arrival of a visitor. The door creaked open, and a young girl stepped into the room, clad in a crisp white uniform and headscarf. She balanced a breakfast tray, resplendent with an array of buns, fresh fruit, savory meats with eggs, and a steaming urn of coffee.

"Good morning, Senhora," the girl greeted with a modest curtsy.

"Good morning," Ivy replied, propping herself up on the pillows.

"I am Izobel. I help you get dressed." Her words, marked by a distinct Portuguese lilt, conveyed warmth as she placed the tray on Ivy's lap.

Ivy's brow furrowed with concern. "Where is Gwen, my maid?"

"She too sick," Izobel replied, adjusting the tray.

"Will she be alright?" Ivy asked, her throat tightening as a wave of panic rose within her.

"She sleep now," Izobel said, her tone gentle yet resolute.

Ivy studied the girl who appeared no older than twelve. She was struck by the unfamiliarity of the encounter. Her only prior interaction with someone of color had been at a traveling carnival, where a group of performers, under the Sultan's patronage, dazzled with fire-eating and knife-juggling tricks. Enchanted by their spectacle, Ivy had eagerly requested an encore, her curiosity piqued by the exotic display.

The memory of that vibrant carnival seemed a world apart from the serene confines of her current setting, amplifying the peculiarity of Izobel's presence. Ivy observed as Izobel meticulously arranged her garments, the girl's delicate hands moving gracefully. Ivy could not help but admire the caramel-toned hue of Izobel's skin; it was a vivid reminder of the beauty she encountered in this new and unfamiliar place.

As Ivy pondered this, an unexpected flash of the mysterious young man with the sun-kissed complexion and striking green eyes intruded upon her thoughts. She swiftly banished the image from her mind, focusing instead on the comforting routine of her breakfast.

Once her meal was complete, Izobel assisted Ivy out of her nightgown and into a fresh chemise. The girl then deftly encircled Ivy's torso with a corset, her fingers nimble and precise as they worked to fasten the busk. Ivy marveled at the deftness of Izobel's touch, finding it remarkably more agile compared to Gwen's. Each movement was executed with a quiet efficiency, adding an unexpected touch of finesse to the morning's ritual.

When Izobel approached with a delicate, ruffled petticoat from her wedding trousseau, Ivy felt a stab of remorse. The thought of being part of a society that demanded this child to serve her like a slave—because she probably was one—filled her with a profound discomfort. Ivy recalled reading a newspaper article during her voyage about Brazil's stubborn refusal to loosen its hold on slavery. It was yet another unsettling detail that marred her new circumstances. However, she dared not ask Allyn if there were slaves at the Aramina estate, knowing it would only complicate matters. She despised feeling so helpless, but at that moment, she was his captive, powerless to alter her situation.

"I can do this; thank you," Ivy said softly, gently pulling away from the girl. She moved toward the standing mirror near the bed and began tying the petticoat ribbons tightly around her waist.

As she looked at her reflection, a wave of shame washed over her. How could she, or anyone else, expect a child to work under such conditions? The ribbons felt like a tangible reminder of her own privilege and the injustices that surrounded her. Ivy's hands trembled slightly as she finished tying the petticoat, the weight of her thoughts pressing heavily upon her. It took a few moments before she could bring herself to face the child. When she finally looked up, she saw Izobel standing beside her, holding a linen gown. The girl's warm smile touched Ivy's heart.

"Izobel help, Senhora," the girl said softly.

"Alright, we can finish this together," Ivy replied, returning the smile.

She gratefully accepted Izobel's assistance, welcoming the girl's sweet disposition. Despite any hardships, Izobel still radiated the glow of childhood, evoking thoughts of Evelyn's sweet innocence half a world away. Curiosity and concern tugged at Ivy's heart. "Izobel," she said tenderly, "are you well cared for? Where is your mother?"

"*Minha mãe*, my mother, she works here," Izobel said, her eyes sparkling with delight.

Ivy let out a soft sigh of relief. "Thank goodness," she muttered to herself. With a warm smile, she continued, "Well, she must be a very good one. I'm pleased to know that you are well looked after."

Ivy bid farewell to Izobel, bestowing upon her a small bag of sweets and coins as a parting gift. She watched as the girl skipped away, her spirit undiminished by the trials of her world. With a final, reflective glance around the room, Ivy picked up her ecru-colored parasol and fan. Drawing a steadying breath, she braced herself for what lay ahead.

Allyn lingered in the lobby, his eyes locked on the delicate hands of his pocket watch, each tick echoing his impatience. As Ivy descended the grand staircase, her presence commanded his regard, and he moved to greet her with a composed yet determined stride.

"Darling, good morning," he said, placing a tender kiss on her forehead. His eyes scanned her with an intensity that bordered on possessive. "I trust you slept well?"

Ivy offered a polite smile, though a trace of concern shadowed her expression. "I did, thank you. However, Gwen appears to have taken a turn for the worse. The physician suspects dehydration due to her seasickness."

Allyn's expression remained unperturbed as he adjusted his cufflinks with deliberate care. "Well, these things cannot be helped. I have arranged for her care until she can return to England," he said with a casual detachment.

Ivy's heart clenched, a wave of panic rising within her. The thought of leaving Gwen behind, her sweet and loyal maid—a friend in her own right—was unbearable. Gwen was her only solace in this unfamiliar land, her last connection to the life she left behind.

"You intend to send her back?" Her voice quivered despite her efforts to regain control. An uncomfortable tightness knotted in her throat, the rawness of her distress settling heavily within her. "Why would you do such a thing?"

"She is unwell, Ivy. Do be reasonable. Forcing her to endure the grueling journey to Aramina would be nothing short of cruel."

"Then let me stay with her," Ivy implored, her voice still unsteady. "We can join you once she recovers. I will not go otherwise," she insisted.

"There is no need for theatrics, my dear," Allyn said, his tone clipped with impatience. "She is under the care of the finest physician in the city. You are my wife, and your place is by my side as we travel to our home."

Ivy's chest tightened her thoughts a whirlwind of disbelief. How could he make such a decision with such cold indifference? Leaving Gwen behind felt like severing a part of herself.

"Besides, I have brought on a maid suited to your needs," Allyn continued his voice firm. "She's waiting at the fazenda."

He withdrew his pocket watch, flicking it open with practiced precision. His brow furrowed slightly as he checked the time. "I have enlisted our most capable men to ensure the journey is as comfortable as possible. Our train departs at half-past nine, and they should arrive any moment now."

As if on cue, the clatter of wheels on cobblestone announced the arrival of the carriage. Allyn's lips curled into a satisfied smile. "That must be them now. Come."

Outside, the driver expertly reined in the horses and dismounted, flanked by two manservants. One of them stepped forward, bowing gracefully. "Senhor Marsden, *eu presumo?*"

Allyn's expression stiffened. "Yes, but I gave explicit instructions that we required a footman who speaks English! None of this native gibberish."

The footman straightened, a hint of amusement in his eyes. "Well, my lord, you are in luck. My English is impeccable."

Allyn regarded him with a stern, appraising look. "I'll be the judge of that," he replied curtly.

Ivy stood waiting with graceful poise by the hotel entrance, her parasol held aloft as a delicate shield against the sun's relentless glare. The rays danced around her, weaving playful patterns on the cobblestones. Her gaze fell upon the striking contrast before her—Allyn's pallid complexion was a ghostly foil to the newcomer's captivating appearance, his skin sun-kissed, a clear indication of a life spent in the open air. His dark hair was meticulously groomed, yet it retained a hint of wildness that intrigued her.

As Ivy observed the man's face, a surge of recognition jolted through her. It was him—the very man she had encountered in the courtyard! Her heart quickened, and she fanned her face, feeling a warm blush spread across her cheeks. The unrelenting sun was no match for the heat rising within her, a warmth that seemed to emanate not from the sweltering summer day but from this man whose presence stirred deep untold emotions.

Her embarrassment heightened when Allyn, with his usual indifference, summoned her and directed the man to assist her into the carriage. Their eyes met, and the stranger's expression shifted from polite detachment to one of amused familiarity. Ivy felt a flutter of apprehension at the silent exchange between them, as though a secret was being shared amidst the bustling scene. Her thoughts were a tangle as she tried to decipher the curious smile that lingered at the corners of his lips, leaving her both bewildered and uncertain about the strange pull she felt.

"This is Mr.—" Allyn began, pausing to scrutinize the newcomer, "May I inquire your name, sir?"

"Fontes," came the reply.

"Mr. Fontes," Allyn resumed, his look sharp and assessing, "I take it you have come to join your relatives at the fazenda?"

"Yes, Senhor," Mr. Fontes confirmed, his tone steady and respectful.

"Mr. Fontes asserts that he possesses an excellent command of English, which should prove useful on our journey," Allyn remarked, his brows furrowed in mild skepticism.

"Think of me as your manservant—of all trades. I am at your service, Senhora Marsden," Mr. Fontes said, extending his hand to Ivy with a flourish.

She nodded graciously and allowed him to assist her into the carriage, her mind awhirl with the implications of this unexpected encounter, pondering the secrets that lay behind his enigmatic eyes.

Once the servants had deftly stowed the luggage onto the carriage, it set off with a rhythmic clatter toward the railway station. Ivy clenched her gloved hands together, casting a lingering glance back at the hotel, her heart aching.

Gwen, forgive me, she thought, swallowing the bitter taste of remorse.

Settled in the train's luxurious interior, Ivy's mind remained uneasily preoccupied with the ambiguous Mr. Fontes. She struggled to quell her apprehension about whether the manservant might reveal their brief encounter in the courtyard. Across from her, Allyn stirred from his nap, his languid form shifting with the gentle sway of the train. Ivy felt a deep-seated relief that he had finally surrendered to sleep after luncheon; his relentless grumbling about the train's sluggish pace had done little to improve the pleasure of his company.

Her sense of relief was further heightened by the fact that Travers had remained behind to finalize the business deal from the previous evening. The prospect of enduring the bickering of two pretentious men was a discomfort Ivy was more than happy to avoid.

After nearly four hours aboard the train, Ivy's eyelids grew heavy with fatigue. Her thoughts meandered restlessly between concerns for her maid's recovery at the hotel, the unsettling episode of her foiled escape observed by Mr. Fontes, and her own dismay at having been so easily deceived about his true identity. She had mistaken him for a gentleman, misled by his impeccable attire. Indeed, his education must have been of the finest sort, though his manners still hinted at a need for refinement. A swirl of questions danced through her mind. The gentle hum and steady rhythm of the railcar provided a soothing balm to her frayed nerves, gradually lulling her into a much-needed repose.

Just as Ivy was on the verge of drifting into a peaceful slumber, the train gave a sudden jolt, followed by a slow and deliberate halt. The abrupt disturbance roused her from her drowsy reverie, and she blinked awake to see a porter enter the passenger car, speaking swiftly in Portuguese.

Allyn lifted his head with an irritated groan, his expression one of displeasure. The train compartment, once a haven of luxury, had erupted into a flurry of activity, the anxious murmurs of fellow passengers swelling like the tide. Ivy watched the scene unfold, her brow furrowing as a flutter of tension settled in her chest as Mr. Fontes navigated confidently through the crowd, his presence commanding attention. Ivy's eyes darted around, trying to make sense of the commotion, when she spotted Mr. Fontes engaging in a brief exchange with the porter before making his way through the throng of passengers, his purposeful stride cutting through the growing chaos.

"Just what the devil is going on here?" Allyn demanded, rising from his seat with an air of indignation, his voice cutting through the growing commotion like a blade.

"Senhor, there's been a mechanical failure," Mr. Fontes announced with authoritative composure. "The conductor has instructed that all passengers disembark here until the matter is resolved."

"And where, precisely, is that?" Ivy queried, feeling a quiver of alarm as her eyes darted toward the window. She took a sweeping view of lush, rolling fields and distant hills veiled in a gentle mist, their outlines softened by the midday sun.

"We're just outside the city of Barra Mansa, madam," Mr. Fontes replied, his tone infused with a protective assurance that seemed to ease her growing concerns.

"You'll need to remain here while I locate a wagon. I'll secure your lodging until they can fix the issue," said Mr. Fontes.

"Absolutely out of the question!" Allyn declared, his voice dripping with disdain. "We are mere hours from Aramina! I demand you find an alternative means of transport immediately."

Mr. Fontes met Allyn's glare with a steady and unwavering expression. "Consider it done, Senhor," he replied, his tone composed and unshaken by Allyn's agitation. With a firm nod, he turned swiftly and exited the compartment.

The day's stifling heat was unlike anything Ivy had ever endured. The afternoon sun blazed with such fervor that it seared through the coach windows, turning the interior into a searing furnace.

Ivy waved her silk fan in a futile attempt to cool herself, but the heat intensified despite her efforts. Her arms soon grew heavy from the constant motion, and she felt as though she were slowly marinating beneath her corset. Outside, the world dissolved into a hazy blur as sweat trickled into her eyes. The lush green landscape and azure sky merged into a blurred watercolor, swirling like a painter's fevered dream.

One of Monsieur Pierre's masterpieces gone mad, she thought, the observation fading beneath the oppressive warmth.

The coach jolted and swayed over the uneven terrain, each bump heightening her discomfort. Colors outside spun in a disorienting whirl until Ivy's vision succumbed to impenetrable darkness.

Chapter Five

vy awoke to a symphony of birdsong echoing softly beyond the window. A gentle breeze danced through the sheer white curtains, brushing against her skin with a tender caress. The cool air was infused with a subtle fragrance of herbs, soothing her senses like a comforting balm. The rustling of palm leaves outside captured her attention, stirring a flicker of curiosity within her. Had they truly arrived at the fazenda? A fleeting thought crossed her mind: perhaps she had slept through the entire journey. If only that were so. Wherever this place might be, she felt enveloped in an undeniable sense of safety.

The room, dimly lit yet inviting, revealed a sparse decor adorned with clusters of dried herbs that hung in fragrant bunches. Memories of her bedroom at Chetwynd Manor surged forth, vivid and poignant, just before she summoned Gwen. She could almost envision her father and sister seated at the breakfast table, their laughter intertwining with the gentle morning light.

She shook off the memories and focused on sitting up. Her head still ached, though the fog was gradually lifting. She attempted to swallow, but her parched throat betrayed her with a cough. How long had she been asleep? Her focus landed on a clay pitcher resting on a nearby table. With a shaky hand, Ivy reached for the pitcher, only for it to slip from her grasp and shatter on the stone floor.

At that moment, a native woman entered the room, her attire entirely white, the fabric gleamed against her nut-brown skin and long, black braid.

"I'm sorry," Ivy muttered, her voice a fragile whisper. The woman hurried out of the room, returning swiftly with a new pitcher. She poured a cup of water and handed it to Ivy, who gratefully accepted it. Taking a long, refreshing sip, Ivy felt relief wash over her. She examined the clay cup with a curious eye, appreciating its simple yet elegant craftsmanship.

"Are you my new maid?" Ivy inquired tentatively.

The woman shook her head, replying in a language foreign to Ivy's ears.

Ivy's brow furrowed in concentration as she studied the woman's face intently. Offering a nervous smile, she confessed, "I'm afraid I don't understand."

A knock at the door drew the woman's attention. She crossed the room and exchanged a few hushed words in her native tongue with someone just outside.

"Senhora, may I have a word with you?" he called from beyond the door, his voice smooth yet insistent.

Ivy sprang from her bed, her heart racing at the familiar sound—it was Mr. Fontes. Conscious of her scant attire, a mere chemise, she quickly draped a blanket around her shoulders and positioned herself discreetly behind the door.

"Yes, I'm here! Can you tell me where my husband is?"

"He's resting in the next room," Mr. Fontes replied. "I'm afraid he's suffering from heat exhaustion and will need ample rest before we can continue.

"Where are we?" Ivy inquired.

"We're in a village about three hours from the Aramina Fazenda," Mr. Fontes explained. "This woman is the village healer. We depart tomorrow at sunset, but if you require anything, she will see to it for you."

With that, he was gone. Ivy pondered whether she too had suffered from heat exhaustion, though it was no surprise that Allyn, being fairer than she, would be affected more severely by the sun. From what she had observed, the days seemed longer in this country.

That evening, she cautiously peeked into the room where Allyn lay sleeping. The air was fragrant with incense, and she saw the native woman gently cooling him with damp cloths. In the corner, his valet, Afonso, weary from the journey, watched on with a tired expression.

Suddenly, a savory aroma wafted to Ivy's nostrils, stirring her appetite. She followed its trail to the kitchen, which was even more rustic than the rest of the tiny abode. A wooden table occupied the center, and a small mud-brick stove stood against the far wall.

The woman followed Ivy, setting a basket of bread on the table and gesturing for her sit. She then served Ivy a plate of rice and stewed meat from a simmering pot on the stove, accompanied by a simple wooden spoon. Ivy expressed her gratitude and began to enjoy the unfamiliar cuisine, finding the cheese bread particularly delightful.

As Ivy savored her meal, finding it surprisingly filling, the kitchen door suddenly swung open, and Mr. Fontes stepped inside.

"Please forgive my intrusion. I've put the horses up for the evening. I can take my plate and go," Mr. Fontes offered.

"No, that isn't necessary. You're welcome to sit if you'd like," Ivy replied, gesturing toward the table.

He nodded and moved toward the wash basin near the doorway. Rolling up his sleeves, he lathered his forearms as the woman went to set a place at the table. An awkward silence followed as he dried his arms with a cloth and sat across from Ivy.

She tried to avoid eye contact, focusing instead on the bun in her hand.

The native woman stood silently, observing them as if expecting a conversation to unfold. It was likely she was perplexed by Mr. Fontes's status, treating him with the same deference one might show to a high-born gentleman. The silence in the room thickened until Ivy finally decided to break it.

"Mr. Fontes, have you worked for the family long?"

He looked up from his plate. "No, not long; however, my family has been with them for almost five years now," he replied.

Ivy sensed the woman's keen interest in their exchange.

"I heard you speaking to her. What is this woman's native tongue?" Ivy asked, glancing toward the woman.

"She speaks one of the many Tupi languages," he replied.

A stirring sound came from the hall, prompting the woman to hurry from the kitchen to attend to it.

"That must be your husband now," he said, taking a spoonful of stew.

"Will he be alright?" Ivy asked.

"Yes, he'll be fine by morning," he assured her. The woman returned to gather their plates, exchanging a few words with Mr. Fontes before standing and looking intently at Ivy.

"She's asking if you would like a cup of coffee," he informed Ivy.

"Yes, please, that would be lovely," she replied. After a moment, she stole a glance at him. There was something intriguing about Mr. Fontes. She had mistaken him for a gentleman the previous night, yet now he played the role of a servant. She couldn't help but wonder if he suspected her intentions—that she meant to flee from her new life in Brazil when they first met.

The woman brought them clay mugs filled with dark coffee, its aroma as soothing as the quaint room itself. Suddenly, low grunting sounds filled the air—unfamiliar noises that grew closer. Ivy's eyes darted around the room, searching for the source.

"Is that some kind of animal?" she asked, concern creeping into her voice.

"Judging by the sound, I'd say howler monkeys. They make those calls when searching for a mate," he replied, taking a sip from his mug. "Or in search of their next prey," he added with a hint of mischief.

Ivy's brow tightened. "What? Are they aggressive?" she pressed, her heart quickening.

"Some are known to be," he said, watching her closely. "I see," Ivy murmured, her thoughts racing beneath her calm exterior.

Mr. Fontes smiled, clearly entertained by her discomfort. "They won't harm you. You're safe here," he said. He set his drink down with a soft thud, his smile remaining as his eyes held hers.

Ivy nodded, lifting her coffee to her lips, acutely aware of the amusement in his expression.

"It's getting late, Senhora. You should rest for tomorrow," he suggested, his voice gentle but firm.

"Very well. Good night, Mr. Fontes." Ivy stood, and his voice reached her as she turned to leave.

"Sleep well, Senhora," he said, his tone lingering as she stepped from the kitchen.

The next day, Allyn was on the mend. He rested until late that afternoon when he finally emerged from the bedroom.

"Please forgive me for not summoning you sooner, my dear. I would have hated for you to witness me in such a wretched state," he said as they prepared to depart the village. As a token of gratitude for her hospitality, they presented the healer woman with a bag of coins, a humble gesture for welcoming them into her home.

They reached the Aramina Fazenda as dusk settled over the land. The fading light bathed the fields in soft hues, casting long shadows across the earth. Ivy's eyes followed the expanse before her, taking in the rows of coffee fields that spanned endlessly toward the horizon, where the sky melted into pale shades of pink and blue. The scene held a quiet, almost serene beauty, its pastoral charm only disturbed by the presence of small, weathered buildings she suspected were slave dwellings. The sight stirred a sense of unease within her—a stark contrast to the beauty she would have liked to capture with her paintbrush. She shifted uneasily in her seat as the wagon turned onto the gravel road leading to the house.

Nestled within a small valley, the estate gradually emerged, resembling a grand vessel adrift in a vast sea of mountains and verdant foliage. Its scale surpassed her expectations, its detailed woodwork lost to the shadows as the fading light settled in.

Yet, the lanterns outside bathed its white façade and blue shutters in a soft, inviting light, painting a serene picture against the darkening sky.

As the coach drew to a halt, Allyn immediately became preoccupied, issuing orders to organize their belongings. He stepped ahead of Ivy and made his way inside, closely followed by his valet. Two man-servants were already unloading Ivy's luggage when Mr. Fontes extended his hand to assist her disembark.

"Congratulations, Senhora, on making the journey here in one piece," he remarked, a hint of admiration in his voice.

"Was there cause to think otherwise, Mr. Fontes?" Ivy replied, arching an eyebrow.

"The journey alone has been known to challenge even the bravest souls. I wish you a pleasant evening, Senhora," he said, before turning his attention to the horses.

Ivy pondered whether he was conveying his true thoughts or merely being insolent. Her mind felt weary, and she dared not engage further with the enigma that was Mr. Fontes!

As Ivy approached the entrance, a house servant emerged. Petite in stature and attired in a pristine white uniform, her specific role within the household was not entirely clear to Ivy.

"*Bem-vinda a casa,* Senhora Ivy—welcome home! Allow me to introduce myself; I am Flávia, your lady's maid," she proclaimed, ushering Ivy inside with a refined attentiveness. "From this moment forward, I shall be at your service," she added, her smile warm and reassuring.

As Ivy stepped over the threshold, the inviting aroma of candle wax and kerosene enveloped her senses. Brightly lit sconces cast a warm glow upon the staircase and hallway, leading to a modest bedroom situated a short distance from Allyn's own quarters.

"It must have been a treacherous journey for you, my lady," Flávia remarked, her voice laced with genuine concern. "Here, allow me to help you out of those clothes," she added, her hands poised with attentive grace as she stepped closer to Ivy.

The bath Flávia prepared was nothing short of luxurious. Ivy delighted in the warm water, breathing in the intoxicating scents of herbs and oils that danced on the surface. The room was softly illuminated by candlelight, casting a golden hue that made the water shimmer like liquid gold. She reveled in the soothing embrace of the bath for as long as she could, savoring each tranquil moment, until Flávia returned with a plush towel draped over her arm.

"Here, Senhora, you must be ready for sleep," Flávia said, her voice a gentle murmur.

"Thank you for this lovely bath," Ivy replied, her gratitude evident in her tone.

"Of course," Flávia responded, a smile playing on her lips as she poured water over Ivy's shoulders, the liquid cascading like a silken waterfall.

Flávia's almond-toned complexion glowed in the candlelit room, imbued with a warm, subtle luster as she tended to Ivy. Soft chestnut curls slipped from her headscarf, gently framing her face. With smooth efficiency, she wrapped Ivy in a towel, helping her out of the tub. After dressing her in a delicate nightdress, she guided her to the comfort of her bed.

As she settled beneath the covers, Ivy felt an unexpected wave of gratitude for having such an amiable maid in this distant place. As she closed her eyes, she recalled the bond she and Gwen had forged over the years and wondered if she and Flávia might form a similar friendship. With that comforting thought, Ivy drifted into a deep slumber.

Her dreams, however, took a darker turn. She imagined Allyn entering her room, his presence palpable even in her sleep. She felt his fingers stroke her hair, his voice a haunting whisper in the darkness: *You're mine now, my dear!* The words echoed in her mind, leaving her to question, upon waking, whether he had truly been there or if it was merely a figment of her restless dreams.

Downstairs, Flávia tapped gently on the heavy oak door of Allyn's study.

"Yes, come in!" he instructed, his voice carrying a note of authority.

She entered quietly, finding him seated at his desk, a crystal glass of brandy in hand, the amber liquid catching the light of a solitary candle on his desk.

"I ensured your wife was bathed and comfortable. She's now situated in the spare room as you requested," Flávia reported softly.

"Very well," he acknowledged, his eyes scanning intently over a document spread before him.

Flávia stood silently, observing him for a few moments until Allyn finally looked up, his gaze meeting hers.

"Was there something else?" he inquired, his voice measured.

"Will you be attending to her tonight? She seemed quite exhausted," Flávia asked with a hint of concern.

Allyn remained quiet, his expression unreadable, before rising from his chair and crossing to a nearby velvet settee, where he sat down heavily.

"I wasn't certain our arrangement would endure—especially once she arrived," she confessed.

"You're simply stepping in until I can bed her, remember?" said Allyn.

"Of course, I do. And I know just what pleases you," said Flávia as she removed her headscarf. Allyn looked on as brown ringlets fell to her shoulders. She continued to undress, leaving her blouse and skirts on the floor. She was entirely naked now as she approached Allyn on the settee. Flávia leaned in to kiss him but was startled when he took a handful of curls, forcing her to look at him.

"And, you'll continue to please me for as long as I ask it of you," he said before releasing Flávia.

"I will do whatever you ask of me, Senhor," she said.

Chapter Six

Ivy awoke the following morning feeling famished, the enticing scent of freshly baked bread beckoning her from the depths of slumber. Rising from her bed, she donned her dressing gown and slippers, then descended the staircase. The wooden floor creaked beneath her as she followed the heavenly aroma, accompanied by the rhythmic sounds of mixing and chopping, toward the far end of the house. Each room possessed a rustic charm, though the furnishings and decor exuded a refined elegance. Yet, Ivy's thoughts were not on a leisurely exploration; her sole desire was to seek out breakfast.

As she stepped into the kitchen, her eyes fell upon a dark, robust woman diligently slicing fruit.

"Good morning—" Ivy began, her voice trailing off as the woman's deep-set eyes widened in surprise.

"Senhora! *Perdoe-me, não te vi aí!*" the woman exclaimed, repeating her apology until Flávia entered the kitchen to calm her. The cook then offered Ivy a bashful grin as Flávia gently guided her away.

"Oh, Senhora, you needn't come in here. Please, come with me," she urged.

"Forgive me. I have yet to learn Portuguese," Ivy replied, following Flávia into the dining room.

"You needn't worry about that, Senhora," Flávia said, pulling out a chair for Ivy at the grand table. Ivy's curiosity was piqued by the arrangement: large leaves served as a runner, complemented by a vibrant display of red and yellow flowers in a vase at the center.

Flávia instructed the servants to return to the kitchen, her expression one of satisfaction when they brought forth a placemat, silverware, and neatly folded napkins.

"Senhor Marsden usually takes his breakfast out on the veranda, but he's still resting from—well, the long journey," she added with a smile.

Ivy felt a wave of relief wash over her; she needed a moment to gather herself before facing him as the Lady of the Fazenda.

"The cook has prepared a full breakfast of eggs and sausage, along with *pão de queijo*. It's a cheese bread you're going to adore!" Flávia declared with enthusiasm.

Just then, a servant entered with a tray laden with assorted fruits, breads, and pastries. Flávia raised her voice at the servant before excusing herself to check on the rest of the meal.

As soon as they were out of sight, Ivy filled her plate and began to devour the fruits. Her palate had never tasted such a fusion of sweet and tangy delicacies. She then bit into a meat-filled pastry and savored each bite after that.

Flávia returned holding a glass decanter of bright orange juice, trailed by two servants bearing silver entrée dishes. They set the gleaming dishes on the sideboard before quietly departing.

Ivy stepped closer, her attention fixed on the polished lids. Lifting the first, she was met with a cloud of steam and the sight of poached eggs, their whites smooth and glistening. The second lid revealed savory sausages beside a tureen of creamy grits, their scent rising to tempt her senses.

Flávia reappeared silently, her presence signaled by the soft rustle of fabric as she approached, her hands folded neatly in front of her.

"Will there be anything else, Senhora?"

Ivy had already taken a mouthful of eggs and sausage when she responded, "Everything is perfect, thank you. I would like to get dressed and explore the fazenda after breakfast." For a fleeting moment, she thought of her mother—undoubtedly disapproving of the Lady of Aramina speaking with her mouth full.

"Of course, just ring this bell, and I shall come at once," Flávia assured, gesturing gracefully toward a small silver bell placed discreetly upon the polished sideboard. She cast a glance at one of the housemaids standing attentively by the door, her expression a blend of expectation and uncertainty. "They may not understand your words," she continued, her voice a soothing lilt, "but I will be there to guide you in making your wishes known."

With her hands pressed together, Flávia exuded a sense of warmth and confidence, her presence a reassuring anchor in this unfamiliar environment. Ivy, with a touch of curiosity, asked, "Might the new footman be in attendance?"

"Ah, Mr. Fontes?" Flávia's chuckle was light and knowing. "He has a certain disdain for wearing livery, finding himself more at ease amidst the open air and gardens. Yet, he stands ready to assist with anything you might require."

"I see," Ivy replied, tugging at her napkin. Her fingers traced its edge with idle intent as she pondered Flávia's words. A flicker of interest sparked at the mention of Mr. Fontes, but she quickly dismissed it as mere curiosity rather than anything more profound.

"I assume there's a butler?" Ivy asked, casually steering the conversation.

Flávia pointed toward a dignified figure moving through the hallway—a white-haired gentleman of graceful stature, carrying a silver candelabra with slow deliberate steps.

"Of course—old Octávio," she said nodding in his direction.

Upon noticing them seated in the dining room, Octávio paused to offer a respectful bow, his demeanor one of quiet authority.

"His English is limited," Flávia continued, "but he comprehends instructions with a keen understanding that surpasses that of the women."

A thoughtful silence descended upon Ivy, her gaze lowering as she absorbed the nuances of her new environment. Reflecting on the complexities of the world she had just entered, she finally asked, "Flávia, are there many slaves working here?"

Flávia's expression grew contemplative. "There's Octávio, Hilda the cook, a kitchen maid, and two housemaids. There's more workers outside in the coffee production, overseen by the Fontes family," she explained, her voice carrying the weight of a complex history.

"I see," Ivy replied again, her tone reflecting a mixture of gratitude and concern. The thought of being served by slaves was unsettling, an unfamiliar reality that felt at odds with her upbringing. "Thank you for speaking with me, Flávia." Ivy felt a flicker of confusion as she absorbed the intricacies of her new surroundings.

"Now, Senhora, I will leave you to enjoy your meal," Flávia said, offering a final, warm smile before exiting the dining room. Ivy remained seated, her thoughts consumed by the daunting reality of navigating a household with enslaved servants. Raised with the belief that those of privilege had a duty to provide opportunities for the less fortunate, the presence of enslaved individuals struck her as almost inconceivable. Perhaps, once she was more deeply involved in household affairs, she might persuade Allyn to grant them their freedom. For now, however, she needed to focus on preparing for the expectations that awaited her. She bit into another delectable pastry, her eyes wandering over the room's mahogany furnishings. Her attention settled on a china cabinet and a matching tea cart, their elegance evoking memories of home. Then something along the wall caught her eye.

"What are these? Old stenciled designs?" she wondered out loud.

Her curiosity awakened, Ivy rose from the table to investigate further. As she examined the wall more closely, she realized the designs were hand-painted. Whoever crafted them possessed a skilled hand, breathing life into the house. Satisfied with her observation, she returned to her seat to finish her breakfast.

Flávia assisted Ivy in dressing for the sweltering weather, suggesting a single cotton petticoat beneath a linen frock. Ivy, who typically wore her hair in a braid, decided to take Flávia's advice and arranged her hair into a chignon under her sunbonnet.

As Ivy descended the stairs, she was greeted by Allyn, who marveled at her appearance.

"Ah, my dear, I was just about to send for you. Come, let us tour our estate," he said, looking exceedingly pleased.

Ivy was surprised to find Mr. Fontes acting as their driver. He met her with a knowing glance and assisted her onto the carriage. Unlike the expected livery, he wore a crisp white shirt paired with black trousers and boots. His sleeves were rolled up to his elbows, revealing well-defined forearms. As he took his place in the driver's seat and began handling the reins, she couldn't help but notice his robust physique.

Probably from years of labor, Ivy mused to herself.

None of the young men she was acquainted with had ever appeared so well-endowed through their attire, at least where muscles were concerned. After all, they were gentlemen. Yet she found herself unable to ignore how his shirt rippled with every movement.

As they traveled along the dusty road, Ivy's attention was drawn to the breathtaking panorama before them. Rolling hills stretched toward the horizon, while wispy clouds crowned the distant indigo mountains. It was as if all the shades of blue on her old paint palette had come to life. A sudden yearning stirred within her to capture this majestic scene on canvas.

"All of this is ours, my dear," Allyn said, taking her hand in his with a possessive tenderness. "Do you love it as I do?" he asked, his voice imbued with pride.

"It's absolutely breathtaking," Ivy replied, a sense of inspiration filling her. "I would dearly love to begin capturing these lovely scenes on canvas as soon as I can procure the proper supplies."

"My dear, you are incredibly talented," Allyn acknowledged, "but wouldn't you agree that your time would be better spent learning to be the mistress of our household and upholding your social responsibilities?"

"I could do these in my spare time—" Ivy began, her enthusiasm undeterred.

"Tonight will be your debut as the Lady of Aramina," Allyn interrupted smoothly. "I've invited some of the most influential landowners to dine with us. If you prove to be a gracious hostess and fulfill all your duties to my satisfaction, then perhaps I'll reconsider it."

As they advanced along the winding path, the fields of coffee crops fanned out before them, their lush expanse shrinking to mere specks along the distant horizon. A handful of enslaved workers toiling diligently in the fields glanced up as they passed, their faces etched with the burdens of their labor.

Ivy turned to Allyn, her countenance a portrait of thoughtful concern. "Does this fazenda employ many enslaved workers?"

"Quite enough to keep things running smoothly," he replied, his tone as indifferent as his expression.

Her brow furrowed with earnestness as she pressed on, her voice soft yet imbued with a tender sympathy. "Yet, if Brazil were to abolish slavery, these men would then be entitled to a living wage and improved conditions, surely?"

Allyn's expression remained as impassive as he shook his head slightly. "My dear, Brazil's economic stability relies too heavily on the current system for such ideas to be feasible. To entertain the notion of change would only invite instability. For now, I suggest you concentrate on your role as my wife and the gracious hostess to our guests this evening," he said, patting her hand with a reassuring and subtly patronizing gesture.

In the distance, several tiny, weathered structures came into view, their dilapidated state making it clear that they were the slave quarters. They were a disheartening sight. Further down, a small group of homes in the lush valley beyond the grand house came into view.

Ivy leaned forward to get a better view of the landscape. "Is that another village?" she inquired, her eyes drawn to the scene.

Allyn shifted his attention to where Ivy was looking. "Ah, that?" he responded, his tone marked by a touch of irritation. "That is the tenant village, where the families who tend to the fazenda reside."

"You mean, indentured servants?" Ivy said, startled by her own outburst.

"They are working off a considerable debt to my father," Allyn explained. "Such arrangements are quite common here, I assure you. You need not concern yourself with their situation," he added dismissively.

Ivy sat quietly, struggling to reconcile the harsh reality of slavery, let alone the presence of indentured servants among them. The thought of such practices weighed heavily on her, leaving her to ponder what more disquieting truths about the estate might yet emerge.

That evening, Flávia expertly arranged Ivy's hair into an elegant coiffure, with a braid artfully cascading over her shoulder. As Ivy descended the stairs in a striking scarlet taffeta gown, Allyn's gaze remained locked on her, clearly captivated by her allure.

Ivy, in turn, observed the array of fashionable ladies around her, their elaborate hair accessories catching her eye. The two younger ladies, Catia and Belhina, were attired in bold hues of teal and fuchsia, their gowns revealing more of their arms and décolletage. In contrast, Gertrudes, the apparent matriarch of the group, wore a darker gown that demurely covered her from neck to wrist.

Their husbands—Senhores Avila, Santos, and Veiga—were noticeably eager to greet Ivy, their enthusiasm clearly fueled by recent triumphs in their business ventures. Senhor Gonzaga, a burly figure known for his reserved demeanor, stood apart as the sole unmarried guest among them.

Ivy's interest waned in the men's fervent discussion of business and politics, preferring instead to focus on the ladies' conversation about their preferred dressmakers and the latest endeavors of their charity organizations. Yet, as the men's debate grew increasingly heated, it became impossible for her to ignore their vigorous exchanges.

"To you, we owe our exceptional success this year!" Senhor Avila declared, lifting his glass in a toast to Allyn.

"Your praise is deeply appreciated, gentlemen," Allyn replied with a gracious nod.

"It's the least I could offer in acknowledgment of your invaluable support in revitalizing Aramina—a task that was no small feat." He then took a deliberate sip from his glass, savoring the satisfaction of the moment.

"You're one of us now!" Senhor Avila declared with a hearty laugh. "Besides, the state in which it was left was nothing short of disgraceful. Any *fazendeiro* who refuses to keep slaves is simply asking for trouble."

The men murmured their agreement, their voices a low chorus of consensus.

"Gentlemen, let us temper our judgments," Senhor Veiga said, raising his hand to calm the room. "The calamity that befell our former neighbors could easily have befallen any of us. I, for one, still consider them friends."

"They brought their misfortune upon themselves and will receive no sympathy from me!" Senhor Santos declared with forceful conviction.

"Indeed," Senhor Santos continued, "they should count themselves fortunate that Senhor Marsden permits them to reside on his estate, rather than being cast into prison or left to wander the streets."

"You are entitled to your own opinions, gentlemen," Senhor Veiga responded with resolute firmness. "However, out of respect for our hostess, let us redirect our conversation to more agreeable topics in the presence of our esteemed ladies."

The men exchanged thoughtful glances and fell silent.

As the men continued their meal, Ivy's thoughts remained fixed on their unwavering endorsement of slavery. The former owners of Aramina, whom they spoke of with such disdain, must have been people of profound principle to reject such a practice. Their refusal to partake in it spoke volumes about their integrity and honor. It suddenly occurred to her that these were the very individuals from the tenant village she had seen earlier that day.

A surge of conviction stirred within Ivy, compelling her to voice her thoughts. "Back at home," she stated, keeping her tone firm and poised, "lords considered it a point of honor to provide their servants with a fair wage for their labor. It was a mark of noble leadership. Forgive me, but the notion of purchasing and owning another person strikes me as antiquated and profoundly cruel." As she spoke, Ivy swiftly recognized that her sentiments might set her apart from the prevailing views around her.

"You must forgive my candor, Senhora Marsden," Senhor Gonzaga began, his resonant voice echoing through the dining room, capturing the attention of each guest. "There was a time when even reputable Englishmen exploited slaves mercilessly." He paused, the gravity of his statement permeating the atmosphere, and Ivy could sense the ripple of discomfort in the guests. "Such topics are perhaps best left unspoken in the company of ladies," he added his eyes narrowing as if scrutinizing their reactions.

Allyn interjected smoothly, attempting to steer the conversation. "Please excuse my wife, gentlemen. She is still acclimating to the realities of our world here. Rest assured, she will soon become accustomed to the nuances of managing a household in Brazil."

"My Belinha was much the same when she arrived from Portugal," Senhor Santos remarked with a chuckle. "She was a young woman brimming with notions gleaned from novels and tea rooms."

Belinha, cutting a piece of meat with the utmost grace, cast a sidelong glance before replying with a coy smile, "Yes, but now I find myself managing the household of servants almost single-handedly."

Ivy marveled at how the young woman, with such delicate grace, managed not only to tackle a hearty cut of meat but also to oversee a household of servants. Despite her reservations, the three ladies appeared amiable enough, and Ivy hoped to guide the conversation toward lighter topics, as Senhor Veiga had suggested. She was keen to avoid provoking further remarks from Senhor Gonzaga.

"Do you have any particular pastimes you enjoy?" Ivy inquired with genuine curiosity.

Belinha paused thoughtfully before responding, "Embroidery and riding my horse."

Allyn, seeming to seize the opportunity to redirect the discussion, added, "Ivy, my dear, also has a passion for painting, do you not?"

Caught off guard by his sudden revelation, Ivy stammered, "Um, yes, I do, very much." She couldn't help but find it peculiar that Allyn, who had previously shown little interest in her artistic endeavors, now chose to highlight them.

Allyn gestured toward a modest painting adorning the dining room wall, depicting a serene Northumberland landscape. "Observe this," he remarked with a touch of pride. "I was gifted this charming work of art on our wedding day. It captures the picturesque scenery of Chetwynd Village, where we hail from."

"How utterly exquisite!" exclaimed Belinha, her eyes widening in admiration.

"She was schooled by a well-respected French artist and is an excellent artist in her own right. Just today, she expressed an interest in picking up the brush again and capturing the beauty of our landscape," Allyn said.

"That is fascinating. Senhora Marsden, your artwork would be the perfect addition to our next charity auction!" said Catia as the other ladies chimed in.

Ivy gave them a coy smile. She was surprised to hear Allyn speak favorably about the subject after their discussion in the carriage. She was glad that things had taken a turn in her favor for once.

"Very impressive, Senhora Marsden," Senhor Gonzaga intoned, his deep, commanding voice reverberating through the softly illuminated room. He paused, letting the weight of his words linger. "However, you might discover that our conditions here differ significantly from those to which you are accustomed.

Supplies for such ambitious endeavors are a rare luxury, and the relentless heat can be unforgiving." His gaze remained unwavering and stern. "It would be prudent to first concentrate on mastering the intricacies of managing a household, as these trials may present challenges more formidable than you might expect."

Ivy, unperturbed, met his gaze with serene determination. "I appreciate your concern, Senhor Gonzaga," she replied with poised cheer, her knife gliding effortlessly through a plantain. "I'm confident in my ability to handle both the climate and the responsibilities. After all, challenges often bring out the best in me."

Chapter Seven

Tristão remained seated near the stables, far from the lively dinner party unfolding inside the house. The evening had settled into a tranquil hush, the twilight sky deepening as soft light spilled from the windows, contrasting with the fading day. A breeze stirred the valley, shifting the dense humidity that clung to the air and offering a brief respite from the thick heat.

His thoughts churned, restless and sharp. He could not ignore the nagging unease that lingered as he watched the house, his mind dissecting every movement inside, every word spoken between Allyn and the visiting *fazendeiros*. What business did they have together? What secrets were being shared in those whispered exchanges? The unknown festered, a gnawing uncertainty that clung to him.

The soft rustle of footsteps through the grass broke his concentration. He stood slowly, his instincts alert, his body tensing in quiet anticipation. It was neither the other male servants nor any of the guests, but Flávia—her form outlined in the dim glow spilling from the windows. The sight of her stirred something in him, a mix of caution and a deep anger he refused to acknowledge.

"Hello, Tristão—it has been far too long," Flávia's voice was warm, laced with an almost aching familiarity, as if no time had passed.

Tristão fought to keep his expression neutral, his gaze averted. He had no desire to look at her, to let her words reach him. "What is it that you want, Flávia?" His voice was a cold impenetrable shield—one he had long perfected to keep her at bay.

Her gaze softened, and a bittersweet smile tugged at her lips. "I am a lady's maid for the new Lady of Aramina. When I heard you had returned to take on the role of footman, I could not resist coming to see you," she said, her eyes sweeping over him—searching, prying, as though she expected to find some trace of what they had once been.

Tristão's jaw tightened, the tension anchoring him against the vestige of their old bond, which he forcefully pushed from his mind. "We have nothing left to discuss," he said, each word a command to himself as much as to her. His hands curled into fists at his sides, the impulse to reach out to her tempting but dangerous. He wouldn't let her in again.

"But there is still so much left unsaid between us," she persisted, her voice a soft plea, almost a whisper. She reached up to touch the gold chain around her neck, her fingers caressing the pendant as though it were a relic of their past. The green stone caught the light, and Tristão's chest tightened. He could almost hear the echoes of the memories attached to it.

"I keep this close to my heart," she whispered, her voice distant with nostalgia. "It never leaves my skin. When I mentioned it resembled your eyes, you had this gemstone set for me. Do you remember?"

Her familiar touch lingered in the air as she reached out, her fingers brushing his cheek with a sultry tenderness that made him want to recoil. The subtle caress, so intimate and knowing, threatened to erode his resolve.

He caught her hand instantly, the movement sharp, a warning he could not suppress. "That means nothing now," he said, his voice betraying the weight of his frustration. The past had no place between them anymore, yet its ghost still clung to him, unraveling the control he fought to maintain.

"You need not run from me, *meu amor*," Flávia murmured, her voice low and coaxing. "All I desire is to be close to you again. I only wish to love you."

The words hit him like a blow. The temptation gnawed at him, but he could not afford to succumb again. "And what of your treachery?" he asked, his voice a steely edge, betraying none of the turmoil.

Her eyes fell, and she seemed to shrink under the shame of her own regret. "I was foolish to run off with Mateus," she said, her voice faltering. "Not a day passed without my thoughts returning to you, yearning for your arms around me. There has been no one else for me, Tristão. I need to know that you can forgive me for my mistakes."

Her words stirred something profound within him, but it was not forgiveness. His heart burned with the fury of old wounds, still raw despite the time that had passed. "Damn you, Flávia!" The words were out before he could stop them, his anger flaring like fire. "He was one of my oldest friends, and now you dare to approach me as though we might reconcile?"

But Flávia was undeterred. She pressed her hand gently over his chest, the softness of her touch a stark contrast to the tempest inside him. It almost made him forget the bitterness and the betrayal, but he could not allow himself to fall back into those old patterns. He knew what she was capable of—her presence was intoxicating, her charm utterly disarming. Once ensnared, there would be no escaping it.

"Your touch is neither welcome nor required," he said, his voice biting as he removed her hand from his chest with a firm but deliberate motion. "If you have any regard for my family and me, then keep a vigilant eye on Marsden and report any whispers of his dealings to me. Loyalty is a principle I hold in the highest esteem."

Flávia's smile remained enigmatic and knowing. "Is that truly the sole purpose of your return? To spy on Senhor Marsden?" she asked, her tone almost teasing, though there was a challenge in it that Tristão didn't miss.

His answer came without hesitation, his resolve hardening in the face of her probing. "The reasons for my return are of no concern to you. However, from what I know of you, I suspect you've already ingratiated yourself with him. I intend to use that to my advantage."

Flávia met his words with a calm, steady confidence. "Just as you have made difficult choices for your family, so have I made sacrifices. Rest assured, my loyalty is steadfast. I will not fail you."

Ivy perched at the foot of the bed, her breath coming in uneven bursts. The evening's events had left her on edge, the weight of expectation pressing down on her as Allyn's wife. He had proudly shown her off to his neighbors. Though she had done her best to keep the conversation light and agreeable, the experience had been quite unpleasant, mainly when the subject of slavery arose.

She dabbed at the perspiration on her forehead, her nerves taut with anticipation. What should have been a mere formality as his companion now loomed before her. The thought of sharing the marriage bed left Ivy unsettled, a heavy knot tightening her chest.

Her hand reached for the bell, but the room swayed, the world tilting around her. With shallow breaths, the dizziness suddenly overcame her, leaving her powerless. Her vision blurred, the light in the room flickering out as the darkness claimed her.

When Ivy slowly came to, she found herself bathed in the soft light of her bedroom. Her mind felt sluggish, her senses foggy, but she felt the weight of concern in the air. A man, his silver hair neatly combed, stood by her bedside. He exuded quiet authority, his presence offering a calming steadiness as she struggled to regain her bearings.

"Father, what has happened to me?" she whispered, her voice weak, barely a murmur.

The man smiled, his eyes kind but shadowed with a trace of worry. "No, my dear, I am not your father. You've had a fall, I'm afraid. Nothing too dire, but it requires attention."

Ivy's attention fell to the leather bag resting on the bench at the foot of the bed. The promise of relief was tucked inside, and she focused on it with quiet desperation.

"Doctor, what steps should we take to ensure her swift recovery?" Allyn's voice sliced through the stillness, his tone betraying a hint of anxiety he could not entirely conceal.

The doctor adjusted his spectacles, his movements measured and composed. "Her body is still adjusting to this new climate. She will need ample rest and plenty of water for a full recovery. Have her maid continue applying this poultice until the swelling subsides. Additionally, I have prepared a tonic powder. Dissolve this in a glass of water for her to drink; it will help alleviate the headache."

The doctor pulled the envelope from his bag, his hands steady as he handed it to Allyn with a practiced nod. His every motion spoke of confidence, of years spent performing these very tasks.

"When might she be able to resume her normal activities?" Allyn asked, his voice softer now, tinged with concern.

The doctor pressed his spectacles back on the bridge of his nose, his expression serious. "Allow her a week. She needs to keep her head elevated and rest throughout the day. Ensure she drinks plenty of water. However, do not hesitate to summon me if she feels faint again."

With that, the doctor carefully gathered his belongings, offering Ivy a reassuring glance before closing the door behind him, with Allyn trailing after.

Left alone in the hush of her room, Ivy sank deeper into the pillows. She welcomed the quiet pull of sleep, grateful as it silenced her thoughts and uncertainties.

Chapter Eight

Ivy spent the next two days largely confined to her bed, finding solace in the absence of Allyn, who remained out late each evening. This respite afforded her precious moments to sketch and pen letters to her family. On the third day, sunlight cascaded through the window, accompanied by the cheerful chorus of chirping birds and the gentle rustle of palm leaves—comforting sounds that filled the air. This room was hers for the time being, yet an unsettling feeling of dislocation persisted in her heart.

Though she would not readily admit it, a pervasive sense of boredom soon enveloped her. Ivy settled onto the floor and began sifting through the contents of her trousseau chest. The room became suffused with the fragrant scent of lace handkerchiefs, their soft folds carefully wrapped in dried lavender, infusing the air with a subtle, calming aroma. Ivy's fingers then gently glided over the delicate hair ribbons, each a gift from her mother.

She then uncovered an old rag doll, packed by Evelyn. A surge of emotion welled within her, but she fought back the tears, allowing herself a brief moment to savor the comforting embrace of cherished memories. Time slipped away as she remained amidst her keepsakes, until the realization of noon's approach shattered her solitude.

At that moment, Flávia knocked softly and entered, bearing a tray laden with tea and sandwiches.

"Senhora! Do you require assistance finding something? Allow me to help," she offered, hurrying to set the tray upon a nearby table.

"It's quite alright, Flávia. I fear I'll go mad cooped up here, and I needed a distraction," Ivy confessed. She rose quickly, her nightgown swishing softly as she paced the room, her bare feet barely making a sound on the wooden floor.

With a warm smile, Flávia began carefully folding items back into the chest. "Before long, you'll be making calls like all the other ladies," she remarked, a note of optimism in her tone.

Despite Flávia's encouraging words, Ivy longed for something of greater substance than paying calls to occupy her in this exotic environment. Nothing felt familiar—not the architecture that loomed around her nor the vibrant sights and scents that wafted through the air. Voices swirled like a gentle, melodious cacophony, their murmurs and songs intertwining in a language that twisted the very sounds she had come to know. Having studied French and Latin, Ivy found herself both captivated and confounded by Portuguese. Its beauty was undeniable, yet it held its own complexities—rules she had yet to grasp fully.

Naturally, she would devote herself to mastering the language, but the notion of burying herself in books or enduring hours in a classroom offered little allure to Ivy. She longed to be enveloped by the vibrant culture of the land, evolving from a passive spectator into an active participant in the exquisite tapestry of life as it gracefully unfolded around her. Yet, painting had always been her sole means of achieving such immersion. The absence of her cherished tools gnawed at her, serving as a poignant reminder of her deep disquiet.

As Ivy roamed through the room, her thoughts meandering in tandem, she found herself captivated by the decorative patterns painted along the walls. Rows of once-vibrant floral motifs, now softened to a delicate teal and pale yellow, adorned the wainscoting and framed the crown molding with their faded splendor. Though time had dulled their colors, the designs sparked a flicker of inspiration within her. As she examined them more closely, it became evident that they were the work of a master artist, each petal and bloom now seeming to call out, urging her to restore their faded splendor.

Ivy could almost see the room transformed, the walls coming alive as fresh paint revived their former elegance, flooding the space with a new, radiant brilliance. In restoring these motifs, she imagined leaving a part of herself etched upon the walls, as the original artist had once done. Each brushstroke would not only breathe life into their beauty but also weave her spirit into the very essence of the room. She believed that through this artistic endeavor, she could find a deeper connection and a true sense of belonging within her new surroundings.

With renewed fervor, Ivy washed her face in the porcelain basin, the cool water cascading over her skin. She reached for a plush towel, pressing it tenderly against her cheeks and forehead, indulging in its softness as it absorbed the moisture.

Seated at her dressing table, Ivy felt Flávia's nimble fingers work with effortless grace, gathering her hair and sweeping it back before securing it with a delicate ribbon.

"You look as radiant as ever, Senhora. I trust the dinner went well a few nights ago?" Flávia remarked as she poured Ivy's tea into a porcelain cup. "You have not mentioned it, especially after you fell ill."

Not quite," Ivy replied, a faint smile touching her lips as she scrutinized her reflection. She rummaged through the table's drawers, her fingers brushing over the contents until they found what she sought. Ivy brought two pots of face powder and rouge to the surface, opening the first with a flick of her wrist. As she dabbed the powder onto her face, her words grew pointed, the puff pressing into her skin with a force that betrayed her irritation.

"The other night, Senhor Gonzaga made it abundantly clear that he deems me unsuitable for the role of lady of the house." Ivy held the puff for a moment longer, her grip tightening before tossing it back into the pot. Reaching for the rouge, she dabbed it onto her cheeks and continued, "He also mentioned that art tools are considered a luxury in these parts and difficult to procure."

"I would not heed that imbecile," Flávia replied, as she smoothed stray strands of Ivy's hair. He is alone for a reason; no sensible woman would marry such a fool. Indeed, rumor has it he was responsible for his first wife's untimely demise."

"I should hope not," Ivy said, her brow furrowing slightly as she massaged jasmine-scented lotion into her arms. The soothing fragrance rose to meet her senses, calming her as it perfumed the air.

"There may be someone who knows where to find such items," Flávia suggested, a glimmer of intrigue in her eyes.

"And who might that be?" Ivy asked, her curiosity piqued.

"The footman, Mr. Fontes," Flávia replied with a knowing smile.

"Can he? Very well, I shall speak with him directly," Ivy declared.

"Permit me—I would be delighted to convey your message, Senhora," Flávia offered, her expression betraying a hint of eagerness at the prospect of facilitating a meeting with Mr. Fontes.

"No, thank you, Flávia. I shall speak with him myself. Once you have helped me dress, please summon him immediately," Ivy insisted, her voice firm as she addressed Flávia, determination settling in her chest.

Flávia nodded, a faint flicker of hesitation in her eyes before she replied, "As you wish."

Ivy waited in the parlor until half past one, her patience unraveling with each passing moment. When Mr. Fontes still failed to appear, she moved with quiet determination into the small hallway adjoining the kitchen and seated herself by the open door. The view beyond was nothing short of captivating. Clouds, bathed in a celestial luminescence, drifted languidly across the azure expanse, casting a delicate, shadowy veil over the lush, verdant valley below. The distant mountains, garbed in muted greys and deep indigos, stood as ancient sentinels, their majestic forms framing the landscape with an air of timeless grandeur.

Ivy closed her eyes, letting the soft breeze soothe her troubled mind, carrying the faint scent of blooming wildflowers and a distant sense of calm. Yet, the certainty of her future with Allyn pressed heavily upon her, the thought of surrendering entirely to him sending a shiver of apprehension. She wrapped her arms tightly around herself to ward off the growing dread.

Since the incident at the ball, Ivy had meticulously avoided any chance to be alone with a man, a deliberate measure to shield herself from the profound fears she struggled to suppress. Now, the mere thought of Allyn discovering the violation she had endured filled her with profound trepidation, the fear of his reaction threatening to dismantle the fragile serenity she had so painstakingly maintained.

The helplessness of these thoughts clawed at her, a feeling she despised. Frustration simmered, driving Ivy to her feet, pacing in restless agitation. She needed an escape, a way to wrest back control. Painting—only painting—could lift her from this unbearable fragility. The resolve took hold swiftly, solidifying with each step. She would face this turmoil directly. She would seek out Mr. Fontes herself.

Ivy felt the sun's warmth penetrating her bonnet as she approached the tenant village just east of the Fazenda home. The quaint white cottages, with their blue shutters, complemented the estate's charm, offering a far more agreeable sight than the austere slave quarters.

Ivy's eyes followed the tenants as they moved through their routines—one woman scrubbing laundry, children playing along the path, their clothes and shoes pristine. There was something in how they carried themselves that seemed at odds with her expectations of their station.

Aside from their evident honor in denouncing slavery, Ivy was left in the dark about the circumstances that had led them to serve on their own land. Their story, she mused, was undoubtedly interwoven with Mr. Fontes' own narrative.

A man emerged from one of the cottages, casting Ivy a curious glance. He removed the napkin tucked into his collar, suggesting that her arrival had disrupted his meal. As she drew closer, Ivy noted his striking resemblance to the footman, surmising they might be related. His emerald eyes mirrored the same deep-set intensity, and his features bore the same chiseled lines.

"May I assist you, Senhora?" he inquired, his expression a mixture of surprise and curiosity. The sun cast dappled shadows across his face, highlighting his furrowed brow.

"Yes, please. Could you direct me to Mr. Fontes—our footman?"

"Certainly," he replied, gesturing toward a building at the edge of their community. "You will find him in the workshop just over there." Ivy directed her attention toward the modest structure, partially concealed by the overhanging branches and foliage of the surrounding trees.

"Thank you," she said, pausing briefly. "May I ask—what is this place?"

The man looked at her with mild confusion. "This is the Fontes family village. We are tenants working and residing on your fazenda, Senhora."

Ivy nodded, her thoughts turning over the concept. While the notion of tenants was familiar—many landowners, including her father, had generally appreciative tenants—she had never before encountered a situation where families were obligated to work under these circumstances.

"I see. And what is your role here, sir?" she asked.

"I am Joaquim Fontes, at your service," he said. "I oversee the coffee production on the estate. If there is nothing further, Senhora, I must take my leave."

"Of course," Ivy replied, her tone gracious and composed. Joaquim offered a polite nod before turning and retreating into the house.

As Ivy gently eased open the door to the workshop, she was greeted by the rich, inviting aroma of freshly cut wood mingled with the subtle scent of varnish. Upon entering, her eyes widened at the sight of exquisitely crafted furnishings displayed on numerous shelves. Ivy was astonished to find such fine works in this modest place, each piece seemingly worthy of the grandest homes of Europe.

The dark, lustrous finishes suggested the opulence of some exotic, luxurious wood that Ivy couldn't quite discern.

Reaching up to caress the smooth, gracefully curved leg of a small table, she was startled by a voice that seemed to emerge from the shadows with a familiar resonance.

"Fascinating, isn't it?"

Ivy spun around, her heart fluttering at the unexpected interruption.

"Mr. Fontes, I did not hear you come in!" she exclaimed, words tumbling out as she turned to face him. The flush spreading across her cheeks felt impossible to suppress, and she turned slightly, feigning distraction to regain control.

"Forgive me, Senhora. I merely wished to express that you happened upon one of our most prized treasures." With a magnetic presence, Mr. Fontes entered the room, his rugged yet polished appearance immediately capturing attention. As he set down his pack, a faint, evocative scent of polished wood mingled with the robust fragrance of bay rum, lingered in his wake.

Ivy turned to face him, her curiosity stirred. "Is that so? Why, then, is this piece so special?" she asked.

"For one thing, the table's twin graces the opulent chambers of Emperor Dom Pedro II himself," he replied, a note of pride in his voice as he swept open the window shade to flood the room with light.

Ivy found herself captivated by the sight before her. The table's rich, dark grain absorbed the sunlight streaming through the window, casting a soft, enchanting glow that danced across its surface.

"I don't believe I have seen wood quite like this before," Ivy remarked, her fingers tracing the smooth finish. "What sort of timber is this?"

"Brazilian rosewood," he replied, his voice as rich as the wood itself. He paused to meet Ivy's gaze, a faint smile playing on his lips.

"It's truly exceptional how one can transform a simple piece of wood into something so exquisite," Ivy commented, in awe of its craftsmanship.

Mr. Fontes selected a log from the pile, lifting it for Ivy to see, his eyes glowing eagerly. "In my hands, this humble timber can become whatever you envision. There's a hidden secret within its grain, just waiting to emerge," he said, his tone carrying a hushed intensity.

A shiver of intrigue rippled through Ivy though she carefully maintained her composure. She stepped back, letting her fingers glide over the polished edge of the table as she moved toward the workbench. There, she surveyed the array of tools and half-finished pieces with a discerning eye, each one whispering of its own potential and artistry.

The more she observed, the clearer it became that he was not merely a servant but a true artisan, each creation a testament to his exceptional skill and dedication, evident in every meticulously carved detail.

"Well, I must admit, I've never encountered a footman with such remarkable talent for crafting such furnishings," she said.

"I do what is necessary," Mr. Fontes replied, his tone adopting a more straightforward quality. "Now, how can I be of service, Senhora?"

Ivy squared her shoulders, grounding herself in the authority she needed to convey. "Mr. Fontes, I waited more than an hour for you in my parlor this afternoon. I take it my message did not reach you?"

He met her look, unfazed by her words. "I did receive your message, Senhora," he replied smoothly, the hint of mischief lingering in his tone. "However, your husband has tasked me with crafting a card table for his study. I was engaged in sourcing the necessary materials to begin. I hope my delay hasn't caused you too much distress," he said offering a curt nod.

As he spoke, Ivy's attention drifted to his shirt, drawn to the fabric halfway unbuttoned, revealing a glimpse of his well-defined chest. She turned away, unwilling to dwell on the sight any longer, but the image lingered, etched into her mind.

Mr. Fontes then stepped beside her, and when she turned to face him, his expression was unreadable, a mask of calm that only heightened the tension between them.

Leaning just a fraction closer, his voice—rich and deep—rumbled in her ear. "See for yourself." Her breath caught as he unfurled a set of plans before her—each curve and intricate design meticulously sketched, promising something grand and beautiful. "This is what you can expect," he said, a hint of pride and excitement coloring his voice.

The proximity—his presence so close—was overwhelming, yet she dared not pull away. He allowed her a moment to take in the details before rolling the draft back into its scroll-like form. Her eyes fluttered when he brushed past her as if she had been roused from a dream, the pull of his presence almost palpable.

She watched as Mr. Fontes reached for a set of chisels and a measuring tape, the tools making a soft, metallic clink as he collected them. Ivy gathered herself together, brushing her hair back and clearing her throat before addressing him once more.

"There is still the matter for which I summoned you," she began, her voice firm.

He turned, his expression unreadable, but a glint of curiosity flickered across his features. "And what might that be?"

"Mr. Fontes, I will require art supplies, and I understand you can help procure them."

He paused for a moment, then raised an eyebrow, his voice carrying a note of intrigue. "For what purpose, exactly?"

"Painting landscapes," she replied. "It is a cherished pastime of mine. I also intend to restore the motifs throughout the house."

"Quite an endeavor you're setting out on, Senhora. Even the most skilled artists must be truly committed to restoring such images."

Ivy straightened, clasping her hands to suppress the frustration bubbling beneath the surface. "I am very committed," she said. "Otherwise, I wouldn't have sought you out myself. Now, will you help me or not?" Her words carried a sharper edge than she intended, but she couldn't afford to temper them—not when he had already seen her at her most vulnerable.

Setting down his tools, Mr. Fontes brushed the dust from his hands before responding. "There's a small mercantile in the village run by a family friend—a master artisan rather than just a merchant."

"And you're certain he will have all the materials I require, considering how remote we are?" Ivy asked, her eyes narrowing slightly.

He curled his lips in what seemed to Ivy a knowing smile—a maddening echo of their first encounter.

"He'll have what you need, Senhora. I assure you, his supplies will be more than adequate for your task."

"Splendid," she said, though her clipped tone betrayed her irritation. "When can I expect you to have the carriage ready? I want to leave sometime today."

"One step at a time, Senhora," he replied, his unhurried tone stoking her frustration. First, he had ignored her summons; now, he was her only hope for securing the supplies. Did he not understand how vital this project was to her?

"Your husband keeps me quite occupied, and there's still much to do before I drive him to Senhor Gonzaga's fazenda this evening. They leave for São Paulo in the morning, as I'm sure you know."

"Yes, of course," Ivy replied briskly, lifting her chin as if to reinforce her words. "My husband always ensures I'm kept well-informed of his business travels." She pursed her lips briefly, a subtle gesture to mask the white lie—Allyn rarely communicated anything important. Steering the conversation elsewhere, she continued. "Since your schedule appears quite full, might you suggest someone else to assist me?"

Mr. Fontes leaned casually against the table's edge, his arms crossed as he studied her. Ivy felt his demeanor shift, mild amusement giving way to something more akin to admiration, though she couldn't quite place it.

"It's clear, Senhora, that you're determined to acquire these materials as soon as possible," he said, his tone warmer now. "I'm at your service. Would tomorrow morning suffice?"

"Yes, that would be fine," she said.

"Very well. The carriage will be waiting by the entrance at seven o'clock."

His eyes rested on her for a moment, a depth of recognition in his expression. His voice softened. "It's my pleasure, Senhora.

Ivy nodded once, then turned and left the workshop. As she walked away, a strange flutter of anticipation stirred within her. There was something else—a subtle change in the air, an unspoken hope she couldn't quite define.

As Ivy entered the house, Flávia approached with concern etched in her features.

"The senhor was searching for you," she said. "He was quite distressed upon finding you absent from your room."

"Yes, I've just spoken with Mr. Fontes about the matter we discussed," Ivy replied with calm assurance.

"Oh, I did inform him, Senhora, but he seemed rather unsettled," Flávia added.

"I shall speak with him now," Ivy said, her resolve quickening her steps as she moved with purpose.

"What possessed you to venture out to the tenants' quarters alone?" Allyn demanded, his voice a mixture of frustration and concern.

Ivy, taken aback by the sharpness of his tone, remained composed in her chair. "My bruise has healed, and I felt well enough to inquire about procuring art supplies. Yet your tone suggests I was in grave peril. Do you not trust your tenants?" she replied, her voice steady.

Allyn poured a generous measure of brandy into his glass and downed it in one swift motion. "It's not a question of trust, but rather the simple truth that those less fortunate may not always act in our best interest," he said, his tone laden with gravity.

"I find it hard to believe that, especially when they seem so dedicated to their work," Ivy countered.

"There have been rumors of political unrest throughout the countryside," Allyn continued, his voice darkening. "The recent drought has left many Northern regions in ruin, driving vagabonds southward. Moreover, there's always the risk of trouble from runaway slaves. We must remain vigilant."

"Allyn, if there is even a hint of danger, why must you leave tomorrow?" Ivy asked, her voice edged with concern.

"My dear, while I may be called away on business from time to time, I assure you that I've taken every precaution to ensure your safety," he replied.

"Is it truly necessary? I doubt I'll feel reassured knowing there are armed guards stationed about," Ivy said, a touch of sarcasm coloring her words.

Allyn's demeanor shifted abruptly as he set down his glass and moved closer to her. "How dare you question my decisions!" he snapped. "Might I remind you that it is not your place to judge what our tenants might do?"

Ivy leaned back, maintaining her composure as he loomed over her. "If you continue to defy me, I will have no choice but to curtail your indulgences," he warned, his tone icy. "I suggest you do not compel me to take such measures."

Allyn poured himself another glass of brandy, the act seeming to soothe his agitation. Ivy remained silent, her demeanor calm. "Forgive me, Ivy," he said, his voice softening. "It has been an exceptionally trying week, and we've yet to enjoy a night together as husband and wife. Can you find it in your heart to forgive me?"

Ivy nodded, a rueful smile touching her lips. "You're right, of course. What was I thinking, venturing out alone?" she replied, shaking her head slightly.

"My dear, you look as though I've wronged you deeply," Allyn said, his voice tender. "I assure you, I am only trying to manage the fazenda responsibly and keep you safe." He knelt before her, taking her hand in his.

Ivy looked at him, her expression softening. "Would you accompany me to the village in the morning?" she asked.

Allyn's face fell. "I have a pressing meeting in São Paulo that I cannot reschedule," he said regretfully.

"I understand," Ivy said, her gaze falling to the floor.

Seeing her disappointment, Allyn sighed. "Never mind the meeting. I will accompany you, if you'll forgive my previous tone."

He pressed a gentle kiss to her hands and then leaned in for a more tender kiss. Ivy returned the kiss but pulled away with a sigh.

"I'm simply exhausted. I think I shall retire now," Ivy said.

"Goodnight then, my dear," Allyn said softly, watching her as she left the room.

Chapter Nine

A restless night had left Ivy weary, her thoughts consumed by the prior encounter with Mr. Fontes. The strange, magnetic pull she felt in his presence lingered, defying her attempts to rationalize it. She had lain awake, remembering his steady gaze and that fleeting, forbidden moment replaying repeatedly. Was it merely her long isolation from men that had swept her into something so absurd? Or was there something more insidious at work, something she dared not name?

The rhythmic jostle of the carriage beneath her helped her steady her mind as the village of Belas Águas came into view. Its alabaster buildings gleamed like polished ivory in the bright light and the hum of activity from the square carried on the warm breeze.

"Thank you for graciously accompanying me today," Ivy said, her tone infused with warm regard intended to soften Allyn's somewhat irritable demeanor.

"Indeed, my dear," Allyn responded with a polite nod, though his tone remained notably devoid of enthusiasm.

Ivy shifted her attention to the lively scene outside, hoping the picturesque charm of the village might soothe the unease still stirring within her. She admired the row of alabaster buildings lining the village square, their pristine façades gleaming like polished ivory beneath the sunlight. Each edifice stood as a paragon of Portuguese colonial architecture, with gracefully curved stucco roofs, elegantly recessed windows, and striking blue borders that appeared to dance with the shifting light.

Yet, the true gem was the church, majestically perched atop a verdant hill, its spire reaching heavenward and casting a serene, watchful presence over the quaint village.

The rhythmic clopping of the horses' hooves and the gentle creaking of the carriage wheels echoed through the bustling avenue, drawing the attention of fruit vendors at the lively outdoor market. Their vibrant stalls, overflowing with a bounty of lush, tropical fruits, injected a vivid burst of color into the scene, creating a harmonious symphony of sights and sounds that embodied the very essence of this idyllic locale.

The merchant's shop stood unassuming past the bustling market square, its exterior modest and humble. The only hint of its presence was the carved wooden sign swaying gently near the front door, a subtle proclamation of its proprietor's name.

Mr. Fontes helped Ivy down from the carriage with a gallant and effortless flourish. His firm yet gentle touch lingered just long enough to stir the same flutter she had pondered over the night before. The magnetic pull Ivy felt in his presence returned, unbidden yet unmistakable. As their hands brushed, a sudden warmth coursed through her—a disconcerting echo of the feelings she had tried to dismiss. It was fleeting yet vivid, a connection that vanished as swiftly as it had appeared, leaving her unsettled and contemplative.

She caught her breath, momentarily disoriented by the sensation, before regaining her composure as they proceeded indoors. With a shared glance that hinted at an unspoken connection, she eagerly followed him inside, her curiosity piqued.

The resounding jangle of a brass bell heralded their entrance, summoning a young man who approached with a broad, cheerful smile that bespoke genuine warmth.

"Is Senhor Da Silva at home?" Mr. Fontes inquired, his tone smooth and polished. "Please let him know an old friend has come to visit," he added with a genial nod.

The young man acknowledged the request with a swift nod and disappeared behind a door. Seizing the moment, Ivy allowed her eyes to wander, taking in the quaint charm of the small room. Woven baskets of every conceivable size lined the gray stone floor, their earthy textures contrasting with the cool hardness beneath.

She spotted a few knick-knacks within a tall curio cabinet—carefully crafted ships suspended in bottles, carved tribal masks, and other intriguing mementos that evoked the allure of faraway lands and forgotten stories.

"One could hardly mistake this place for a shop, could they?" Allyn remarked with a hint of disdain as he surveyed the scene with a critical eye.

Before Ivy could respond, the sound of hearty laughter filled the room as an older, robust man emerged. His frame, exuding a vibrant energy, was matched by a face that split into a grin stretching from ear to ear, his small eyes twinkling with unrestrained joy.

"Look at you! I can hardly believe my eyes!" Senhor Da Silva exclaimed, his voice ringing with genuine delight as he moved to draw Mr. Fontes into a hearty embrace. The warmth of their reunion was unmistakable, their easy camaraderie reflecting years of close friendship.

"I'm just relieved I managed to catch you before you set off on another one of your adventures," Mr. Fontes replied. The bond between the two men was evident, showcasing a deeply cherished friendship.

"Ah, I've finally given up that way of life," Senhor Da Silva said, his tone infused with contentment and an almost child-like exuberance. As they spoke, Ivy looked on, eager to uncover the stories etched into the face of this curious figure. He quickly turned his attention toward her as she stood near one of the cabinets.

"Senhor Da Silva, allow me to present Senhora Marsden of the Aramina Fazenda," said Mr. Fontes, his voice imbued with reverence as he made a formal gesture.

Feeling the weight of the moment, Ivy nodded gracefully, determined to maintain her poise despite the flutter of nerves in her stomach.

"What a pleasure it is to make your acquaintance," Senhor Da Silva declared with a graceful bow, his eyes twinkling with genuine admiration. "I have encountered but two other women of such exquisite beauty in these parts—my dear wife and this young gentleman's mother," he said with a nod toward Mr. Fontes. His heartfelt words resonated with Ivy, leaving her deeply moved and filled with quiet gratitude.

Allyn edged closer behind Ivy, his presence a subtle yet unmistakable shadow that cast a hush over the room, heightening the tension.

"And here, I present to you my esteemed *patrão*, the Lord of Aramina," Mr. Fontes declared, his voice rich with measured respect.

"Welcome to my modest establishment, Senhor; I am at your service," said Senhor Da Silva with a gracious nod. His smile was warm yet subtly guarded, a flicker of caution in his eyes.

Allyn Marsden, exuding an air of superiority, acknowledged the welcome with a curt nod, his eyes devoid of any genuine appreciation. "Mr. Fontes," he commanded, in a frigid tone, "attend to the supplies with all due speed. I have pressing matters at the plantation and cannot afford to linger."

Mr. Fontes took Senhor Da Silva aside. Their conversation slipped effortlessly into Portuguese until Senhor Da Silva turned his attention to Ivy.

"May I inquire if you have a list for me, Senhora Ivy?" he asked with an air of cultivated courtesy.

"Indeed, you may, Senhor Da Silva. Here it is," Ivy responded, her smile exuding warmth and poise. Senhor Da Silva then offered a courteous nod and guided them toward a curtained door.

As Ivy stepped across the room's threshold, she was immediately enchanted by the scene before her. Expansive wooden cabinets lined the walls, showcasing an exquisite array of canvases, easels, and brushes, each item meticulously arranged as though part of a hidden painter's trove. Her gaze was irresistibly drawn to the central alcove, where a stunning display of glass jars shimmered in the soft light. Each jar held a spectrum of pigment powders, their colors unfurling in a mesmerizing kaleidoscope—cobalt blues, radiant oranges, sunny yellows, and delicate lavenders intertwining in a visual feast that left Ivy spellbound.

With exacting precision, Senhor Da Silva set about gathering the items on her list. Ivy watched with keen interest as he wrapped each parcel in fine, crisp paper and secured them with lengths of twine. His fluid, precise movements were reminiscent of a maestro conducting a grand symphony. The weathered lines of his round face, each a testament to a rich life, and his dark, lengthy braid streaked with silver imparted a sense of gentle wisdom. His warm eyes, alight with a lively twinkle, hinted at countless untold stories. Ivy delighted in his striking resemblance to the jolly Father Christmas from her childhood cards, though he lacked the snowy beard and red attire. His white apron and effortless presence in the workshop of wonders evoked a similar warmth. When he completed his task, two large wicker baskets overflowed with meticulously wrapped brushes, pristine canvases, and a few paint tubes from a prior batch.

Finally, when he and Mr. Fontes loaded the baskets and easels onto the carriage's rear, Senhor Da Silva promised Ivy that he would craft a batch of exquisite and exotic colors tailored to her discerning tastes. "If there is a particular shade you desire, Senhora," he declared with a confident smile, "I shall create a pigment especially for you." He bid her farewell with a nod and a warm clasp of her hand.

As Mr. Fontes helped Ivy back into the carriage, his touch lingered for a heartbeat longer than necessary, a subtle pressure in his palm that sent an unexpected thrill coursing through her. The sensation was not unlike the flutter she had felt the day before—a surge of excitement that fluttered low in her chest, making her pulse quicken despite herself. She forced calmness to her demeanor, but inside, something stirred, urging her to acknowledge it, even as she tried to bury it beneath her composure.

Allyn, seated beside her in the carriage and exuding an air of disinterest, inquired, "I trust you have secured everything you needed?"

"I believe I have everything I need for now," Ivy replied, her tone reflecting a quiet sense of satisfaction.

Once settled, Allyn's presence beside her did little to dispel the stirring thoughts that invaded her mind. The sound of wheels turning against the cobblestone road echoed in the quiet space between them. As the carriage rolled back to the house, Ivy felt a profound inner triumph surround her, draping her in a cloak of accomplishment. Beneath her serene exterior, however, subtle empowerment simmered, marking this trip as a personal victory in securing her artistic provisions.

The moments with Mr. Fontes—the warmth of his touch, the proximity of his presence—stirred something within her, a mix of excitement and unease that she could not quite reconcile. Ivy's heart quickened at the thought of him, a reaction that unsettled her, especially after everything she had endured. Why did she feel this pull, this strange magnetism toward a man she barely knew? The doubts rose; the fears of being vulnerable and hurt again crept in, but she couldn't deny the thrumming excitement that refused to be ignored. It both frightened and thrilled her in equal measure.

Chapter Ten

The residence at Aramina, though not particularly grand or exquisite, possessed a unique charm. Its design borrowed elements from the village's architecture, blending colors and styles in an eclectic manner that transcended the simplicity of a farmhouse. Surrounded by lush greenery and vibrant blooms, it exuded the allure of a chateau. Each room, adorned with subtle refinements, seemed to create an ambiance that beckoned inhabitants to leave behind their remote surroundings, and embrace the genteel charm of a quaint European village.

If she had to remain a captive, she could at least find solace in the beauty of her confinement. Yet, the house felt far from home. She hoped to infuse it with life using the paints she had gathered. With Allyn due to return in a few days, she wanted to make this place feel like her own in some way.

The manservants had cleared the path for Ivy to begin her work upstairs. Upon entering the farthest spare bedroom, she was immediately struck by the large wardrobe dominating the space. A thick layer of dust suggested it had been untouched for some time. Ivy took a rag and wiped it down, revealing a smooth, dark rosewood finish beneath. She also noticed the letter 'F' delicately etched into the doorknob design.

Ivy pushed open the double doors with serene resolve, her glance sweeping over the seemingly vacant space.

However, as she was about to close them, an unusual sight captured her attention. A rectangular parcel lay carefully on the wardrobe's inner wall, arousing her curiosity. With a steady hand, she reached for it, lifting it from its resting place. As she set it down, a shiver ran through her, and the hairs on the back of her neck rose at the sudden surge of intrigue.

For a moment, Ivy hesitated, her fingers tracing the outline of the parcel's wrapping.

The mystery of what lay within seemed to pulse with a distinct allure. Nevertheless, the lure of the unknown proved irresistible. With a deliberate motion, she swiftly unwrapped the folds of paper.

Before long, a framed portrait revealed itself. The dark-haired woman depicted exuded an air of elegance, her expression a beguiling blend of allure and restraint. A letter 'A' was gracefully inscribed atop the opulent frame, its gilded embellishments shimmering with intricate gold leafing that suggested a concealed grandeur.

There was something utterly captivating about her, a quality that drew the eye with irresistible magnetism. Perhaps it was how the painter had immortalized her piercing emerald eyes, capturing their depth and intensity with unparalleled skill.

A soft thump echoed through the quiet space as Ivy drew the painting from its wrapping. She glanced down and spotted an oval pendant on the floor, its thick glass gleaming softly in the light. Framed in intricate filigree, it hung from a silver chain. Inside, tiny magenta petals were woven with a dark lock of hair, creating an intricate pattern. The craftsmanship mesmerized Ivy, stirring her curiosity. The dark hair did not match Allyn's, suggesting it may have once belonged to the lady in the portrait.

Ivy held it up beside the portrait. The resemblance was undeniable; it seemed the dark-haired lady wore the very same one around her neck, adding a mystique to her already compelling allure.

She carefully wrapped the necklace in a silk handkerchief, tucking it into a velvet-lined jewelry box nestled within the depths of her dressing table drawer. After safely concealing the pendant, Ivy felt a surge of inspiration ignite her spirit. She retrieved her paint palette, dabbing vibrant dollops of umber, yellow, and white with eager enthusiasm.

As the evening progressed, Ivy became entranced by the rhythm of her brush strokes, each movement a dance upon the plaster canvas. The motifs transformed under her deft hand, each curve and hue reflecting her burgeoning creativity. Time slipped away as she immersed herself in her work, her surroundings fading into a blur of color and light.

By the time twilight deepened into night, Ivy had breathed life into every spare room, as well as the hallway. Her new apron bore the vivid traces of her artistic endeavor—splotches of red, yellow, and ocher painting a testament to her industriousness. Her hair, now an untamed cascade of color-streaked chaos, resembled the end of a paintbrush more than anything else. Nevertheless, Ivy remained blissfully indifferent to her disheveled appearance. Her room finally felt like a refuge, filled with the heart of her spirit and imagination.

Ivy stood poised before the open French doors, her easel and canvas arranged with an artist's precision as if she were on the cusp of conjuring a masterpiece. Beyond her, an enchanting panorama of verdant splendor bathed in the soft glow of morning. The fragrance of dew-kissed earth, mingling with the delicate scent of flowers, wafted through the air, each breath a tantalizing promise of artistic inspiration.

With a soft sigh, she closed her eyes, savoring the crisp mountain air that gently brushed her cheeks. The majestic scene extended a silent, intimate welcome to this idyllic retreat, enveloping her in an atmosphere of serenity.

"Ahem."

As her eyes sprang open, she was immediately drawn to the doorway where Mr. Fontes stood—a rugged figure framed by the threshold. In each hand, he carried a wooden toolbox, and his bemused smile softened the intensity of his features. Ivy's heartbeat quickened in a visceral reaction to his presence. However, an unexpected sense of ease washed over her rather than the usual discomfort she experienced alone in a man's presence.

"Forgive the intrusion, Senhora," he intoned, his voice a low, velvety timbre. "Here are the pigments you requested, carefully blended by my own hand." He gestured toward one toolbox. "The milk paints are in these tins," he said, then indicated the second box with a slight nod. "And these contain the oil paints I've prepared for you."

"Yes, you may place them on the table. Thank you," Ivy replied, keeping her voice composed despite the flutter of anticipation in her chest. Her fingers betrayed a subtle tremor as she deftly brushed back the wayward strands of hair that had slipped from her ribbon. As she straightened her posture, she realized her dressing gown buttons had come slightly undone, exposing more cleavage than was proper before a manservant. She swiftly secured them with a practiced, discreet gesture, ensuring that no hint of impropriety would intrude upon the moment.

"If there is nothing further, I shall take my leave," he said, giving a brief but respectful nod.

As he turned to go, an impulse took hold of her, urging her to delay his departure.

"Mr. Fontes," she called out. "Would you happen to know the name of that mountain range? I see them daily, but I have yet to ask Flávia."

She gestured toward the horizon, feeling a flicker of warmth in his regard. Despite the lingering reservations in her mind, rooted in a deep-seated distrust of men, she could not deny the growing sense of calm his presence instilled with each encounter. It was as if the rugged landscape before her mirrored the strength and tranquility that emanated from him—unspoken yet profoundly felt, challenging the walls she had carefully built.

He entered the foyer and positioned himself with arms crossed by the French doors, where the light played upon the dark sheen of his hair, accentuating the emerald depths of his eyes. "So, you've developed quite an admiration for our mountains?" he remarked, his glance sweeping over the canvas with an appreciative eye.

"They're quite lovely," said Ivy.

"The Serra Mantiqueira has a way of captivating anyone fortunate enough to behold them," he remarked, a hint of reverence in his tone. "There is a legend among the natives, where they are known as the mountains that weep."

"Do they truly—weep I mean?" The question lingered between them, a soft invitation. Her lips tugged upward almost against her will, the faint curve betraying the curiosity she had not meant to reveal. Then, as if something in the air had shifted, a warm sensation spread across her chest—subtle and unfamiliar. The moment settled around her, but she quickly pressed her fingers to her dressing gown as if to steady herself.

"They do," he replied with a playful glint in his eyes. "An array of streams weave through the landscape, their winding paths adding an air of authenticity to the legend."

The gentle allure of their conversation began to create a comforting intimacy between them, one that Ivy could not ignore. With a quiet effort, she shifted her focus back to her work, a twinge of propriety stirring within her, urging her to regain control.

Determined to reestablish her composure, Ivy meticulously opened several jars of paint, carefully transferring their contents onto her palette.

"You've done a marvelous job blending these colors," she remarked, assessing each hue.

"I learned from the best," Mr. Fontes replied, a faint smile touching his lips. "Senhor Da Silva taught me some of his techniques many years ago."

"Did he?" Ivy mused, thoughtfully dipping her brush into a pool of vibrant paint. "I went through his first batch of mixed pigments within days, but I'll need a broader palette to fully capture the hues of these blossoms. Even when blending red and white with blue paints, the pink shades remain elusive."

Her brush hovered above the canvas as she gestured with a hint of frustration. Mr. Fontes leaned out of the open French doors, plucking a cluster of vibrant blooms from a bush just outside, where the garden stretched toward the distant mountains. "Senhor Da Silva has a remarkable gift for transforming natural pigments into something extraordinary," he remarked, turning the blossoms over in his hand. "Perhaps I'll take him a few of these and see what magic he can work."

"Do you suppose he might be inclined to share some of his secrets with me—about his pigment methods, I mean?" Ivy inquired, the question escaping her lips as she felt a rush of intrigue surge within her.

"That remains to be seen. He's typically quite secretive about his methods. However, he does appear quite taken with you. Yesterday, he even asked when you might return for another visit," he said, a hint of amusement in his voice.

"Good heavens!" She laughed, startled by her own sudden outburst. "Might you be so kind as to drive me into the village tomorrow morning?" she inquired, her voice light with enthusiasm.

"I'm not so sure that is a good idea—at least for now," he replied, his tone firm yet tinged with a hint of concern.

Her eyes narrowed with restrained irritation. "Is it because of those buffoons my husband insists on having loitered about the grounds?" she quipped, her tone edged with both annoyance and amusement.

A glimmer of humor danced across his features as he leaned casually against the doorframe, arms folded with an air of relaxed authority.

"I imagine your husband would not be pleased in any regard," he observed, his tone measured yet subtly imbued with a trace of mischief.

Ivy drew a sharp breath, startled by the unexpected surge of audacity within her. The brush in her hand met the canvas with a forceful sweep, mirroring the defiant spark kindling in her heart. "Well, I'm not so sure I care!" she declared, the intensity of her words surprising even herself. However, as swiftly as her boldness had ignited, it receded, leaving a trace of vulnerability behind. "But you're probably right," she conceded softly, her defiance dissolving into a sigh of reluctant acceptance.

Turning back to her canvas, she dipped her brush into the paint with deliberate, rhythmic strokes. "I should not keep you from your other duties," she said, her voice calm but subtly inviting, as though offering him the chance to linger a moment longer if he wished.

"I'll leave you to your work," Mr. Fontes said, offering her one last, lingering look. "I'm keen to see how these colors will bring your scene to life. The Serra Mantiqueira, with all its wild, untamed splendor, may forever elude capture, but I have every confidence that you'll unveil its true spirit." He paused, his eyes steady and intent, carrying both challenge and admiration. Then, with a noble stride, he walked past the blooming garden. As he moved, the majestic mountains in the background framed his retreat, blending him seamlessly with the verdant landscape as if he were a natural extension of its formidable presence.

Left in the quiet wake of his departure, Ivy's eyes lingered on the spot where Mr. Fontes had disappeared, her thoughts momentarily suspended between his words and her own artistic musings. Returning to her easel, she studied her half-finished landscape, her attention drawn once more to the flowers she couldn't quite capture with the colors on hand. Frustration crept in as she realized they still lacked the vibrancy she envisioned.

Turning her focus away, her eyes wandered across the room until they landed on the faded motifs along the dining room's border. The once-vibrant designs, now muted and lifeless, beckoned her. Perhaps, she mused, this was something she could bring back to life while awaiting the perfect hues for her landscape. With renewed purpose, she took a brush from the nearby wicker basket and dipped it into the thick yellow paint. She slowly began painting life into the faded flowers.

Time slipped away unnoticed as Ivy became lost in her work. Before she knew it, bowls brimming with blended colors lined the floor, creating a vibrant path that led from her workspace out into the hall. Her wooden palette, once bare, now overflowed with a dazzling array of hues, each more striking than the last—a testament to her dedication and creativity.

At last, she stepped back to admire her handiwork in its entirety. The walls, once drab and lifeless, were now adorned with a profusion of bright yellow orchids, twisting green vines, and mauve roses that seemed to bloom right from the plaster. It was as though the very spirit of the garden outside had spilled indoors, flourishing under her careful hand. The worn taupe walls had become merely a backdrop, a canvas upon which life had been restored in full, vivid color.

A pleased smile curved Ivy's lips as she took in the scene, pride swelling within her. She stood for a few moments, basking in the transformation. The sun, now casting long shadows across the room, had shifted its position in the sky, silently reminding her that the afternoon was well underway. Before she could glance at the clock to confirm the time, Mr. Fontes' familiar voice interrupted her reverie.

"This is truly lovely, Senhora. Just as when my—" he paused as if moved by a distant memory before he resumed with quiet composure, "as when they were first brought to life." As he walked closer to the wall, the wistfulness in his voice revealed the stirring of something long forgotten. The revived motifs seemed to have touched a place within him that he rarely allowed himself to revisit.

"You knew the original artist?" Ivy asked.

"I certainly did," he replied, his expression softening with a hint of nostalgia.

"She must have been quite extraordinary," remarked Ivy.

With a gentle nod and a faint smile gracing his lips, he replied, "Her influence on this house was truly profound." His eyes shone with quiet reverence, reflecting cherished memories Ivy could only envision.

For a fleeting moment, Ivy's heart fluttered—an exhilarating yet strange sensation as she found herself surprisingly at ease in his presence once more. It was the first time since that ill-fated ball that she no longer felt the need to remain on guard. Yet this newfound comfort also stirred a lingering wariness. Had she not once been similarly enraptured by Henry's charm, only to discover the scoundrel beneath?

The thought was enough to pull her back from the brink of her feelings. Seeking distraction, she turned away, rinsing her brushes in water as if the simple task could clear her mind as effectively as it cleansed the bristles. She allowed herself a graceful return to the conversation, hoping to obscure her rising apprehension.

"As I mentioned earlier, I am quite intrigued to see what other hues your friend might bring forth." She continued with a controlled breath, maintaining a pleasant tone despite conflicting emotions.

"If it originates from nature, Senhor Da Silva can capture it perfectly. We have the very source right here." With a flourish, he drew the same pink flower from his trouser pocket, its petals still vibrant from the morning's pick.

"What I am most eager to learn," Ivy said, her eyes fixed intently on the flower from where she stood at the table, "is how he achieves such marvelous hues."

He chuckled softly, a glint of mischief in his eyes. "Ah, but Senhor Da Silva guards his methods with a closely held secrecy. Only a select few are privy to his craft. I daresay Senhor Marsden might not relish the thought of another day-long expedition away from pressing matters," he said with a mischievous grin.

"Would you consider driving me there?" she asked, her voice a deliberate blend of poise and purpose. She made a quiet effort to steady her tone, each word chosen carefully to conceal the eagerness rising just beneath the surface. She glanced in his direction, watching for the slightest hint of assent, but when she saw none, she continued. "It would spare my husband the trouble of another trip into the village." She paused, drawing a breath before adding, "And perhaps Senhor Da Silva could be persuaded to craft a pigment to capture the delicate hue of these petals within this piece. I've never encountered such a shade in nature."

She held it up, her eyes examining its intricate design. "The craftsmanship is rather unusual, yet undeniably exquisite, wouldn't you agree?"

Mr. Fontes stepped closer, his eyes narrowing as he took the necklace from her hand. "Where did you happen upon this?" he inquired, his voice suddenly more intense. Ivy noticed the subtle shift in his demeanor, a tension that hadn't been there before, and it only deepened her intrigue.

"It was in an old wardrobe, upstairs," Ivy began, her voice steady despite her apprehension that she might have inadvertently offended him, "alongside a portrait of a woman in one of the spare bedrooms. Have you seen this before?" Her eyes searched his face for a flicker of recognition.

For a moment, Mr. Fontes was silent, his attention locked on the necklace in his hand, lost in contemplation. At last, he shook his head, a quiet determination settling over him.

"It doesn't matter," he said, his voice steady, infused with gentle authority. "This is your home, and everything within it rightfully belongs to you." With a deliberate gesture, he returned the necklace to Ivy's hand, his fingers lingering just long enough to convey an unspoken connection. Offering a courteous nod, he then turned and took his leave.

The pendant evidently held a significance far beyond its physical beauty, possibly linked to someone dear to him. A pang of guilt stirred within Ivy as she replayed the scene with Mr. Fontes, wishing she had chosen her words with greater care. The distant sound of footsteps interrupted her thoughts, followed by Flávia's voice calling softly from the hallway.

"Senhora, I have drawn your bath," Flávia said as she entered the room. "The water is ready and waiting."

Ivy glanced down at her hands, still clutching the brush, noticing the streaks of paint staining her dress. Her thoughts tugged in opposite directions, torn between her duties and her emotions.

"Oh my—" Ivy exclaimed, before dashing to the mirror in the parlor. Orange, yellow, and umber smudges marred her cheeks, forehead, and hair.

"I promised the ladies I'd host an afternoon tea—and it's already three o'clock!" she said, her voice rising in urgency as she turned to Flávia. "You must help me become presentable at once."

"Don't worry, *minha amor.* I'll have you ready in no time," Flávia reassured her with a comforting smile.

Once Ivy emerged from the tub, refreshed but still anxious, Flávia set to work. With deft fingers, she parted Ivy's hair at the crown, twisting the top section into an elegant bun. Keeping a vigilant eye on the clock, she braided the remaining length into a cascading plait that fell gracefully just above Ivy's waist.

She watched in admiration as Flávia skillfully wove beads and silk rosettes into the braid, adding a touch of delicate charm. Finally, Flávia helped Ivy into her silk jade green dress, which featured sleeves perfect for the warm climate. Ivy felt relief and satisfaction as she surveyed her reflection, ready to host her first afternoon tea as the lady of the house.

"You've done it—thank you!" Ivy exclaimed, hugging Flávia in gratitude.

Over tea, Ivy learned much about her guests, hearing of their origins in Portugal and the circumstances that had brought them to Brazil for marriage. "Thank you ever so much for having us over, my dear," Gertrudes said with heartfelt appreciation.

"Indeed," added Belhina, with a touch of nostalgia. "We rarely have the opportunity to pay as many calls as we did back in Lisbon."

Catia, cradling her teacup delicately, sighed softly. "At times, it feels as though my old friends and relations have nearly forgotten I exist."

"It is not a task suited to the most delicate of ladies to forge a life far from the world she once knew," Gertrudes remarked with a touch of somber wisdom. "The heat is relentless, yet the call to aid those less fortunate in this land is equally formidable."

Moved by concern, Ivy asked earnestly, "How can I be of help?"

"For one, you could channel that divine talent of yours for capturing nature's splendor onto canvas. I daresay your landscapes would make a splendid contribution to our Ladies of Lisbon charity auction. Previous art donations have been selected by representatives from the most esteemed institutions," Gertrudes suggested with a hint of enthusiasm. "We would also be honored if you would consider assisting with our upcoming annual charity ball. The proceeds from these events support those suffering from the devastating famine, providing them with much-needed food and clothing."

"I would be delighted to participate," Ivy replied with heartfelt eagerness. "You can count on me for both endeavors!"

Ivy was quietly pleased with the success of the tea gathering. It was her first time hosting a social event as a married lady, and she felt confident her mother would be proud. The companionship of the other women had been a comfort, their collective efforts in goodwill serving to preserve their decency in this wild and unfamiliar land. Ivy was determined to absorb all she could from these women if her future was to be bound to this place alongside her new husband.

Yet, beneath her outward composure, a sense of unease lingered. The encounter with Mr. Fontes and his reaction to the pendant troubled her deeply. He did not carry himself like any manservant she had ever encountered, and that, in itself, vexed her.

Her fingers traced the intricate carvings of the parlor's ornate furniture, admiring the craftsmanship that far surpassed anything she had seen back home. The Fontes family's artistry was unparalleled. The more she dwelled on the misunderstanding, the stronger her conviction grew—she needed to make amends with him, if only to ease the weight of her conscience.

Ivy draped a cloak over her shoulders, the sumptuous fabric whispering gently into the night as she slid open the veranda gate.

The path to the tenants' quarters lay ahead, shadowed and narrow. As she stepped forward, the thought of a nearby armed guard gave her pause. She hesitated, allowing a few tense moments to pass before darting down the path.

Suddenly, a pang of fear gripped her, and she wished she hadn't taken such a reckless chance. A feeling of confinement washed over her—like that of a prisoner, always under the watchful eye of a captor, fearing discovery at every turn. But despite the fear gnawing at her resolve, Ivy pressed on, knowing there was no turning back.

The village lights emitted a warm, captivating radiance that seemed to beckon from a distance. Despite Allyn's misgivings, Ivy struggled to understand how such a humble community could harbor ill will toward landowners, especially when they shared in the labor that sustained the estate. Despite Allyn's cautions, Ivy entered the village with unwavering resolve. From watching her father manage Chetwynd Manor, she grasped the vital bond of mutual dependence. The idea of discord in what should be a harmonious partnership seemed inconceivable.

As she walked along the dim pathway, a faint gleam from a lantern flickered into view through the workshop window.

As she reached the workshop, she knocked softly, the sound barely more than a whisper against the door. Receiving no answer, she tested the handle, finding it yielding beneath her touch. Her pulse quickened, a relentless drumbeat in her ears as she eased the door open. It groaned softly, and she slipped inside, her eyes adjusting to the dim glow of a solitary table lamp illuminating a large, cluttered workbench.

Clutching the necklace from her cloak pocket, Ivy approached the lamp's fragile light, her fingers lingering on the delicate piece. It seemed to pulse with hidden significance, as if it harbored secrets that might reveal themselves to Mr. Fontes. She fumbled for a pencil and began to scrawl a note, her nerves betraying her in the faint tremor of her writing.

Just then, the door creaked open behind her, and Ivy whirled around, her heart leaping into her throat. There, silhouetted in the doorway, stood Mr. Fontes. The door clicked shut as he stepped into the workspace..

"Senhora, what brings you here at this hour?" His voice was a mix of surprise and curiosity, his gaze drifting over the workbench cluttered with tools and materials.

"Mr. Fontes, you have a remarkable talent for appearing at the most inconvenient moments," Ivy said, her breath still uneven from the shock.

He moved toward the workbench with a deliberate stride, his expression growing more curious. "I'm here to work. And you? Have you developed a sudden interest in wood-crafting?" The hint of mockery in his tone was subtle but unmistakable. Ivy attempted to brush it aside, intent on her goal—to extend an olive branch and perhaps ease the strain that had come to define their interactions. Yet, her frustration slipped through.

"You aren't like any manservant I've ever encountered. While we're on the subject, perhaps you may enlighten me as to why you refuse to wear livery." Feeling exasperation rise within her, Ivy kept her gaze intent upon him.

However, Mr. Fontes moved past her, adjusting the lamp's wick until it cast a warm, golden glow across the room. Ivy instinctively stepped aside, the soft light revealing the growing tension between them, undulating with the flickering flame.

"By that, you mean why I'm not behaving like a compliant footman? Honestly, Senhora, I haven't the time for such a discussion. And trust me, you would find it of little interest," he replied, methodically laying his tools out in a row.

"Do not presume to know what interests me," she retorted with a commanding tone.

At her words, he set down his tools and faced her, his expression growing stern.

"If you wish to understand my role in your newly inherited kingdom, listen closely," he snapped, irritation evident in his voice. If you must know, I perform menial tasks day in and day out like a trained dog, while you enjoy the luxuries that come with your position. Is that clear enough for you, Senhora?"

The room fell into a heavy silence. Mr. Fontes shook his head, then turned away from Ivy, his hands planted firmly at his sides as if bracing against his emotions.

"How dare you?" Ivy's voice quivered, as she struggled to maintain her poise. Anger surged through her, but a more profound ache threatened to break free beneath it. She pressed her lips together, forcing back the tears, unwilling to let him see her unravel.

The pendant burned hot in her clenched fist. Frustration welled up, the urge to hurl the pendant at Mr. Fontes almost overpowering. Instead, she set it gently by the table lamp, her gesture one of restrained anger.

As she made her way to the door, Mr. Fontes called after her. "Senhora, please, wait!"

Ivy pivoted to face him, her eyes tracing the subtle transformation in his expression as the rigidity that had previously tightened his shoulders seemed to dissolve.

"You've noticed that I don't quite fit the mold of a typical servant," he mused, settling himself onto the corner of the workbench. "That is because I am not really a servant," he added, his voice, once edged with resentment, now carrying a warmth that subtly shifted the tone between them.

"What do you mean?" Ivy asked, drawing in a steady breath.

"I'm here merely to help my father earn a modest living on an estate that was once our own. We are now tenants, overseeing the coffee production for Senhor Marsden—to settle our debts," he confessed, his voice carrying a quiet regret.

Ivy nodded thoughtfully. "Mr. Fontes—my husband believes there are those who would stop at nothing to see his downfall. Are you among them?" she asked, watching him closely.

"Do you believe I am?" he responded, his gaze locking onto hers with such piercing intensity that she felt compelled to look away.

Ivy shook her head, then pushed the necklace toward him, setting it on the workspace when he didn't take it from her outstretched hand. "I came to return this and to apologize for taking it. I'll be leaving now." Without waiting for a reply, she turned toward the door.

"This pendant—belonged to my mother," Mr. Fontes said, his voice tinged with quiet reverence.

Ivy paused, then slowly turned to face him.

He gently brushed his thumb over the smoothness of the glass as though coaxing the memories it held to the surface.

"Amidst the chaos and sorrow, it was misplaced, left behind," he murmured. Ivy could almost feel the weight of his sentiment settling into the room, drawing her in.

"I should have realized it was precious to you," she said, the sting of guilt knotting in her chest.

"Was she the artist behind the wall art?"

"Yes, my mother, Aramina," he replied, a subtle shift in his demeanor—a glimmer of brightness in his eyes.

"I found the painted likeness of a woman wearing this pendant in that same wardrobe. She was stunning—That was her, wasn't it?"

"Yes," he answered.

Ivy's heart stirred with sympathy. She felt the weight of his words like a ripple in the air. Her body softened involuntarily, releasing the tension that had gripped her since entering the room. She lowered her head slightly, allowing the quiet to blanket the moment. "I am deeply sorry," she whispered, dabbing at a stray tear that had fallen.

"May I?" she asked, gently grasping the pendant. With deliberate care, she opened his hand and placed it in his palm. "This is yours, as is the portrait," she added, her hands lingering a moment longer, closing around his in a soft, wordless connection.

As they stood, hands still joined, their eyes met in an unspoken exchange. A rush of emotion swelled within her—a mixture of warmth and confusion that left her momentarily unmoored.

Feeling her cheeks flush, Ivy withdrew her hand and broke the silence. "Is that... your lock of hair?" Her voice trembled slightly, but she steadied herself, clasping her hands together.

"The strands were gathered from each of her five children and interwoven into this pattern," Mr. Fontes replied. Ivy noted the wistfulness in his expression as though the past was both a source of comfort and sorrow.

"It is remarkable," she said, admiring the design before her. Suddenly, the air seemed to shift, suffused with a newfound understanding between them, and Ivy felt a quiet calm settle over her.

"Well, I should be going. I would be most grateful if you could escort me back to the veranda."

"Of course. Follow me," he said.

Leaving the workshop, they veered off the main path, Mr. Fontes leading the way with quiet confidence, his steps sure and steady as he guided her down the hidden route.

Ivy felt the thrill of the unknown tug at her, but there was no fear, only curious excitement. Though the thick darkness surrounded them, she knew she was perfectly safe with him. His hand, strong and steady, encased hers, grounding Ivy as they navigated the winding route. His grip was smooth, yet there was a subtle roughness in his fingers from the woodwork he often did—its presence comforting and reassuring, a reminder of his strength and skill.

As they neared the veranda, a flicker of light from a nearby lantern cast a gentle glow, and Ivy's breath caught in her throat. In the soft illumination, she could see the planes of Mr. Fontes' face. His features, already striking in the dimness, were now somehow more mesmerizing—his jawline sharp, lips set in a way that gave him an almost untouchable air, yet his eyes, warm and earnest, softened that impression.

He turned to her then, his expression unreadable, but his voice softened, low and purposeful. "Do you still wish to visit Senhor Da Silva? Meet me at the stables at eight o'clock tomorrow morning." His tone dropped further as if revealing a secret. "That's when the guards change shifts. Most will be at breakfast."

"And what of those who remain?" Ivy asked, her voice lowered to match his.

"I will keep them occupied with some gossip and some of my sister-in-law's pão de queijo," he replied, his grin widening. In the soft light of the lantern, Ivy caught the faint glimmer in his eyes, a hint of mischief that made her pulse quicken.

She chuckled softly at the image of him charming his way through the morning. "Thank you, Mr. Fontes, for everything tonight," she said.

He met her eyes, an unspoken understanding in his expression. "You may call me Tristão," he said, his voice shifting, no longer that of a servant but that of a friend.

"Good night, Tristão," Ivy said, the words leaving her lips with a softness she had not expected.

"Good night, Senhora," Tristão answered with a respectful nod, his eyes lingering on hers for a heartbeat longer before he melted back into the shadows, leaving Ivy in the lingering glow of the lantern's light.

Chapter Eleven

The dew clung to the grass in glistening droplets as Ivy approached the stables, her footsteps muffled by the lush verdure. She lingered within the cool shadows, eyes tracing the lines of the stables until Tristão emerged from the house, his presence a quiet assurance. A brief exchange of morning greetings passed between them before he moved to prepare the horse and dainty, open-roofed barouche, its sleek lines and delicate craftsmanship setting it apart from the more common carriages. The light morning sun caught its polished finish, and Ivy could not help but notice how its elegance mirrored the tranquil beauty surrounding her.

"We must depart before the men complete their breakfast," he advised, his tone brisk yet courteous. "We'll take the back road, avoiding the field," he added, assisting her into the carriage with fluid skill. As they set off toward Belas Águas, Ivy savored the invigorating morning breeze, grateful for its refreshing touch.

Tristão sat in contemplative silence for a long moment, the rhythmic clatter of hooves the only sound between them. Then, with deliberate care, he brought the horses to a gentle halt, turning toward Ivy with a gravity that caught her attention. "Senhora, about last night, I had no right to raise my voice. My father often reminds me to mind my place, and I fear pride got the better of me. I hope you'll accept my sincere apology."

Ivy's heart fluttered unexpectedly at his words. She was taken aback, not by the apology itself, but by the sincerity in his voice—the rare vulnerability he showed. A swell of warmth spread through her, and she was struck by how his usual confidence softened in that moment, revealing a side of him she rarely saw.

She held his earnest expression; her lips slightly parted as a surge of emotions stirred. His words felt like a gentle balm to a wound she had not realized was still there.

"I have already forgiven you," she replied, her voice soft but firm, as if her words were as much for herself as for him. She felt her breath steady as their silence stretched for a heartbeat longer than usual, the air between them warm and unspoken in its understanding.

Tristão's smile was faint, but it was enough to light something within her—a quiet assurance, just like the morning sun that began to shine brighter above them.

The carriage swayed gently over the uneven road, the rhythmic clatter of hooves mingling with the soft murmur of the stream. Ivy's hands rested on her lap, her fingers brushing the smooth fabric of her gloves as she soaked in the crisp morning air. The earthy scent of damp grass and fertile soil felt grounding, a perfect complement to the quiet contentment settling within her.

Tristão brought the horses to a steady halt, his movement drawing her focus. She followed his gaze to the stream, its surface catching the sunlight, sparkling like scattered jewels across the water.

"This stream," he said, his expression alight with enthusiasm, "winds its way to one of the most breathtaking waterfalls in the valley. I must take you there on our return."

Her chest lifted slightly, and her smile spread instinctively, the flutter of excitement in her chest matching the bright anticipation in his tone. "That sounds wonderful," she replied. The thought of such beauty, shared in his company, felt like a rare and precious reprieve, one she was quietly grateful to accept.

When they arrived at Senhor Da Silva's shop, the familiar charm of the space welcomed them once more—an alluring blend of sights and scents. The tall cabinets filled with exotic items blended with the earthy aroma of spices and exotic woods, creating a vibrant backdrop for their visit. He led them to the rear of the shop, where his true passion resided: his workshop, a haven of craftsmanship. Here, the air was thick with the energy of vibrant pigments and finely honed tools, a creative atmosphere that once again captivated Ivy.

Tristão extended the pendant for the artisan's discerning eye. "We'll need a color to match this hue," he said, his voice steady and resolute, as Ivy watched intently.

"Ah, yes, these blossoms come from the Quaresmeira, a tree native to our region," Senhor Da Silva replied, his eyes gleaming with recognition. Adjusting his tiny spectacles, he peered closely at the pendant. "I remember this filigree frame quite well. It was a unique creation I brought from Portugal many years ago. Your mother commissioned me to craft the design within the glass pendant," he added, nostalgia threading through his words.

Ivy moved closer, her interest sparked. "Can you replicate that exact color?"

"Allow me to prepare the ingredients for you, Senhora," he promised, offering Ivy a reassuring smile before stepping into a narrow closet. The shop fell into a hushed stillness, only the soft sound of cabinets opening and closing echoing faintly.

Ivy glanced at Tristão, their eyes meeting instantly, the connection between them palpable and unspoken. There was something in how he regarded her—an intensity that made her breath catch. She felt something stirred within her, both vulnerable and undeniable, as though his look were a touch upon her skin, caressing her in a way that left her pulse quickening.

She tried to look away, focusing on the jars of pigments on the shelf, though her thoughts lingered on him. Every inch of her seemed attuned to his presence, her body unconsciously leaning slightly toward him, drawn to something she could not name.

A soft rustle interrupted her reverie, and she looked up just as Senhor Da Silva reappeared, cradling several jars filled with dried magenta petals—delicate fragments in ethereal shades of purple and pink, reminiscent of twilight skies, each one a vibrant reminder of nature's vivid beauty. These unique hues contrasted the muted palette of English flora Ivy knew so well.

"I was in the process of making pigments from that species. It has been many years since I last attempted it, but perhaps your arrival at this very moment was fated," Senhor Da Silva mused, preparing his worktable.

Ivy stood entranced, watching him transform into an alchemist, utterly absorbed in his craft. His hands moved with practiced precision, grinding a blend of roots and mysterious earthy fragments, coaxing the raw essence of nature from their hidden depths.

Sensing Tristão's watchful presence, Ivy turned to him, her lips curving into a smile. "Would you care to join us, Mr. Fontes?" she asked, her tone light yet inviting.

As Tristão neared the table, Senhor Da Silva handed him a mortar and pestle, a familiar and unspoken bond sparking between the two men. Intrigued, he began grinding clay into ocher pigment.

With a gentle nudge, Senhor Da Silva encouraged Ivy to add a vibrant floral pigment into a concoction of natural gum Arabic and crushed Brazilwood. Their movements soon synchronized, seamlessly blending their efforts. As the colors blossomed and swirled into something extraordinary, Ivy felt a surge of excitement, as if they were unveiling hues the world had long awaited. The very air around them seemed to hum with potential, and Ivy couldn't shake the exhilarating thought of creating something entirely new—especially with Tristão by her side.

Ivy could not contain her laughter as she withdrew a mixing spoon from one of the tins, inadvertently sending a flurry of tiny blue droplets flying onto Tristão's face and his crisp white shirt. The surprise in his eyes quickly morphed into an amused grin, and she felt a delightful flutter in her chest at the sight.

Senhor Da Silva, ever the jovial spirit, joined in the merriment, his laughter ringing out like music as Tristão, with a playful glint in his eye, retaliated by flicking a brush laden with lavender droplets back in her direction. The soft splatter of paint against her cheek and the silky strands of her dark auburn hair—braided and adorned with a few wayward wisps—only heightened her joy. She couldn't possibly feign offense; instead, she savored this whimsical exchange, feeling utterly carefree. With a playful flick of her wrist, she wiped away the paint, her smile blooming like the vibrant colors that surrounded them.

As she assisted Senhor Da Silva in meticulously filling and sealing the tins, Ivy sensed Tristão's eyes lingering on her once more. The depth of his attention sent a delightful shiver down her spine, mingling with the colors that danced in the air around them.

When their eyes finally met, Ivy offered him a coy smile, her heart quickening in response to the silent connection weaving between them. In that moment, the world faded, leaving only the soft thrum of unspoken tension. Tristão held her stare, an irresistible magnetism hinting at untold secrets waiting to be discovered.

Just as Ivy felt herself drifting further into this enchanting moment, the sound of gentle clatter broke the spell. Senhor Da Silva, a knowing smile tugging at the corners of his mouth and a glint of mischief in his eyes, called lightly,

"Senhora Ivy, be sure to seal those cans tightly. We don't want our beautiful creations to dry out before their time."

Ivy blinked, feeling the moment's magic settle around her like a fleeting dream. With each lid she secured, she sensed Tristão's presence nearby, the warmth of his aura brushing against her skin. Though the moment had transformed, the memory of their shared glance lingered in her thoughts, igniting a delightful flutter in her chest and a deepening desire to unravel its significance.

As they turned to bid farewell to Senhor Da Silva, Ivy felt a twinge of reluctance in her heart. The older gentleman's eyes sparkled with genuine delight, and a warm smile graced his face.

"My dear friends," he said, his voice resonating with sincerity, "Please do visit us again soon. Your presence breathes life into the shop."

With a final exchange of pleasantries, Tristão offered Ivy a firm hand, assisting her as she stepped into the barouche and around the crate. The touch of his hand lingered in her mind, a gentle reminder of the connection they had forged. As she settled into the carriage, the anticipation of the journey ahead settled comfortably between them as they set off.

As they journeyed back to the fazenda, Ivy could not help but smile, her perspective transformed by the beauty surrounding her. True to his word, Tristão led her along the scenic route, where a stream widened into a serene pool, cascading into a magnificent waterfall that plunged into depths of azure. He stopped to assist her down to the banks, and Ivy was awestruck, absorbing every sound and sight. She watched the water rush over green and pewter rocks, creating a cascade of blues before it flowed gently into the lagoon.

She closed her eyes and let the roaring sound wash over her, its steady pulse unraveling the tension that had remained within her for far too long.

When she opened her eyes, she caught Tristão's intent expression, the sunlight glinting off his untamed hair and illuminating the warmth of his emerald eyes. They exchanged smiles, standing together for a moment that felt suspended in time before reluctantly returning to the carriage. The ride home was silent, yet Ivy sensed a deepening connection between them. He was no longer the servant she had perceived that first night in Rio de Janeiro; he had transformed into something more, something she could not yet name.

Ivy resolved that this enchanting place beckoned her return, a sanctuary where she longed to immortalize its splendor on canvas. A newfound passion ignited within her, and she eagerly anticipated the moment she could once again breathe in its breathtaking beauty.

Chapter Twelve

March 15th, 1881

Dearest Evelyn,

I trust this letter reaches you, Mother, and Father in the best of health and spirits. I hope by now you've received the notes I sent during my voyage, though I must offer my sincerest apologies for the lapse in writing since my arrival. Adjusting to the subtropical climate proved more difficult than I anticipated. I confess to a few fainting spells, much to the local doctor's amusement, though he is a kind and attentive old gentleman who has seen me through the worst of it. Fortunately, with the shifting season, I find my health much restored—so rest assured, there is no need for concern.

Now that the fainting spells are behind me, I have wholeheartedly thrown myself into a new passion: painting everything in my line of sight. You may remember the summer we spent in Monsieur Pierre's class, where he showed us the art of breathing life into landscapes with the smallest of brushstrokes. He once said I showed promise as an artist—albeit with that familiar sting of condescension, for I am a woman, after all. The views here are nothing short of breathtaking, yet it is not the landscape that has captured my imagination but rather a more intimate outlet for my talents.

I have found a new calling that does not demand the precision of Monsieur Pierre's techniques. Instead, the faded walls of the fazenda house, and even some long-forgotten furniture, now serve as my canvases. I draw inspiration from the magnificent Portuguese tiles adorning the house, their designs whispering stories of a bygone era. Equally enchanting is the flourishing flora and fauna that thrive in this lush valley, offering endless patterns and colors to my eager brush.

Yet, what truly ignites my passion is the restoration of the hand-painted motifs that time has rendered almost invisible. Reviving these delicate works has become my greatest joy, as if I am breathing life back into forgotten memories etched upon the walls.

My bold color palette looks nothing short of magnificent against the taupe plaster walls. Oh, Evelyn, you should see the transformation I've wrought upon the furniture—tables, desks, and even a grand bed have become my latest creations. When the curtains are drawn open and the sun casts its full light upon the floral designs, the entire house seems to bloom with life, as though the walls themselves are breathing.

I've been fortunate enough to procure exquisite paints from a talented artisan in the nearby village. He uses local ingredients to craft his oil and milk paints, and with a twinkle in his eye, he speaks of a secret ingredient he refuses to share with anyone. He is a delightful character, and I must say, I owe my introduction to none other than our manservant, Mr. Fontes—Tristão, as I've come to call him. Perhaps Providence placed him in my path to ensure that life here would not become the dreary exile I once feared.

Should you wonder about my duties as lady of the house, rest assured, dear Evelyn, I have grown rather adept in my role. Though settling in was no easy feat, I have found my days pleasantly occupied with tasks that keep me rooted. After breakfast, my first concern is ensuring that all runs smoothly downstairs. We are without a head housekeeper, given the modest size of our household, so I take it upon myself to oversee the pantry, ensuring that we never run short on supplies. Our household is a curious mix—only two of the servants receive wages: Flávia, my maid, and Afonso, Allyn's valet. I confess it pains me to report that the others are either enslaved or bound by indentured servitude, their fates tethered to this fazenda in ways that unsettle me deeply.

Our butler, Octávio, a seasoned and dignified man, ensures that the household staff remain on task. Yet with all these duties, you may wonder what it is my husband occupies himself with. Allyn is often absent for weeks at a time, engaged in meetings with business partners and investors. When he does return, his attention is consumed by the coffee fields. He spends long hours with the overseer, Joaquim, ensuring all is well in the fields. I must admit, his determination to make this fazenda thrive is unwavering, driven, no doubt, by a desire to prove himself worthy in his father's eyes. His goal, as you might imagine, is to secure his place as steward of Marsden Hall when the estate is restored. That is where my next role comes in—as the future mother of their heir. It is no small task to be part of this grand plan, but I take solace in knowing that our home is secure, and Father's good name will endure through it all.

On another note, dear Evelyn, I hope that by the time this letter reaches you, dear Gwen will have safely returned home. The doctor in Rio de Janeiro sent word that she is well enough to travel, which offers some comfort. Leaving her to convalesce alone in that hotel—at Allyn's request—was a source of deep sorrow for me; it weighed heavily on my heart. I can only imagine how much she must have missed the warmth of our little family and the comforts of home. Please convey my fondest regards to her and let her know that she is always in my prayers. Her gentle spirit and warm presence are dearly missed here, and she is most welcome to write as often as she likes.

These are my thoughts and experiences over the past month. I long to hear from you, Mother, and Father. For now, I must say goodbye and await your news.

With all my affection,
Your loving sister,
Ivy

Ivy folded the letter with care, sealing it neatly in an envelope. She sat still for a moment, her thoughts drifting. Then, with a slight sigh, she reached for another piece of paper, dipped her pen, and allowed her emotions to spill onto the page:

For the first time in what feels like an eternity, I sense a flicker of life within me, a spark I had long believed extinguished. I am not certain what to make of it, but I find myself drawn to him, compelled in a way I never anticipated. Each moment spent in his presence awakens an unfamiliar yearning as if something about him— something I cannot yet name—calls me to understand more. I must admit, my husband has never evoked such feelings within me, nor could he ever come to know of them.

She stared at the bold confession, the ink still wet on the page. The words felt like an unbearable weight, too dangerous to exist. With a sudden resolve, Ivy tore the paper into small pieces, scattering the fragments as if to erase the truth she had momentarily allowed to surface.

Meanwhile, Allyn sat at a polished desk in his room at a grand hotel in São Paulo. He dipped his pen into an inkwell and began to write in smooth, confident strokes.

March 15, 1881
São Paulo

My dearest Ivy,

You have been on my mind constantly, to the point where I can scarcely concentrate on business without thoughts of you. I trust you are feeling rested, and I hope you anticipate my return as much as I do.

The business here has been prosperous, and we've secured promising projects for the year ahead. Thanks to Travers and myself, Brazil will soon stand shoulder-to-shoulder with the rest of the world in innovation and superior transportation. I met with the gentlemen from our first evening in Rio and send their regards. They are all eager to visit us at Aramina in the coming months. Travers assures me I'll be back to resume my duties at home by April, but for now, I remain here, securing our future. I look forward to finally embracing the life we have yet to fully share as husband and wife and planning all that is to come.

Your dear husband,
Allyn

A soft knock echoed against the door, prompting him to call out, "Come in!"

A well-dressed young lady glided into the room, her presence both striking and familiar. She bore an uncanny resemblance to Ivy, though her warm beige complexion set her apart. Loose, tight auburn curls framed her face and cascaded gracefully over her shoulders.

"From this moment on, you will answer to the name Ivy," he declared, his tone cutting as the door clicked shut behind her. She nodded, her head bowed, avoiding his piercing stare. "And tonight, Ivy," he continued, his voice steady and commanding, "you will comply with every demand I make."

Chapter Thirteen

$\mathcal{I}$vy stood on a step ladder, palette and brush in hand, delicately dipping it into the wet dollops of paint. With meticulous strokes, she applied the final touches to the floral motif that graced the ceiling above her. The house felt more serene with Allyn away, and she relished the newfound freedom his absence afforded her. Yet, with each passing day, an unsettling sense of disquiet slowly began to rise within her, like a storm gathering on the horizon. He had been gone for weeks, and she knew all too well what he would expect upon his return. The thought of sharing a bed with him filled her with dread, especially now, when she bore a secret—a secret that trembled on her lips, too fragile to be spoken.

Ivy rubbed her forehead, striving to push aside these unwelcome thoughts. Why did this feel so daunting? Women in society entered into arranged marriages without complaint, and many sought the company of strangers with brazen ease. Yet the very idea of his touch sent ripples of anxiety coursing through her.

As she dipped her brush again, a shadow crept over her thoughts—a memory that seemed to materialize from the encroaching twilight. In her mind's eye, the image of that harrowing night resurfaced: the suffocating darkness of the room, the scent of sweat, the echo of her own muffled cries, and the relentless grip of cold hands pinning her down. The flash came unbidden, striking her like a gust of icy wind, and for an instant, it was as if she were back there, fighting desperately against a faceless attacker.

Why didn't I fight harder? The thought pierced through her, leaving a bitter taste in its wake.

She shook her head firmly, pulling herself back to the present as the room grew darker still. Glancing at the clock in the parlor, she noted the time—it was nearly half past six. The servants had already retired for the evening at her request, leaving her in solitude.

Her thoughts drifted to Tristão. There was something in how he looked at her—an unspoken understanding that lingered in his gaze, as though he could perceive the weight she carried. Though she dared not admit it to herself, the prospect of sharing her completed motifs with him brought a flicker of warmth to her heart. It felt as though these small triumphs were beginning to weave him into the fabric of her life, almost as if he had become an essential part of her world without her even realizing it. Most importantly, she found herself eagerly anticipating their subsequent encounters, a welcome balm to her troubled thoughts.

Ivy pondered the notion that this art might evoke cherished memories of Tristão's lovely mother. With every delicate brushstroke, fragments of the earlier encounter resurfaced in her mind. She recalled the unmistakable tension that filled the room when Flávia entered to deliver a tray of refreshments for Tristão and one of the manservants, who had been clearing out the dining furniture for Ivy to paint the ceiling motifs. Flávia had a way of commanding attention, yet Tristão seemed to instinctively turn his gaze and body away from her presence. Ivy couldn't help but wonder if there was an unspoken history between them, a thread of the past they were both trying to conceal. Yet, the thought of broaching such a delicate subject with Flávia made her anxious. How, after all, was a lady to inquire about her maid's romantic entanglements without overstepping the boundaries of propriety?

Suddenly, she didn't know how to feel about the idea of Flávia and Tristão having made love. It had been weeks since their outing to Senhor Da Silva's shop, and Ivy longed to recapture the freedom she had felt by the waterfall. More than that, she feared those precious moments would vanish for good once Allyn returned. He and Ivy's consummation had been delayed for so long, and he certainly made it clear by his last letter that he was ready to begin living as man and wife at Aramina.

Ivy suddenly felt the need to save that fleeting sense of self. She threw off her apron and reached into the wardrobe for her jade cloak. She tiptoed down the stairs and left through the back kitchen door. Once outside on the veranda, the smell of impending rain filled the crisp night air. Ivy listened for the guards but only heard the wind rustling through the trees and plants that surrounded the fazenda. She stopped when she saw a guard walking in the distance and waited until he disappeared around the house before hurrying down the path toward the tenants' village.

Tristão was surprised to see Ivy at the door and invited her inside.

"Are you alright, Senhora?" he asked, his expression a mix of concern and curiosity.

"Yes, only I've run out of fresh paintbrushes and rags. I thought you'd have some out here," she said.

"Certainly, just give me a moment," he replied with a curious glance.

The rain poured harder now, streams of water coursing down the windowpane, their paths weaving like vines under the dim light. A silence lingered between them as Tristão busied himself, adding supplies into a small crate.

"My husband is due to return any day now," Ivy remarked, hoping her voice would not betray the apprehension she felt creeping in.

Another clap of thunder rumbled in the distance.

"Please, make yourself comfortable. We may be here for quite some time," Tristão urged, gesturing toward a chair. Reluctantly, Ivy settled into her seat, watching as he rummaged through an old cabinet and retrieved a bottle of pale liquid. He eased into a chair behind the workbench, the bottle resting casually in his hand. Ivy noted the label: Cachaça. With a swift twist of the cap, he released a faint, sweet, earthy aroma in the air.

"Care for a drink?" he asked, the bottle poised effortlessly in his hand.

"No, thank you," Ivy replied.

Tristão stretched his legs across the table, radiating a relaxed confidence that filled the space between them. The unspoken tension thickened as the rain continued its steady rhythm against the roof, a muted backdrop to the unease swirling in Ivy's thoughts.

The world beyond the workshop faded away, cocooning them in a hushed intimacy where the air was infused with the rich scent of damp earth and distilled spirits, grounding them in the shared moment.

"It's rather cozy, wouldn't you agree? Though hardly the ideal setting for a lady's comforts," he remarked with a slight grin, lifting the bottle to his lips. As he took a sip, the smooth liquid lingered on his palate, and he leaned back, savoring its warmth. "I've spent countless nights toiling away in this space," he continued, a hint of nostalgia in his voice as he reflected on the many hours spent here.

"I can tell," Ivy said, her look briefly drifting to the bottle in his hand.

A sudden chill swept through the night, making Ivy's hands tremble. She instinctively brought them to her lips, seeking warmth, but paused as she caught Tristão watching her with quiet interest. In a heartbeat, she tucked them into the pockets of her cloak, a fleeting sense of vulnerability washing over her.

"The weather is known to be fickle in these parts," he remarked, setting the bottle before her. "Here, this will do the trick. It's guaranteed to warm you."

Not wishing to appear timid, she accepted it without hesitation and took a cautious sip. The liquid surprised her, holding a sweetness she had not expected, far more delicate than the spirits back home. She swallowed, a slight cough escaping as the warmth bloomed in her chest.

"Thank you," she said, clearing her throat. "I've never tasted anything quite like this. Is it a type of rum?"

"Not quite. It's crafted from sugarcane juice rather than molasses." After a moment, his expression shifted to one of thoughtful consideration. "Senhora—"

"Please, call me Ivy. Now that we've shared a drink, we can skip the formalities," she said with light-hearted candor.

"I have a question that has been weighing on my mind," he began, his voice steady yet deliberate. "I hope you will not misconstrue my intentions." His eyes remained locked onto hers, imbued with a quiet intensity as if his words bore a significance he could scarcely set aside.

"Oh?" Ivy arched an eyebrow, savoring another sip as warmth coursed through her limbs. "What is it that you wish to know?"

"That night in Rio," he began, his voice thoughtful, "when we first met in the courtyard..."

Ivy stiffened slightly. "Yes? It was rather awkward, to say the least, wouldn't you agree?" Her eyes darted away from his as if seeking refuge in the shadows of the workshop.

Tristão focused on the bottle cap on the table, shifting it from finger to finger, allowing a few moments of silence between them before selecting his words.

"Had I not known better, I might have wagered that the lady scaling the gate was seeking a way to slip away unnoticed." Now keenly fixed on her, his eyes seemed to probe for answers she was reluctant to share.

A jolt of vulnerability surged through Ivy at his words. This man had witnessed her at her most desperate, alone in the courtyard on that first night in Rio de Janeiro. Now, his question felt like an intrusion, pressing upon a truth she was not ready to reveal.

A wave of anger and apprehension surged within her, igniting a fierce flame in her chest. "Slip away—you mean escape?" Her voice rose, laced with indignation. "Sir, I cannot fathom where you might have gotten the notion that I needed to flee on the very night of my arrival!"

Ivy sprang from her seat in haste, her sudden movement upsetting a small wooden toolbox perched on the shelf. She let out a startled cry, immediately summoning Tristão to her side, his expression darkening with concern as he gently cradled her injured hand.

He caught sight of the crimson line on her hand, a stark contrast to her porcelain skin.

"It's from the chisel," he murmured, his voice steady yet carrying a quiet concern. "Only a scratch, but it needs proper care." Without hesitation, he retrieved a brown bottle of tincture and a set of dressings from a nearby cabinet.

As he carefully removed the dropper, their eyes locked, and the world around them seemed to fade into a distant hum. Ivy felt the warmth of his presence enveloping her, and for a fleeting moment, the intensity of his gaze held her captive. He tended her wound with a tenderness that sent a warm sensation down her spine. The tincture stung slightly as it met her skin, but it was Tristão's quiet attentiveness that pierced through her.

With each gentle touch, as he wrapped the bandage around her hand, the space between them narrowed, charged with an unspoken connection that neither dared to break. Once finished, he lowered her arm, his fingers lingering for a heartbeat longer than necessary, his gaze still fixed upon hers.

"Forgive me, Senhora," he said softly, a hint of regret in his tone as his eyes flickered to the scattered tools on the floor. "My nephew often neglects to put things back in their rightful place."

Even as he spoke, neither seemed inclined to pull away, the air thick with a palpable tension that made the moment feel timeless.

Ivy nodded and turned her attention to the window. A white, glaze-like film coated the pane, filtering in delicate beams of moonlight that danced across the room. A wave of shame enveloped her for her earlier outburst.

"No, I should apologize for my earlier behavior," Ivy murmured. "I haven't quite been myself since arriving here."

"There's no need for you to apologize," he replied, calm and reassuring.

She met his glance for a moment, then instinctively shifted her focus away, feeling the unspoken charge between them hum softly in the air.

"Thank you, but I'm quite alright," she replied, her words tight with restraint as she fought to keep her composure. The urge to speak more, to convey the weight of what she felt, pressed on her, but she kept it at bay. "You've been exceedingly gracious in obliging my every request," she continued, her voice barely a whisper, strained but steady, as she struggled to maintain control.

Ivy felt Tristão move closer, though she kept her focus on the window. His presence was undeniable, the shift in the air around her growing more pronounced as he drew near.

"Though this place is beautiful, I've felt like an outsider, yearning for the comfort of companionship. At times, the solitude has been nearly unbearable."

For a fleeting moment, she wondered if the words had truly left her lips or if they remained mere echoes of her unspoken thoughts. A warm tear traced her cheek, but she quickly brushed it away before Tristão could glimpse her moment of fragility.

Moments passed, and they found themselves face to face in the moonlight, stripped of all formalities. He stood close enough that the intoxicating scent of bay rum enveloped her senses, its allure a seductive embrace. His eyes gleamed like radiant gemstones in the dim light while his full lips appeared to beckon her closer. She closed her eyes, inhaling the fragrance of his hair, reveling in the closeness he offered—more intimate than she had allowed anyone before, both physically and emotionally. *I want him to kiss me. Please kiss me!* Her head swirled with the intoxicating scents and sensations igniting within her.

"I—I must go," she whispered, looking into his eyes again.

"No, stay here with me," he urged.

"I can't. If he finds out I've been here, he might—" she faltered, glancing away.

"I sense that you want this as much as I do. Don't worry—you're safe with me, Ivy," Tristão whispered, his voice low and compelling.

He held her face gently, pressing his lips to hers. The very touch ignited a spark within her, awakening sensations she had long kept at bay. She savored the fullness of his lips, feeling as though he enveloped her essence, rendering her a willing captive to his allure.

Ivy felt an unexpected lightness in her body as if floating above the ground. Yet, the voice of propriety rang loud in her mind, warring with the rising tide of fear. But it was not the fear she had anticipated—the fear of intimacy. Instead, it was the dread of losing herself to his embrace. If she surrendered entirely, she could never return to her place beside Allyn Marsden. How could she abandon the splendor of paradise for a life that felt trapped in limbo?

As these thoughts lingered, she felt his lips deepen their kiss, a fervent escape from the weight of her duty, her name. Now resting at her waist, his hands seemed poised to draw her further from the world she knew.

Just then, a distant rumble of wheels echoed through the air. Ivy's eyes snapped open, her gaze locking with his. The concern etched on his face was unmistakable. With a quiet exhale, he released her, his posture subtly shifting back to a more formal stance. The sound of approaching grew steadily louder. Tristão moved swiftly to open the door, just enough to glimpse the coach lanterns swinging as it made its way toward the house.

"That's Senhor Gonzaga's coach. He must have brought Allyn home. I must get you back immediately!" he exclaimed. He reached for his cloak and grabbed the lamp from the workbench.

They reached the veranda just as the approaching coach rumbled to a halt in front of the house. The lanterns cast flickering light across the scene—servants hurriedly unloading Allyn's luggage, their movements frantic, while the guards shifted their attention to the commotion. For a fleeting moment, Ivy and Tristão were invisible, slipping unnoticed toward the kitchen door.

The intensity of their narrow escape pressed against her chest, his lingering presence in the doorway sparking the exhilaration flickering beneath her apprehension.

From the front of the house came the sharp clatter of footsteps and raised voices—guards barking orders, servants scurrying to obey.

Without thinking, Ivy reached for Tristão's hand, her fingers trembling as she brought it to her cheek. The roughness of his palm was a grounding contrast to the chaos outside.

She leaned into him, brushing her lips to his in a fleeting kiss—an unspoken testament to the storm raging within her—she uttered, "Thank you." Her voice trembled, barely a breath.

Knowing that Allyn was nearby sent a jolt through her, but she couldn't bring herself to pull away just yet. Tristão's unwavering presence, the warmth of his lips still lingering on hers, became her only refuge amidst the storm.

Tristão's fingers traced the delicate curve of her face before he drew back, casting a final, longing glance at her. Then he slipped away into the shadows, vanishing down the path.

There were echoes outside as Ivy sneaked into her room upstairs, through the back staircase. She removed her cloak, shoved it into the wardrobe, then unfastened her dress as best she could. After pushing it beneath the bed, she took a towel from a hook and dried the still wet parts of her hair.

Muffled footsteps echoed through the walls as Ivy hurriedly slipped into her white linen nightgown and leapt into bed, pulling the covers tightly around her. Her heart thudded in her chest, the footsteps growing louder as they drew nearer, ascending the staircase and finally passing her room.

She had evaded Allyn once more. He was likely too drenched and weary from his journey to wake her.

She smiled, still feeling light-headed from Tristão's lingering caresses that warmed her skin. Flashes of his captivating eyes, inviting lips, and intoxicating scent surged through her imagination.

Suddenly, she began to yearn for more of his touch, even if just for a moment. Urges that she had suppressed since the ball pulsed through her. She began to unfasten the front of her nightgown, running her fingers down her stomach, enjoying the sensation. Oh, how she wanted more of him: conversations, smiles—his touch. Her head swam with images of his long dark tresses, green eyes, and luscious lips. How could this be? How could he have erupted these feelings within her? Soon, her fingers found their way down the inside of her thighs. She trembled and craved him even more. Her white silken gown was now loose on her body, exposing her peach-colored nipples, stiff with excitement. Her tongue swept across the bottom of her rubescent lips at the climax of her arousal. She exhaled softly and lay entwined in the satin bed sheets for some time.

Biting her lip, she allowed a smile to blossom, her heart racing with the thrill of uncharted desire. Was this the sensation that making love with him would awaken within her? Would the gentle caress of his hands upon her body ignite the profound yearning coursing through her tonight? She could scarcely fathom how long she could endure the absence of his presence, longing for the warmth of his touch.

One truth echoed distinctly in her heart—it was Tristão she desired!

Chapter Fourteen

llyn sat at the table on the veranda, his eyes lifting from the newspaper as Ivy approached. "Good morning, my dear. You look quite lovely today," he said, a cold smile stretching across his features.

"Thank you. I've had my fill of rest, so I thought I might join you for breakfast," Ivy said, allowing the servant to draw out her chair gracefully. As she settled in, she unwrapped her napkin and added, "I trust your business trip was successful. Is that a British paper?"

"Um, yes—courtesy of a potential client who brought it with him from London," he replied, a smug expression settling on his face. "Though it is almost a month old, I suppose it is more suited for wrapping fish than reading."

At that moment, a servant girl appeared, balancing a tray laden with fresh pastries. Ivy's spirits soared at the sight of Izobel, the young maid who had attended to her during her stay at the hotel in Rio de Janeiro.

"I brought her as a present for you, my love," Allyn interjected, a smirk playing on his lips.

Her heart quickened, a flush creeping up her neck. "A present? Allyn, do tell me you haven't gone and purchased her!" she exclaimed, her voice rising in disbelief.

"Of course not, dear. I recall how you spoke of the girl with such affinity. She still belongs to her father, the owner of the hotel. I've merely arranged for her to stay on as a maid—or a companion, perhaps," he said, looking quite pleased with himself.

Ivy watched as a servant sent Izobel back inside of the house.

"I'll only accept her as my companion, but what of her mother?"

"She remained at the hotel, in service to the owners," he remarked as he skimmed through his paper.

"Allyn, how could I possibly keep her? The child needs her mother."

"I brought her solely to please you, my dear. Let us not have any displays of ingratitude." Allyn's expression became tense and unyielding.

"Please understand, I am genuinely grateful to you. However, regardless of who owns Izobel, I cannot condone slavery. Given that it has been abolished back home, we, as British citizens, should steer clear of it entirely. So, I hope you will forgive my discomfort with the notion," Ivy expressed.

"My dear, this is a country of slaves! So, I'll ask you to refrain from lecturing me about what is ethical!" he snapped, slamming his hand on the table.

Ivy tried not to flinch.

"As for the girl," Allyn began, setting down his teacup with a soft clink, "she is the hotel owner's illegitimate daughter. That alone should afford her a far better lot than most." He glanced at Ivy dismissively. "Send her back whenever it pleases you; it matters little to me." Pausing, he leaned back in his chair, reaching for his knife. "Though, I will remind you," he added, slicing a piece of sausage, "that her freedom is her father's decision—not yours."

He looked down, giving his full attention to his plate and newspaper. The quiet stretched between them.

"Allyn," Ivy murmured, breaking the silence, "I did not mean to offend you. Please accept my apology. I only meant to—"

"You need not trouble that lovely little head of yours with such trivial matters," he cut in sharply, his voice threaded with condescension. "I suggest you focus solely on your role in this house—and, of course, on pleasing me."

With a self-satisfied look, he continued, "I'm having your things moved into my room. We will no longer sleep separately. Now, finish your breakfast so we can enjoy a pleasant day together."

Ivy obliged him, though her appetite had all but vanished. A wave of relief washed over her when Allyn finally finished his meal and excused himself to review papers in his study.

Once he was out of sight, Ivy beckoned to Izobel, who stood by the door, and invited her to join her at the table. For the moment, she relished the idea of having a young companion.

Together, they savored an assortment of fresh fruits and meat pastries. Ivy felt a warmth spread through her as she watched Izobel smile, her laughter momentarily lifting the weight of the morning's tension.

Allyn stood at his study window, watching Ivy as she sat at the veranda table.

"You look as though you could use some attention," said Flávia, pressing her torso against his back. She then wrapped her arms around him and began unbuttoning his waistcoat.

"Flávia, I do not recall summoning you," Allyn said, pushing her hands away.

"But you want me, no?"

"I don't like it when you try to take charge. You're trying much too hard."

Flávia turned to see that Allyn had been watching Ivy through the window.

"You want her but have been too afraid to bed her?"

"That's my concern! If you wish to keep the special lodging I've secured for your sick mother, I suggest you follow my lead! Do you understand?" he sneered.

"Yes, Senhor, of course!" she replied, her voice trembling slightly.

Allyn straightened, his manner cool and refined as he strode toward the door, his expression lingering just long enough to leave Flávia visibly unsettled.

"If you wish to be of service," he remarked, his tone cool and measured, "then keep a vigilant eye on my wife."

"You mean for me to spy on her?" she asked, her voice steady yet her eyes narrowing. "For what purpose?"

His mouth curved ever so slightly. "My work keeps me away, and I find her recent defiance... distasteful."

Flávia tilted her chin, a trace of defiance flashing in her own expression. "As you wish, Senhor."

He paused, casting her a sidelong glance. "What time shall you be preparing my wife's bath?"

"Approximately nine o'clock, Senhor," she replied.

"See to it," he murmured, a faint smirk touching his lips, "that I might enjoy the view."

Flávia offered a faint, composed smile. "Of course, Senhor. Whatever you desire."

That evening, Ivy's spirits were uncharacteristically high as Flávia arranged her hair and adjusted the fine details of her gown for dinner.

"You seem particularly cheerful tonight, Senhora," Flávia observed, speaking to Ivy's reflection in the mirror with an inquisitive smile.

"Oh, I've managed to accomplish quite a bit of painting around the house," Ivy replied, a faint grin lighting her face.

She observed as Flávia's eyebrows arched in surprise. "Ah, what a commendable endeavor you've undertaken, Senhora. It is rare to see a lady of refinement venture to pick up a paintbrush, even as a mere pastime. I would have thought embroidery or the piano to be more conventional pursuits for someone of your stature," she remarked.

"Yes, I've also learned those things." Ivy nodded. "But painting—it is something altogether different. It feels like it's mine, and it brings me such joy. Not just a hobby," she continued, glancing around the room at the colorful patterns adorning the walls. "More of an expression."

Flávia's expression softened. "Ah, Senhora, perhaps you have fallen in love. With your art—or maybe with someone?" Her voice trailed off, leaving a silence that hummed with unspoken implications. Ivy's heart skipped at the suggestion, the hint of truth making her pulse quicken.

"Your husband is home now," Flávia added with a touch of mischief, deftly arranging the final blooms in Ivy's coiffure. "Surely, you can enjoy each other's company before business steals him away."

"Yes," Ivy replied distantly, toying with her string of pearls, her mind far from Flávia's words.

"Ah, you look exquisite, *minha amor*," Flávia remarked, her voice warm with admiration.

Ivy barely acknowledged the compliment, her mind burdened with swirling thoughts that spilled forth in a whisper. "Flávia... tonight, my husband and I will finally share a room since our wedding. We have yet to be truly together as husband and wife. Do you have any suggestions that might—hasten the experience?"

Flávia paused, a glint of knowing amusement in her eyes. "Ah, *minha amor*, haste is rarely what a man seeks. Are you concerned he may lack tenderness in his approach?"

"That's precisely it," Ivy admitted, her fingers trembling slightly. "I've only read of such things, never... experienced them."

Flávia chuckled, her grin widening as she set a comforting hand over Ivy's. "Do you wish me to speak candidly, dear one?"

Ivy turned toward Flávia, a spark of curiosity igniting within her. "Yes, please do."

With an air of conspiratorial confidence, Flávia sat by Ivy's dressing table, eyes dancing. "In my experience, no man can resist the effects of a strong drink for long. So, serve him wine before and during dinner," she murmured, leaning in, "though beware, *minha amor*, for such indulgence may leave him less gentle than you might hope. If fortune is with you, he may even succumb to sleep before the night truly begins."

Ivy nodded, relief and trepidation mingling in her expression. "You've been so kind, Flávia. Thank you." She clasped Flávia's hand warmly, gratitude evident in her voice.

Flávia glanced down, swallowing softly as she felt a pang of guilt, her gaze flickering away before meeting Ivy's eyes again. "You are most welcome, *minha amor*," she replied, her words catching slightly as she forced a reassuring smile.

Later, Ivy paused just outside the dining room. Tonight, she'd resolved to woo Allyn, hoping that the heavy dread might begin to lift once she had fulfilled this duty. Nevertheless, Ivy knew her heart yearned for only one thing—to feel Tristão's arms around her again. Taking a deep, steady breath, she stepped inside, her heart fluttering with a complex mix of anticipation and resolve.

At dinner, the warm glow of candlelight flickered against delicate crystal and polished silverware, bathing the entire dining room in liquid gold. A sumptuous spread awaited them at the table, each dish more enticing than the last. Emboldened by the intimate setting, Ivy aimed to shine, allowing her laughter to flow like a gentle melody. Each movement was deliberate, crafted to captivate Allyn. "Oh, darling, must we truly return to England?" she murmured, playfully. "I daresay the climate of this country is beginning to suit me rather well."

Allyn gave a low, indulgent chuckle, his voice tinged with the rich indulgence of his drink. "Ah, yes, my dear," he replied, his expression sweeping over her with an assessing fondness, "now that your fainting fits are a thing of the past, your cheeks have taken on a quite charming hue." His pale eyes gleamed with the easy confidence that came after one glass too many, as he leaned toward her.

Ivy joined his laughter, a practiced sound that shielded her thoughts. She sipped her wine slowly, maintaining her composure with careful restraint. Yet, within, her heart tugged toward England, toward the family who awaited her across the vast ocean. Even so, she felt an undeniable pull to this land, a place forbidden yet enchanting, its vastness steeped in a beauty she hadn't anticipated. The charade was held through the evening, through dessert, as Allyn's movements grew loose, his conversation laced with inebriated arrogance.

As the last course was cleared, he leaned back and broached a subject Ivy had been dreading.

"Our heir, Ivy, once he's of age, will take command of the entire Marsden estate." He waved his hand grandly, his words swelling with pride.

She tilted her head in deliberate contemplation, keeping her voice smooth as she ventured, "And the fazenda? Surely it, too, will carry the Marsden name for generations, will it not?" Ivy felt her throat tighten at the thought of bearing his child, quickly masking her disquiet with another sip of wine.

He laughed, waving off her words. "Oh, hardly," he replied, pausing for a generous sip, savoring his drink as smugness crept into his tone.

"This little endeavor is merely my father's notion of a training ground before I return to manage the family estate in England. Once I show him the ease with which I handle matters here, he'll be begging me to come back and assume my rightful place."

Her heart gave a small, painful lurch at his indifferent words, a harsh reminder of his intentions.

"We have come a long way to reach this place, Allyn," she replied, a touch wistfully. "Now that I've settled in, I find its beauty quite alluring."

He gave a casual shrug. "Perhaps it will fetch a handsome profit," he replied, unbothered. Then, with a shift in his tone, he slid his hand over her wrist, idly brushing over the delicate pearls adorning it. "But enough talk of business. I would far rather discuss our sleeping arrangements this evening." His tone dropped, his eyes narrowing with that gleam Ivy had come to recognize—a gleam both bold and possessive.

She knew this moment would come. Her fingers tightened subtly around her glass as she brought it to her lips, willing herself to maintain her composure. "As you wish, Allyn," she murmured, a faint, controlled smile gracing her lips. Yet, a dryness clung to her throat, an unwelcome reminder of the dread she kept buried beneath her poised exterior.

When dinner concluded and the table was cleared, Ivy seized the moment to test the waters.

"Allyn, my dear," she murmured, a teasing glint in her eye and her voice smooth as silk. A playful smile danced on her lips. "I've yet to have the pleasure of seeing your bedroom. Why not show it to me?"

Allyn's eyes sparkled with a look of self-satisfaction, a smirk settling over his features. "I'd be most delighted to oblige," he replied, raising his glass and savoring another swallow of brandy. "But first, my dear, you must take your bath."

Her brows arched slightly as she leaned closer, her tone edged with a mock flirtation. "Alone, you mean?"

"Yes, yes," he said with a careless chuckle, already swaying on his feet as he rose. "Go on, my darling. I'll await you in my room." He reached for her hand, helping her from her chair with a bit too much eagerness. Escorting her down the dim hallway to the stairs, he paused, leaning in close, his breath warm and acrid with brandy and cigar smoke. His shirt had come undone, his collar askew, and his hair lay rumpled in careless disorder. He placed a wet, clumsy kiss on her cheek, the unpleasant musk of alcohol clinging to him.

Ivy endured his advances, though her mind drifted elsewhere, to an image of Tristão, the memory of his lips lingering like a half-forgotten melody. Allyn's hands roamed her frame, sliding from her waist up along her sides, stopping just shy of her breasts before he finally pulled away, apparently satisfied with his effort.

"Go bathe, my dear," he said, his tone heavy with expectation, pressing a kiss to her hand before she ascended the steps. He withdrew, stumbling slightly as he made his way back into the dining room, presumably in search of more brandy.

As he vanished from view, Ivy released a quiet, measured sigh, allowing her composure to settle once more.

She brushed the remnants of his kisses from her cheek and rang for Flávia, who arrived promptly to assist her. As she began to unbutton Ivy's gown, a cool calm enveloped her, pushing away the remnants of the evening's discomfort.

"You may as well take your time and indulge in a long bath," Flávia murmured with a knowing smile, her voice soft yet mischievous. "The senhor is likely fast asleep by now, lost in his brandy-laden dreams."

"I just want this over with," Ivy muttered, her voice emerging louder than intended, betraying her frustration.

Flávia's gaze sharpened. "Is that so?"

Ivy hesitated, then softened her tone. "I mean, I should want it, shouldn't I? After all, we must consummate the marriage..." She trailed off, the conviction in her voice wavering.

Flávia laughed softly, a glimmer of amusement in her eyes. "*Minha amor*, I have yet to meet a woman eager to take a drunken man to bed. It is too much effort, truly," she chuckled, her voice a soothing balm.

Ivy managed a small smile. "It is just... back home, most girls marry much younger than I did. I suppose I am tired of fearing what might happen—or what he might do." Her voice dropped to a whisper.

Flávia brushed a gentle hand through Ivy's hair, her touch tender. "*Minha amor*, it will be as it must. I cannot promise he will be gentle, but if you find yourself in the arms of a man you care for, his touch may light a fire within you, one that warms rather than frightens." She gave Ivy a reassuring squeeze, her expression soft and understanding.

"You've been endlessly kind to me, Flávia. I don't know how I would manage without you," Ivy said, her voice softened with genuine gratitude as she clasped Flávia's hand warmly.

Flávia offered a warm smile, gesturing toward the bath. "Come along, Senhora. The water is ready, and a fresh towel awaits you." She gathered a few small glass decanters, pouring fragrant oils and salts into the steaming bath. "This blend of lavender, sage, and rosemary will make your skin so smooth that no man could resist you," she teased, her eyes twinkling.

As Ivy allowed Flávia to help her out of her corset and chemise, she felt a strange calm settle over her. Stepping into the tub, the steam enveloped her, and the floral notes filled the air, easing her tension. She dipped her head back, letting the water cradle her as she closed her eyes, savoring the scents and the luxurious stillness.

"Allow me to prepare your nightclothes, *minha querida*," Flávia said, her tone warm and reassuring as she moved toward the door. "Rest easy for now—I will return shortly."

Ivy sat for several minutes before sensing a flicker of movement, and when she opened her eyes, she thought she glimpsed a shadow shifting from behind the room divider. Faint footsteps echoed, unmistakably close, as if someone had crept through the door. The candle across the room wavered, its flame flickering as though stirred by a phantom breeze. She sat up, heart pounding, her gaze darting around the room. Only silence and emptiness met her eyes.

"Flávia?" Ivy called out, her voice slightly tremulous.

The door opened, and Flávia peeked inside, her face as calm as ever. "Yes, *minha amor*? Shall I help you wash your hair?"

Ivy hesitated, then nodded. "Please. Did you notice anyone in the hall just now?"

Flávia's brow arched in slight confusion. "No, there is no one else here." She glanced around the room, and Ivy forced a small, dismissive smile.

"Never mind," Ivy murmured, brushing aside the lingering unease.

Flávia moved behind her, lifting Ivy's damp locks and gently massaging an aromatic soap into her scalp. Ivy breathed in deeply, feeling the floral essence work through her senses. She leaned back, her bare shoulders glistening in the soft candlelight, while Flávia's fingers moved with practiced ease, sending shivers of relaxation down her spine.

"Does that feel good, *minha amor*?" Flávia whispered.

"Yes... that feels wonderful," Ivy said with a sigh, her voice barely above a murmur.

Flávia continued the pampering, massaging Ivy's arms and shoulders with scented oils that left her skin luminous. When she was done, Flávia wrapped Ivy in a plush towel, patting her hair dry as Ivy allowed herself to bask in luxury, knowing such peace was fleeting.

"Come, my dear, let us get you dressed in the bedroom," Flávia murmured, gently guiding Ivy from the warmth of the bath, her hand light yet steady at Ivy's elbow as they made their way toward the room.

Finally, Ivy dressed in her sheer lace nightgown and robe, feeling as if she wore nothing at all. She stepped into Allyn's bedroom, taking in his slumbering form sprawled across the bed, his shirt rumpled, his breathing deep and steady. Ivy slipped off her robe, folding it neatly over the chair. Despite her resolve, she found herself wishing he might remain lost in his drink-induced dreams.

Sliding into bed beside him, she was relieved when he shifted slightly, turning away with a quiet, sleep-laden murmur. Light snores soon filled the silence. Ivy lay still, the turmoil within her a strange blend of relief and disappointment. Her mind drifted, envisioning Tristão's warm smile, the strength of his arms that could make her feel safe, even now, as she lay beside another man. Turning to face the window, she closed her eyes and let her thoughts wander to him.

Tristão lay in bed, staring at the ceiling, his mind a restless storm. He endeavored to focus on the tasks that awaited him the next day, yet everywhere he turned, Ivy's face haunted him—her supple lips brushing against his, her sweet scent lingering like a melody in the air.

When he resolved to return and mend his fractured relationship with his father, he had never imagined Ivy would factor into his life. It was sheer happenstance that brought him into her presence at such an unanticipated moment in Rio de Janeiro.

The Marsdens had long aroused his suspicion, and he had sworn to reclaim what was rightfully his family's. That had been his sole focus until he encountered the lovely Lady of Aramina, whose refined elegance and shared confidences lingered in the quiet corners of his memory.

Friends? he mused, disbelief curling in his thoughts. A friendship between her and a man who had seen his family's fortune stripped away. Not likely. He was merely an artisan of carpentry or a footman at best—not a companion worthy of her.

Just then, vivid images of Allyn's hands on Ivy flooded his mind, igniting a surge of something possessive within him.

Tristão sat up, his feet striking the floor with a resolute thud. He curled his fist, stifling the impulse to drive it into the wall in frustration. Instead, he buried his head in his hands, struggling to banish the tormenting images from his mind.

Friend, lover, or confidant, it made no difference. She was a married woman as far as the world was concerned.

A harsh truth that struck him with a searing clarity: he could never truly have any part of her.

Tristão's thoughts wandered to the fiery cascade of her hair, its hue reminiscent of rich wine aglow in the waning light of day. It spoke of something untamed, a reflection of the fire he sensed in her spirit, yearning to be set free. And then there were her emotions—ever-changing, elusive—stirring beneath the surface with a quiet intensity, as though even she struggled to predict their course, like a storm that shifted without warning.

He pressed his fingers to his forehead, attempting to ease the weight of thoughts that had become all-consuming. Still, that face—an exquisite blend of defiance and tenderness—remained imprinted, an indelible mark on his mind. Her eyes glistened like polished amber when she laughed, their warmth drawing him in, a magnetic pull that held him captive in its radiant glow. Though she masked it well, he could sense a quiet restlessness beneath her composed exterior, a longing for something more—something just beyond reach.

That longing seemed to fuel her every effort to preserve nature's beauty on canvas—an artistry, unlike any woman he had known, one that stirred memories of his mother's artistic soul.

The sight of her—her laughter, fire, and unspoken yearning—conquered him entirely, more than he cared to admit. It was a power that gripped him with an intensity he could neither deny nor control, and he feared that he had fallen under the spell of her kiss.

Tristão could not endure staying there as anything more than a servant, helplessly watching as she wasted her days with a man who did not deserve the honor of calling her his wife. To be near her, yet denied the privilege of her touch, was a torment he could hardly fathom. The seething ache to claim her as his own seized him, heightened only by the cruel reality that she was bound to another.

He would have to leave-- return to Portugal and not lay eyes on her again. The mere thought of it sent a shudder through him as his hands gripped his hair in frustration.

"Ivy, you demand all of me!" The words, though quiet, burned with a rawness that echoed deep within him.

Chapter Fifteen

The following day, Allyn rose long before dawn, leaving Ivy to bask in the peace of her slumber. Had he, perhaps, convinced himself that they had shared a night of passion? If so, it might afford her a brief reprieve from his presence—a thought that granted her a rare sense of ease.

When their paths finally crossed later that afternoon, Ivy found him lost in thought; his brow furrowed as he immersed himself in the study. Ivy wondered if, in his intoxicated stupor, he had erased their uneventful evening from his mind—or perhaps he harbored a quiet resentment toward her. His aloof, distant manner offered no clues, leaving her unable to decipher even the faintest trace of his true emotions. In any case, Ivy allowed herself to entertain the hope that Allyn might leave her in peace for a few days, offering her a window of respite.

She turned her attention to her painting, striving to immerse herself in the task of bringing fresh blossoms to life on the kitchen walls. However, Ivy's thoughts drifted with restless longing despite her best efforts to focus. Her heart ached with a silent yearning to see Tristão again, yet with Allyn still at home, she knew a clever ruse would be necessary to slip away unnoticed.

Then, inspiration struck her like a spark in the darkness: why not begin a new landscape for the upcoming Ladies of Lisbon charity auction? It would provide the perfect excuse for time spent away from the house. She would ask Izobel to deliver a discreet note to Tristão, requesting that he wait for her. In her mind's eye, she could already see the secluded pool, its waters glimmering beneath the cascading waterfall—an idyllic setting for her secret meeting.

The plan formed with startling clarity. An innocent, unassuming picnic would serve as the ideal pretext to venture out. Allyn would surely decline; he had always disliked the outdoors, finding the sun too harsh for his pale complexion. The thought of an escape in Tristão's presence quickened her pulse, the idea of a clandestine rendezvous hidden in plain sight stirring a thrill deep within her.

Ivy's suggestion lingered, the silence heavy with unspoken judgment. Allyn furrowed his brows, his expression hardening with irritation as though the idea barely warranted consideration. "A picnic?" he echoed, his tone laced with disbelief, his eyes betraying a flicker of suppressed frustration.

Ivy's pulse quickened, but she forced herself to remain steady. "I simply need to capture the landscape for the auction," she said, the words coming out more matter-of-fact than she intended. "The waterfall would be perfect for the scene I envision."

She watched as his lips pressed into a thin line, his irritation unmistakable. The silence stretched thick with tension. His jaw clenched, his eyes narrowing in a way that made Ivy's stomach tighten—she could feel the weight of his unspoken thoughts, as though her request demanded more from him than just his time.

"I plan to paint three, maybe more, for the ladies' auction," Ivy said, keeping her tone measured, though her words carried a subtle firmness. "Of course, if your schedule is too full, Izobel would happily accompany me." She glanced his way, careful not to look too directly, as if meeting his eyes might spark unnecessary resistance.

Allyn's hesitation was brief. "Fine, I will join you. However, Mr. Travers will be here at a quarter to five," he said, his words clipped as if reluctantly conceding. "I shall need to return well before then."

Disappointment rolled over her, but she quickly quelled the sensation.

She would find a way to wait for Tristão, and the mere idea of it soothed her.

"Wonderful," she replied, her smile a subtle shield, guarding the scheming thoughts hidden beneath her poised demeanor. "I'll have the cook prepare a lovely picnic for us."

Her voice remained steady, but inside, her mind was already on the one person whose presence she truly craved, and nothing, least of all Allyn, could change that.

The splashing of the waterfall against the pewter stones played a symphony to Ivy's ears, each droplet a note resonating with inspiration. The enchanting green pool beckoned her, a siren call urging her to translate its beauty onto the canvas. She felt a burning urgency, her brush poised and ready to capture the moment before it slipped away like a fleeting dream.

Allyn lay sprawled on his side, absently plucking grapes and exuding an air of boredom that seemed almost tangible. He propped himself up, casting a glance at his gold pocket watch. "My darling," he drawled, "we have been out here for nearly an hour, but I fear I must return to the house and attend to some business matters."

"I will be fine. Izobel is here to help with carrying supplies when I am ready," Ivy replied, striving to sound more composed than she felt, the undercurrent of anxiety bubbling beneath her calm exterior.

Allyn nodded, his expression slightly softening as he tucked the watch back into his vest pocket. He leaned down to plant a brief kiss on Ivy's cheek, a cold gesture that lingered like a chill in the air long after he turned away and strolled down the path, leaving her with a sense of unease.

Once Allyn was out of sight, Ivy turned to Izobel, her heart racing. "Did he receive the note?" she asked, her voice barely above a whisper.

"Yes, Senhora, but he no respond," Izobel replied with a shrug.

Ivy's mind raced as apprehension gnawed at her. "I suppose I'll have to wait and see if he arrives before Allyn begins to question my absence," she mused, the weight of her plan pressing heavily upon her. *But I must see him!* The thought echoed in her mind, insistent and compelling, igniting a flicker of hope amidst her growing anxiety.

Grateful for Izobel's presence, Ivy enveloped her in a quick hug before they settled together on the blanket, sharing sandwiches and fruit, the cheerful spread a stark contrast to the turmoil swirling within Ivy's heart.

When Allyn returned home, he withdrew into his study, arranging his thoughts with the same meticulous care he applied to his papers, each document placed with intention as if each held a distinct significance.

The soft, deliberate sound of footsteps broke the room's stillness—Flávia's familiar approach. She entered carrying a tray, her movements delicate yet purposeful. Upon the silver surface rested a decanter of rich, ruby-hued wine, its scent drifting subtly between them, accompanied by a modest selection of dried fruits.

"I thought you might appreciate some regional wine this evening," she said, her voice carrying a note of care.

As she set the tray before him, Allyn noted their brief exchange of glances, her eyes meeting his as she poured the wine. He sensed her silent appraisal, a scrutiny of his mood that infused the air with unspoken tension.

"Your associate sent word," she murmured, extending a sealed envelope from the tray. She slid the envelope into his grasp with a practiced hand, studying his reaction.

Allyn muttered as he read, then crumpled the paper in frustration.

"Blasted delays in São Paulo," he spat, tossing the paper aside, his irritation flaring instantly.

Flávia stepped closer as her fingers brushed his when she placed the glass beside him.

"Is there anything I can do to ease your mind, Senhor?" she asked in a low, soothing whisper, her fingers brushing his hand as he took the glass—a subtle invitation for his attention.

Allyn dismissed her advance, draining the glass in a single motion before pulling out his pocket watch. "Where is Ivy?" he said with a look of concern. "I worry she has been out of doors too long."

Flávia's expression tightened briefly, a flicker of chagrin escaping before she masked it with a playful smile. Her voice shifted to a teasing lilt. "Ah, but you have scarcely visited me of late. I wondered if perhaps my company had lost its charm—or if she has extinguished the fire I once held."

"I do not have time for this, Flávia!" he snapped, his patience fraying. "State your purpose or leave me to my work."

"My only wish is to please you," she replied softly, the faintest trace of desperation creeping into her words. She hesitated before adding, "You asked about your wife."

"Yes, what about her? Has she returned?"

Flávia leaned in closer, lips curling into a faint, bitter smile. "What if I told you that your precious wife has found... other company in your absence?"

Allyn's pen stilled, his gaze locking onto Flávia as her words ignited a fury within him.

"What did you say?" he murmured, ire rising in his voice.

"I... may have seen Senhora Ivy with Mr. Fontes—the footman. It seems he drove her to the village," she paused, lowering her eyes momentarily. "I may have noticed them walking together after hours. I did not want to believe it myself."

Allyn's eyes narrowed, a storm brewing within him. "Are you suggesting," he said, gritting his teeth to quell the surge of rage within him, "that my wife has lowered herself to some sordid affair with a footman? You deemed it wise to withhold this from me?"

Flávia took a step forward. "I wanted only to be certain, Senhor. I would never mislead you," she murmured, refilling his glass with a slight tremor in her hand. "If it pleases you, I can continue to observe for your sake."

"Enough stalling," he demanded, his voice slicing through the air with a ferocity that left no room for hesitation. "Tell me precisely what you saw—and do so now." His fingers gripped her arm, a silent threat.

Flávia's face flinched with something akin to panic, but she quickly regained control. "I wanted to be certain, Senhor, that their meetings were not inappropriate," she uttered, her voice faltering.

Allyn studied her face for a few moments, savoring the power he wielded over her. "So, you've proven yourself by ensuring that my household has no secrets from me," he sneered. "But mark this: you had better tell me the truth." He loomed over her, his voice a harsh growl. "Betray me, and I'll ensure you have no place here—or anywhere!"

Fear glimmered in her eyes, but she held her composure. "I have always been loyal, Senhor. I have spoken nothing but the truth."

His grip softened, yet the simmering intensity within him remained unyielding. "Then prove it," he commanded. "You will follow my instructions precisely when the time is right."

"And what will be my reward, Senhor?" Her voice was a fragile whisper that barely reached him.

Allyn's grimace shifted into a smile. "Do this," he murmured, brushing his hand over her cheek, "and I will see your mother comfortably provided for while you enjoy a life befitting a mistress—no more work for you."

"When would you have me act?"

A sense of triumph coursed through Allyn as he leaned back in his chair, propping his legs onto the desk, while he lit a cigar.

"As I said, when the time is right," he remarked, his words irrevocably sealing their pact.

Chapter Sixteen

midst the lush green valley, Ivy sat poised before her easel, her surroundings a scene worthy of the finest painting. The serene lagoon lay just beyond, its aquamarine waters gleaming in the late afternoon light, framed by the distant waterfall and the gentle murmur of the breeze. However, her focus drifted now and then, her gaze slipping toward the winding path through the trees, hoping to see Tristão's familiar silhouette approaching, bringing with him the soft stir of anticipation.

A large umbrella provided shelter from the sun's warm embrace, casting a delicate shadow over her as she worked. The wide brim of her hat tilted perfectly to shield her eyes, and a loose ribbon trailed down her neck, fluttering as if in anticipation of his arrival. Her soft cream dress billowed around her legs, its fine fabric hinting at subtle luxury, while a faint smudge of paint adorned her cuff—a small mark of her devotion to this private passion. As Ivy's hand moved with practiced grace, her brush wove layer upon layer of vibrant hues, bringing the valley's beauty to life upon the canvas.

Here, amidst the lushness of nature, her spirit felt freed from the stifling confines of her hollow union and the weight of her duties as Lady of Aramina. In this secluded paradise, she was not merely a figure of propriety but an artist in her element, immersed in a delicate interplay of color and the soft chorus of birdsong. Only one thing would make it perfect: if he, too, would step into this scene, completing the vision she dared to imagine.

Then, a disruption broke the peace. The splash of water at the far edge of the lagoon echoed, followed by the unmistakable sound of someone moving through it. Startled from her reverie, Ivy glanced up to see a figure breaking the surface, water droplets glistening as they fell from his dark hair. She squinted against the sun, a smile curling her lips as the figure drew closer, revealing the familiar, striking features of Tristão.

Setting her brush aside, Ivy untied her apron and rose from the small stool. "Izobel," she called to the young maid, who had been quietly absorbed in her own painting.

"He's here! He received my letter." Ivy's heart raced with excitement. "Please take my things back to the house and stay in your room until I return." She lowered her voice, her gaze darting toward the lagoon. "I would rather the servants remain unaware of my whereabouts."

The girl eagerly complied, gathering Ivy's belongings and heading toward the cart awaiting on the path.

Free from her obligations, Ivy wandered down toward the water, the ground soft beneath her feet. She found a place to sit on the large, smooth stones lining the pool's edge, slipping off her shoes and letting her feet dip into the cool waters of the lagoon. Her gaze lingered on Tristão as he swam with effortless grace, his muscular frame cutting through the water, droplets beading on his sun-kissed skin. A quiet intimacy enveloped the moment, an indulgent stillness settling over her as she admired his every movement.

Minutes slipped away in peaceful observation until he dove beneath the surface. Ivy's breath caught, her pulse quickening as the seconds stretched longer than they should have. She scanned the shimmering surface, searching for any sign of him, a growing worry coiling in her stomach as she waited for him to reappear.

She was just on the verge of seeking him out when Tristão emerged at the water's edge, mere steps away from where she stood.

No words passed between them. With a silent command, he reached for Ivy, and in that instant, she surrendered every pretense of decorum, immersing herself in the water's cool embrace, its depths pulling her closer with every step. She followed him without hesitation through the curtain of mist toward the hidden cave beyond, its shadows whispering of a world apart from everything else.

Once inside, its jagged, shimmering walls enclosed them, creating a haven where only the heat of their desire remained, and the outside world was no more. Amid its iridescent walls and cool air, Ivy stood uninhibited, every restraint swept away by the fire between them.

She flushed as his wet arms wrapped around her waist, pulling her firmly against him. Her heartbeat thundered in her chest, each pulse matching the intensity of his kiss. Breathless, she melted into him, returning his fervor with a passion that had long slumbered within her, now awakened and all-consuming.

The waterfall's roar reverberated through her, its powerful rush silencing all her anxieties, leaving only desire in its wake. Tracing the contours of his body with her lips, she explored the strength of his masculinity, each lingering touch deepening the connection between them. Her breath brushed softly against his skin, from his chest down to his navel, every exhale stirring the air between them.

A low moan of pleasure escaped Tristão as his fingers tangled in the softness of Ivy's cascading locks.

Desiring every inch of her, he moved to unbutton the bodice of her dress, its fabric parting to reveal a smooth, boned corset that molded her form. Loosening its laces and unclasping the front, the garment slipped free, falling at Ivy's feet.

Tristão beheld how the damp chemise beneath it adhered to the fullness of her curves, the sheer fabric whispering against her skin in the dim light. Reaching in, he drew Ivy close, slowly lowering the chemise to her waist. A shiver of arousal ran through her as the caressing sensation brushed against her nipples, coaxing a sigh from her lips as her body responded with a subtle, involuntary tremor.

She brushed her lips against Tristão's, then arched backwards in his arms, a silent invitation for him to savor her yearning breasts.

He delighted himself in their suppleness causing her to cry out in sheer ecstasy, with a craving inside of her that she knew only he could satisfy.

Tristão heeded that craving, pleasuring her with his tongue and then opening her up to him. Ivy held onto him tightly as he extinguished the fire inside of her, moaning and crying each time she felt him thrust himself against her ache. Their sounds softened, swallowed by the rush of the water surrounding them.

Soon, they felt the climax of their deepest desires, and nothing else existed in the world beyond the cave. She lay nestled in his arms, her damp ringlets spilling over his chest like tendrils of silk. Was this truly real? How had this man managed to break through her barriers, stirring a rapture so profound it left her breathless?

As he glanced upward, his eyes following the droplets of water falling from the rock ceiling, Ivy's mind wandered. Was he contemplating something? Something about their future, perhaps? What future could they possibly share, when every moment between them defied the boundaries of what was allowed? Their love was forbidden, yet undeniable.

The late afternoon sun, soft and golden, pierced through the glistening veil of water that concealed them from the rest of the world. It cast an almost magical glow around them, cocooning them in their own hidden sanctuary. Ivy, wrapped in the warmth of Tristão's body, savored every inch of his presence—the intoxicating heat of his skin, the powerful sensuality that radiated from him, igniting her very soul. She reached out, her fingers gently caressing his face, a gesture that was both tender and possessive in its intent.

Tristão stirred, his body shifting slightly under her touch. A slow, languid smile spread across his lips, one meant only for her.

"*Minha querida—*" he whispered, the words falling from his lips like honey, sweet and intoxicating to her ears.

They kissed, surrendering to one another, drinking in the essence of their shared passion. Ivy was captivated by his fortitude and the fierce spirit that emanated from him. Hours seemed to slip away, or perhaps time itself had paused in this enchanted haven. Though she was acutely aware of the impending moment when she would have to leave Tristão's embrace, she felt torn—she had everything to lose, yet in his arms, she felt more alive than ever.

Shaking off those turbulent thoughts, Ivy immersed herself in the beauty of the present. She pressed soft kisses against his chest, each one igniting a more profound craving for his very being. Holding him tighter, she savored the intimacy of their connection, fully aware that soon, she would have to relinquish this blissful moment.

"Is something troubling you?" he asked, his voice low as his fingers gently swept a stray lock of hair from her face, his touch lingering as though offering a quiet comfort to Ivy.

"I find myself hoping for the outside world to dissolve, allowing this perfect moment to endure," she replied, her fingers tracing the sculpted contours of his chest as if etching the memory into her soul.

As tranquility enveloped them, Ivy felt an irresistible pull to delve deeper into the enigma surrounding Tristão.

"You once alluded to the fact that the fazenda and everything within it rightfully belonged to your family. How did it come to rest in the hands of the Marsdens?" she inquired softly.

"That is quite a lengthy tale in itself. Are you certain you wish to hear it?" Tristão asked, his fingers deftly reaching for his trousers. He slipped one leg through, then the other, settling into a more comfortable position.

"I would, please," Ivy replied, her curiosity stirred.

After a brief pause, Tristão gathered his thoughts and acquiesced to her request.

"The arrangement between them was dubious from the outset. Old man Marsden acquired Aramina at a public auction, striking a deal with my father to revive coffee production in exchange for my family's labor as indentured servants. Now, five years into this agreement, I can't shake the feeling that the Marsdens may not honor their end of the bargain," he said, shaking his head with a hint of dismay.

"Not when your entire family is shouldering the workload. That would be dreadful," Ivy remarked, her brow furrowing with concern.

"Precisely," he replied, a knowing glint in his eyes. "Since returning from Lisbon, Marsden has had me tackling various odd jobs. The title of footman merely serves to make my presence somewhat bearable," he added with a wry smirk as he slipped on one of his boots. "However, I've long suspected that old Marsden orchestrated the way events unfolded. I could never quite prove he was behind our failed investments, though," he continued, securing his other boot with a hint of frustration.

"I'm so sorry. Your family must have been devastated." Ivy took in a deep breath, feeling a surge of sympathy wash over her. "But why did your father place his trust in Lord Marsden?" she inquired, her fingers working to fasten her chemise.

Tristão glanced away momentarily, lost in thought, before reaching for his shirt. "There was a drought—one that ravaged the northern lands," Tristão began, his brow furrowing under the weight of memory. "My father, feeling a deep obligation, opened our doors to those fleeing in search of work. Many arrived starved, some gravely ill, and with them, the sickness spread."

Ivy drew closer, wrapping her arms around him in a comforting embrace, silently encouraging him to continue.

"Even as the crops began to wither and fail on our land, my father refused to surrender to despair. He held steadfast." Tristão's voice thickened with emotion. "When my mother fell ill, her family urged him to take her back to Portugal before her condition worsened." He paused, drawing a breath as memories surged, threatening to overtake him.

"But when we lost her, he was utterly shattered." Tristão's eyes darkened with pain.

Ivy tightened her grip ever so slightly, "Oh, it pains me to think of what your family has endured," she whispered, pulling him closer in a quiet offering of solace.

He hesitated momentarily before surrendering to her embrace, his arms wrapping around her as if drawing strength from her warmth. A heavy breath left him, his hold lingering before he finally pulled back, his face shadowed with the weight of memory.

"By then, the Marsdens had tripled Senhor Gonzaga's investments and expanded their holdings. My father, reluctant, yet hopeful, invested with them, believing I might one day reclaim the land once our debt was paid."

He glanced at Ivy, his expression softening. "He promised my mother that we would restore this land to its former glory, and so here we are." Tristão brushed his thumb gently against Ivy's cheek, his smile a blend of tenderness and bittersweet remembrance.

"Until that day arrives, we must rely on the furniture we sell to secure our livelihood. Wood artistry has been a cherished tradition in the Fontes family for generations, a great honor to uphold." He paused, turning slightly to glance at Ivy over his shoulder, entwining his fingers with hers—a silent reminder of their connection.

"Yet now, Lord Marsden has enlisted the obscure Croydon & Co. as silent partners, taking a considerable slice of our profits to keep us in our place, it seems."

"But for what purpose?" Ivy inquired, her brow knitting with concern.

"Perhaps it's simply to ensure we never earn enough to escape our indentured servitude and buy Aramina back from them," he replied. "Our home is woven into the very fabric of our being. The Marsdens knew there would be no other workers to tend to the coffee production as we do—even when he brought enslaved people to work beside us. Still, my father, uncles, and brothers are the heart of it," he continued, a subtle blend of pride and melancholy in his voice.

"And you," Ivy murmured, her hands gently cupping Tristão's face.

"This place—this fazenda—was my parents' paradise on earth," Tristão breathed, his voice rich with reverence. "It was as though this land held the key to their entwined destinies... and mine as well."

Through the cascading curtain of water, they glimpsed fragments of the world beyond—a tranquil landscape shrouded in mist, with the sun sinking behind the mountains, setting the sky ablaze with fiery auburn hues that mirrored the depth and intensity of their bond. It was as if nature bowed in silent homage to their shared moment.

Tristão leaned in slowly, capturing Ivy's lips in a kiss that ignited a soft spark within her. Until his touch stirred her senses, she had never imagined that such profound passion could blossom in this quiet corner of the world—at least not for her.

For Ivy, Tristão was as much a part of the land as the rolling hills and endless vistas; his soul intertwined with the very essence of this place. At that moment, she felt a deep yearning to stand by his side, sharing forever in the splendor of the land and the man who called it his own.

Taking her hand, Tristão led her away from their sanctuary. Her heart ached for nothing more than the world they were forging together. However, duty loomed over her like a storm cloud, reminding her she must return to the expectations of her role as Allyn's wife. Before they reached the path, Tristão abruptly stopped and turned to Ivy, his intense expression stirring a flutter of anticipation within her.

"I need you to do something for me," he implored, his voice low and earnest. "I know this is a considerable burden to place upon you, but I may require you to be my eyes and ears within that house. Senhor Gonzaga's visits have grown more frequent, and I trailed him to a clandestine meeting with Travers. They are conspiring, but the full extent of their plans eludes me."

"Of course, I will help," Ivy responded, her heart racing as she grasped the gravity of their predicament. "But what does Senhor Gonzaga want with your family?"

"From what I've gathered, he has coveted our property for years. You must tread carefully; I cannot bear the thought of you in harm's way. Promise me you'll stay vigilant."

"I promise," she declared, her determination solidifying like steel in her veins. "But when can I see you again?"

"Not for at least a few days," he replied, regret etched across his features as though the very thought pained him.

With a surge of longing, Ivy reached for one last intoxicating kiss, desperate to imprint this moment in her memory before parting at the path's edge. As she turned to re-enter the world they had temporarily escaped, an armed guard approached, his presence a stark reminder of her precarious reality.

"You really shouldn't be out here alone, Senhora," he said, concern flashing in his eyes as he took in her disheveled hair and wrinkled dress.

"There is no need to worry," she replied, her voice steadier than she felt. "I was painting the waterfall and lost track of time. If you'll excuse me, my husband is expecting me."

The guard studied her momentarily, his expression wary as he stepped aside. Ivy walked on, slipping through the veranda gate, her heart still thrumming with the warmth of Tristão's embrace. Each pulse carried a mix of passion and peril concealed beneath her calm, composed demeanor.

Chapter Seventeen

Ivy stepped into the dim kitchen, hung her hat, and set her shoes down with deliberate care to preserve the quiet. She had just turned toward the stairs when a voice sliced through the stillness.

"You've been away for hours, my love. I cannot fathom what could have kept you until after sundown."

Ivy froze, her breath catching to see Allyn emerge from the shadows of the library and enter the hall. She moved toward him, her steps deliberate despite the tightness in her chest.

"Allyn, has Travers already gone?" she asked, searching the dimness of the vacant room behind him.

Her hand rose instinctively to tuck a stray strand of hair behind her ear but stilled halfway as a chilling thought seized her—had one of his guards seen her, or was it possible Allyn had sensed the bond she shared with Tristão? She studied his face, searching for any hint of recognition, but his expression remained composed and unreadable. The silence deepened, and Ivy wavered, caught between fear and frustration. Was he withholding judgment or silently piecing together her secrets? A knot twisted in her stomach, its grip tightening with each passing second.

Ivy swallowed, the dryness in her throat making the motion stiff and forced. "What is this all about?" she asked, her voice faltering slightly, the unease inside her tightening, impossible to conceal.

Her mind spun with a thousand thoughts, each more unsettling than the last. Her heart raced a flurry of confusion and fear clawing at her chest. She could feel the weight of Allyn's silence pressing on her, suffocating in its intensity. And just as the tension became unbearable, Allyn spoke.

"He was detained. Take a seat," he said, his voice cold and measured, each word deliberate as if carefully calculated to unsettle Ivy further. His eyes pierced through her, making Ivy feel as though every thought, every secret she tried to guard, was laid bare before him.

Allyn strode to the large mahogany sideboard at the far end of the room where a decanter of sherry and two glasses rested upon a silver tray.

"Hm, just look at you. I can scarcely imagine what sort of activity would leave you so... unrecognizable," he mused, uncorking the decanter on the sideboard. He grew silent as he poured two glasses of amber-hued sherry.

"I—I went for a swim," Ivy replied, feigning ease. "The pool was too beautiful to resist."

"A swim?" he echoed, his tone disapproving. "Undressed, where anyone might have seen you?" His eyes assessed her coldly before capping the decanter with a crystal stopper, his piercing stare fixed upon her as he handed her a glass.

"I merely dipped my feet but slipped in by accident," she said, offering a nervous smile. "Though I did have the presence of mind to stay near the—"

"I won't mince words," Allyn interjected, his voice hardening. "I've heard you've been keeping company with that manservant in my absence."

"I don't know what you mean," Ivy replied, her heart hammering in her chest.

He sank into the armchair, his movements slow and controlled. Ivy hesitated, then followed suit, taking a small sip from her glass.

"I know about your time with Tristão, the manservant," he said, his tone calm yet foreboding, his penetrating regard holding her captive.

Ivy shifted, grounding herself as tension mounted.

"Honestly, Allyn, he only accompanied me to the village for supplies," she said, setting down her glass on the table between them. "You were unavailable, and I was in urgent need of pigments. He kindly offered to drive me so that I could pick them out myself. He's not an artist, so I couldn't very well rely on him to select the right ones." She kept her tone light, but her heart raced. Noticing that his face remained unmoved, she continued. "Mr. Fontes is familiar with the landscapes, so he was most helpful in pointing a few out on the way home," she added, offering a faint smile that wavered beneath his unrelenting stare.

Ivy picked up her glass and took another sip, hoping to steady her nerves, but Allyn's piercing look never wavered. He placed his glass down with a controlled hand and then rose from his seat. Ivy watched him carefully as he paced before her.

"Let me ask you this," he said, his tone chilling. "Have I not been patient with you, respecting your... hesitations as a new bride? And all the while, you've been frolicking with the help?" Without warning, he slammed his fist on her armrest, causing her to flinch. "Tell me it's all lies," he demanded.

Allyn's stare darkened further, an unrestrained fury simmering in his eyes. Ivy had only seen this intensity once before, long ago, at the ball where he and Henry clashed over family grievances. A shiver ran through her, but she held steady.

She stood abruptly, forcing him out of her way. "How dare you? It was a misunderstanding! For goodness' sake! Do servants have nothing better to do than spread gossip in this house?"

Allyn paused for a moment, collecting himself, before speaking again.

"In case you have forgotten, my dear," he sneered, "my family's wealth spared yours from scandal and disgrace." He adjusted his vest and cravat.

"How could I forget?" Ivy replied, catching her breath, "I am here, aren't I?"

Allyn's eyes blazed with fury. "Remember this, Ivy— you're mine. Not his. Not anyone's but mine. Furthermore, if he discovers you've been holding back from me, he'll stop at nothing to claim you first!" His jaw tightened, fists clenched in restrained anger.

Ivy took a step back, her heart pounding. "Allyn, I'm your wife," she said, frustration thick in her voice. "You've had countless chances to claim me, yet you've avoided it at every turn. I won't stand here and endure this any longer." Without waiting for his response, she turned toward the door.

He moved quickly toward her, closing the distance with a single step. "Ivy, please!" His voice cracked with raw urgency as he gripped her arm. "Do not turn away from me. I'd be lost without you!"

The abrupt shift in his demeanor took her by surprise as he knelt before her, taking her hands and pressing a kiss to them with unsettling tenderness.

"If you weren't happy," he said softly, "you would tell me, wouldn't you?"

The question caught her off guard, and she hesitated. "Yes, of course, I'm happy, Allyn," she replied, forcing the words past the tension gripping her.

A flicker of satisfaction crossed his face. "Good. Because if you were cavorting with another man..." He let the words hang darkly in the air. "That would be grounds for divorce. The arrangement our fathers made would be void, and we both know what that would mean."

Ivy's stomach twisted, but she remained composed. "I haven't been out with anyone, Allyn. Please, believe me," she said, her voice trembling despite her efforts to control it.

Allyn's face softened, yet a chill lingered in his expression. "I know I've left you alone often. I'll remedy that. The other fazenda owners may sacrifice their marriages for business, but I refuse. I'll give you more of my time." He took her hand and kissed it, his lips lingering. "And I shall have all of you. Be ready tonight," he commanded.

Ivy nodded, dread settling heavily in her chest. "I'm going to rest for a while. Could you kindly ask Flávia to send up some tea?"

Allyn nodded, watching her with an unreadable look as she turned and left the room.

Chapter Eighteen

ristão shut the door behind him with a soft, resonant thud, the sound filling the stillness of the workshop. He turned to find Flávia, her slender form casually leaning against his workbench, her face half-hidden in the deepening shadows of dusk.

"What are you doing here?" he asked. The question slipped from his lips sharper than he intended, his irritation flaring.

She shook her head, her stare hardening. "You're a damned fool, Tristão," she said, each word laced with cold disdain.

"I don't have time for this, state your piece and leave," he muttered, brushing past her. He picked up a wooden tool caddy, methodically gathering the tools strewn across the workbench, one by one.

But Flávia was relentless, stepping closer until she stood directly in his path. "Don't act like nothing's happened. Don't pretend you haven't had the senhora in your arms," she hissed, a flash of jealousy in her eyes. "I've seen how you look at each other—it's obvious, Tristão."

"Shouldn't you be elsewhere, working?" he asked moving around her and continuing with his task.

"You chose her—the lady of the house—over me?" she scoffed.

Her words struck him, though he remained silent, his hand hovered briefly mid-reach over a chisel before his

fingers tightened around it. The muscles in his jaw tensed—
a fleeting break in his otherwise unshakable demeanor.

"Admit it, you never saw us as equals but look at you
now. You're nothing more than a servant."

He slammed the chisel onto the workbench and spun
to face her, his patience unraveling. "What exactly are you
after, Flávia? For the whole fazenda to hear your
groundless lies?" He set down his tools with deliberate
force, then ran a hand through his hair, his fingers gripping
the back of his neck as he tried to steady himself.

She studied his face for a long moment, a cruel
satisfaction playing across her lips. "So, it's true," she said,
her words cutting deep. "When will you realize you don't
belong here anymore? You're just another pair of hands.
No better than the rest of us!"

Tristão felt his expression softening as a sudden wave
of clarity washed over him. Though her words stung, the
familiar ache of old wounds had faded for him, leaving only
a quiet space behind. Yet she still clung to the person he
was when he needed an escape from his surroundings.

"I never thought I was above you, Flávia," he said
seeking to pierce the wall of her anger. "I did care for you
once, but we were never meant to last."

Her fierce expression gave way to a look of genuine
concern. "And what do you think will happen to her if you
are caught? Senhor Marsden has the power to ruin her,
Tristão. Toss her aside, leave her and her family with
nothing! And what of your family? Do you think he'll
overlook their connection to you?" Her tone rose,
desperation spilling into her words. "If you are smart, you
will leave this place. Forget what once was. Take your
family and go." She paused, her breath quickening. "Think
before you go near her again. Tonight, she'll be with him.

I even drew her a bath so she can wash you off and prepare for the man with a right to her." Her words cut like a blade.

Tristão shook his head slowly, as he drew in a long, breath. "Yet, there you stay by his side, bound to whatever promises he's fed you. Your loyalty to him stinks of betrayal. I was a fool to think you'd bring me anything but trouble," he muttered. His hand shot out, pointing toward the door with a decisive, commanding gesture. "Don't come back here with your poison again. Is that clear?"

He paused for a moment, the air thick with tension, before his eyes sharpened, filling with a fierce resolve. "As for this fazenda," he continued, his voice firm and resolute, "I will never give up on Aramina. Not ever." His words rang out with finality, a vow made not just to Flávia, but to himself as well.

With that, he turned his back to her as if severing the last tie between them. The silence that followed was heavy, charged with the weight of his declaration, leaving no room for doubt or further argument.

"She belongs to him, Tristão. He'll do whatever it takes to keep her, no matter the cost. Please, just be careful." Her voice softened, almost breaking, as she turned and strode to the door.

With one last look, she pushed her way out, leaving Tristão standing alone in the fading light. Her words lingered in the air, reverberating through him like distant thunder, unsettling and impossible to ignore.

Ivy sat at her dressing table, her fingers trembling slightly as she adjusted the silver brush in her hair, trying to calm the unease within her. The soft flicker of the oil lamp did little to steady her nerves. A light rap at the door broke the silence, and Flávia entered, her presence a brief respite from the mounting tension. She moved with quiet grace, leaning over to turn down the lamp.

"Did you need anything else, *minha amor*?" Flávia asked softly.

"No, thank you." Ivy's voice was steady, but the tension in her shoulders betrayed her.

Flávia paused, studying her intently. "You look frightened."

"Perhaps it's just nerves," Ivy replied with a sigh, her breath coming too quickly. "We still haven't been together, but it will happen tonight."

Flávia's expression softened with curiosity as she approached, sitting beside Ivy and gently taking the brush from her hand. "I thought for certain he would have claimed you by now. You've had such a glow about you recently. But..." She hesitated, brushing a strand of hair away from Ivy's face. "You'll be fine if you let him have his way. It will be easier that way."

Ivy stiffened slightly but smiled, masking the discomfort with a light tone. "I'll try not to forget." She then looked at Flávia, her concern growing. "Are you alright? You seem sad."

Flávia hesitated, her eyes clouding over with an emotion Ivy couldn't quite name. "It's just... I miss my mother. She's been ill, and I worry about her."

"I'm so sorry," Ivy said, her voice softening. "If you'd like, we could arrange a week off. Izobel and I can manage, and perhaps another girl could fill in on your days off to visit her."

Flávia's eyes widened, and she blinked as if struggling to comprehend Ivy's offer. "You'd do that for me, Senhora?" Her voice was barely above a whisper, a mix of surprise and gratitude.

"Of course. You're my friend," Ivy said, her tone warm and sincere as she cupped Flávia's hand gently in hers.

Flávia smiled faintly, the weight lifting from her shoulders as she stood. "Thank you, *minha amor.* Good night."

With a kiss on Ivy's forehead, Flávia withdrew, leaving Ivy alone in the dimly lit room. The eerie glow of the oil lamp seemed to grow heavier, the shadows stretching unnaturally across the walls. Ivy's thoughts drifted, and for a fleeting moment, she longed for Tristão to appear, knocking on the window, to sweep her away from the prison of this night.

Her reflection in the mirror betrayed her once more. She could feel the weight of her duty pressing down on her, but beneath it all, a hidden longing stirred—an unspoken fear that she might never again find a moment's peace.

As Ivy rose from her dressing table, she reached for the oil lamp, her fingers hovering near the flame as she drew a steadying breath. She turned the wick slowly, watching as the light faded, casting the room into gentle darkness. The shadows grew around her as she moved to the small table, where a dimly lit lantern awaited. Lifting it carefully, she slipped out the door and ventured toward Allyn's quarters, her heart thrumming in the stillness of the hall.

Upon entering, she found the room empty, its silence unnerving. The heavy bed curtains, half-drawn, loomed like a giant cocoon in the lamplight. She approached, setting the lantern on the nightstand, its muted glow barely illuminating the shadowed bed. She shrugged off her robe and eased onto the bed's edge, the crisp linens cool beneath her.

Footsteps echoed faintly down the hallway, and she stiffened, her pulse quickening. Deep down, she knew she must feign indifference—that nothing had transpired earlier, nothing that Allyn could perceive. Her heart ached, but she reminded herself of the necessity; she had glimpsed Allyn's possessive anger often enough to know that any suspicion could bring danger to Tristão and his family.

To protect all she held dear, she would have to play her part tonight as the dutiful wife, burying her true feelings as deeply as the shadows now concealed her face.

Ivy lay perfectly still, her breath catching as Allyn's cold fingers trailed down her back, the touch sending an involuntary shiver through her. His lips, searing and insistent, skimmed over her neck, each caress stirring an unwelcome sensation that burrowed deeper with each passing second.

"That was wonderful, darling, absolutely wonderful," he murmured, his hand sliding possessively along her waist, then settling over her hip. "You were well worth the wait."

She held her breath, bracing for some accusation, some dark suspicion, that she had been unfaithful, but none came. He offered no hint that he doubted her; instead, he seemed thoroughly pleased, languidly savoring his triumph. Ivy clung to the hope that his desires were satisfied for the night, that she would be spared his attention until tomorrow.

Relief washed over Ivy as she felt him slip into the heaviness of sleep. However, she lingered cautiously, her heart pounding in her chest, then eased herself from his grasp. He rolled onto his back, still deep in slumber, oblivious to her quiet escape.

Chapter Nineteen

ristão stood within the stables, grooming a spirited mare with gentle strokes, the rhythmic sound of hooves on straw filling the air. As Allyn approached on horseback, Tristão set down his brush and stepped into the warm afternoon light. Allyn sat resolutely in his saddle, an oppressive figure of authority against the serene backdrop.

"Is there something I can assist you with, Senhor?" Tristão inquired, his demeanor a calculated blend of respect and poised readiness. He straightened his posture, a fleeting flicker of disdain passing across his features before composing himself.

"It has come to my attention that you have been utilizing the barouche to escort my wife into the village while also transporting supplies during my absence." Allyn's voice, firm and commanding, carried a hint of irritation as he sat tall upon his horse, looking down at Tristão. "Neither she nor you possess my permission to employ that carriage for such menial tasks."

He paused, allowing the weight of his words to settle in the air. "Should any harm have befallen the carriage, I would ensure that your entire lot bears the burden of the expenses, for it is only fitting that those who presume to misuse my possessions are held accountable."

With a firm grip on the reins, he leaned slightly forward, his expression unwavering. "Effective immediately, she shall no longer require your services," he declared, the finality in his tone leaving no room for dissent.

Tristão absorbed Allyn's words, maintaining an air of composed dignity. "In my role as a footman, I sought only to be of assistance," he replied, his voice resolute despite the tension. "I could not abide the thought of her undertaking such a journey unaccompanied or confined to that uncomfortable wagon." His posture remained firm as he met Allyn's scrutinizing stare.

"Be of service?" Allyn sneered derisively. "My wife, a lady of stature, has no reason to venture anywhere with a manservant. Even here in the depths of Brazil, I will not tolerate it. Do I make myself clear?" Allyn's voice dripped with contemptuous authority, his words cutting through the air like a blade.

"You can expect no further trouble from me, Senhor," he said, meeting Allyn's piercing scrutiny with a defiant stare.

"You'll do well to remember, I am the master here, and you and yours are but my working tenants," Allyn stated, his lips forming a wry grin that hinted at both amusement and superiority.

"As you wish, Senhor," Tristão responded with a firm nod. He moved forward to accept the reins as Allyn dismounted from his horse, handing them over with a touch of briskness.

Allyn lingered as Tristão guided the horse toward the stables, his eyes narrowing slightly. With deliberate precision, he removed his gloves, the motion slow and calculated, before following behind. "Between you and me, Ivy is a woman of undeniable allure. Auburn curls, alabaster skin—and that scent..." He paused, inhaling deeply as though he could still feel the trace of her presence lingering in the air.

Tristão halted mid-step, his jaw tightening in a controlled display of restraint.

Allyn's voice dropped lower as though savoring the indulgence of his words. "Yes, my Ivy embodies every man's ideal of beauty—a dream made flesh, though such pleasures are mine alone." He cast a sidelong glance at Tristão, whose rigid posture betrayed the simmering anger beneath.

Satisfied that his warning had landed, Allyn turned on his heel and marched toward the house.

Tristão remained for a moment, reflecting on Allyn's remarks, until Joaquim's voice broke through, direct and probing.

"I must return to my duties," Tristão replied, brushing past him.

Joaquim quickened his pace. "Don't treat me like a fool! I've seen her wandering around our quarters at night!"

Without a word, Tristão continued on his way.

"You'll bring ruin upon us all!" Joaquim shouted, the force of his words echoing in the silence.

A letter arrived at Aramina, its envelope elegantly inscribed with the distinguished script of Mr. Travers and addressed to Allyn. Ivy's fingers trembled with anticipation as she fought the urge to pry into its contents. A flicker of hope ignited within her; perhaps this missive would herald Allyn's imminent departure. Weeks had elapsed since she last felt the warmth of Tristão's embrace, and her heart ached with an intense, unfulfilled longing to reunite with him.

As Allyn strode onto the veranda, the sunlight danced upon the polished wood, casting a gentle glow on the scene. Ivy's heart quickened, a tumultuous rhythm echoing in her chest as he approached and kissed her forehead.

"A letter has arrived for you," she announced, gesturing gracefully toward the table where the missive lay. "It's quite delightful outside today. I've instructed the maid to prepare tea for us to enjoy in this serene setting." She returned her focus to the canvas before her, adding strokes of dark paint to the landscape, unfurling in vibrant hues.

Allyn settled into a chair, a smile playing at the edges of his lips, conveying both contentment and expectation. "Ah, enjoying tea is my second most favored pastime with my enchanting wife," he remarked, a subtle note of entitlement threading through his tone. "It feels most gratifying to be home and share a bedroom as husband and wife, don't you agree?"

"Indeed, it has," Ivy replied, her voice a delicate thread, betraying the tremor of her inner turmoil. She paused, dabbing her brush into the wet paint, as if the colors might absorb her thoughts and conceal her true feelings.

"Now, if only you would set aside your paints and spend time with me, it would be perfection. Honestly, Ivy, you've had ample opportunity to paint during my absence," he chided, his tone assuming a firmer edge as a cold flash of dismay darkened his features.

At that moment, a house servant stepped onto the veranda with a tray of refreshments. She placed it gently on the table, quietly arranging the tea and delicacies before retreating without a sound. Ivy expressed her gratitude, wiping her hands with a damp cloth as if to wash away the tension in the air.

"You are quite right, darling. Just look at these delectable cakes and sandwiches," she exclaimed, taking her seat at the table, her tone lightened by a playful lilt, though her expression briefly hardened, betraying the delicate façade.

"Yes, yes," Allyn murmured, his attention momentarily diverted as he perused the letter. "It appears Mr. Travers requires my presence in Valença. It's just to the east, so I shall be away for a few days. I know I promised we'd spend time together, but once I have handled a few affairs, I'll be entirely yours," he declared, folding the letter with a decisive snap and tucking it neatly back into the envelope.

"Very well," she replied, feigning disappointment while artfully masking the relief swelling within her.

"I suppose I shall find ways to occupy myself in your absence," she added, her playful tone edged with an undercurrent of detachment.

"See, darling, you'll have ample time to devote to your little projects while I am away," Allyn declared, a satisfied smirk playing at his lips. "Besides, the accommodations on this occasion are rather...primitive. Hardly suitable for someone of your station. Next time, I will be sure to make arrangements worthy of you." His words, wrapped in false concern, rang hollow in her ears, though Ivy smiled dutifully.

As he reached for his cup, a fleeting thought crossed her mind: Perhaps he had a mistress waiting for him in the city. The idea stirred no pang of jealousy, no spark of anger. It simply did not matter to her. If anything, it might explain his newfound eagerness to leave. Ivy felt a cold satisfaction settle in her chest at the notion, her relief mingling with the faintest sense of triumph.

Allyn angled his cup in her direction with an assertive gesture that was less a request and more an unspoken command. It was a move Ivy had come to recognize as his way of reminding her of her place: the ever-dutiful wife who existed solely to fulfill his needs.

As she reached for the teapot, his hand closed around her wrist with startling firmness. "My dear," he said, his voice low and measured, "you have every liberty to engage in your artistic pursuits, but I trust you will remember your place as my wife."

Her breath caught momentarily, but she forced herself to remain composed. "Yes. Naturally, I will," she replied, the words sliding off her tongue as smoothly as the lie she tucked away behind them.

Allyn released her wrist, leaning back with a satisfied air as if her response had fortified his confidence in her obedience. Ivy, however, had already dismissed him in her mind, her thoughts occupied with how best to savor his absence.

As she poured the steaming liquid, she willed her hand to remain steady, praying Allyn would not notice the faint quiver in her grasp. She could not allow him to glimpse the unease rippling through her—or the quiet anticipation stirring beneath it, an emotion she barely acknowledged herself. The thought of being in Tristão's embrace consumed her thoughts; her heart caught between longing and restraint as Allyn lingered in her presence.

Something deep within her yearned for Tristão, an ache that had only sharpened with each night spent beside Allyn. Her soul longed for the solace only Tristão could offer, the sense of home she had never truly known until him. But how could she reveal what had transpired—what had, at last, bound her to her husband?

The surge of joy she experienced at the prospect of reuniting with him quickly dissipated, replaced by a sobering truth—profound changes had transpired since their last encounter. Her body was no longer solely hers; it belonged to Allyn, a painful burden that pressed heavily upon her heart.

Now, she feared that disclosing their union to Tristão would tarnish the tender moments they had shared and fracture the trust that bound them. How could she explain the agony of being tethered by marriage to someone whose touch failed to ignite the fire of longing she felt for Tristão?

Her soul had become entwined with Tristão's, yet Ivy felt as though Allyn had appropriated it for his own satisfaction, claiming something that was not rightfully his.

No, she would keep this knowledge close, guarding it as fiercely as she protected her heart. This would be hers alone, at least for now.

For two long days, Ivy waited, her heart a tempest of hope and despair as she anticipated a response from Tristão. Each attempt to capture the breathtaking panorama of the mountains on her canvas only deepened her yearning. Every stroke of her brush echoed with his absence, each hue a reminder that he was woven into the very fabric of her surroundings. Frustration seeped into her soul until, in a moment of desperation, she sent Izobel back to him once more, carrying a note that begged him to wait for her at the workshop.

"He sent it back, Senhora," Izobel said, her arm outstretched, the unopened note a silent testament to Ivy's heartache.

"Is that so?" Ivy replied, vexation lacing her voice. She donned her hat, securing a scarf beneath her chin, and strode purposefully from the fazenda, determination propelling her forward.

As she pushed open the door to the workshop, the sight of Tristão sharpening his tools struck her like a bolt of lightning.

"Ivy, why have you come?" he asked, surprise etched across his rugged features.

"Why haven't you responded to my letters? Allyn left days ago to meet with his associate." She searched his face, waiting for a flicker of acknowledgment, but he resumed his work, silence stretching painfully between them.

"It has been weeks since I have seen you! You could at least acknowledge my letters!" Ivy's voice rose, frustration spilling over.

Tristão paused, his brow furrowing as he met her gaze. "And if he intercepts these letters? He could use our words against us. It's too much of a risk," he said sternly.

"What do you mean?" Ivy's heart raced. "So, he might have suspected something at first. Maybe he heard gossip when you drove me into the village. He was jealous for a moment, but I'm sure I eased his mind."

"For a moment?" he retorted, his voice low and steady. "I'd wager he suspects far more than that. It's best we end this now."

Ivy stared at him, shock rendering her momentarily speechless. "No!" she declared, shaking her head vehemently.

"Yes, Ivy. He will find out. He's too clever! And we mustn't forget you are still his wife!" The weight of his words hung heavy in the air.

"No, not in heart or spirit! You know my heart," she pleaded, placing her hand tenderly on his face. He covered her hand with his, but after a moment of deep breaths, he turned away, anguish etched into his features.

"I want nothing more than to be with you. You consume my thoughts every hour of every day! I can't breathe without your touch!" Ivy's voice trembled with desperation.

"Ivy, it's too dangerous! What about your situation?" he pressed, urgency seeping into his words.

"What about my situation?" she demanded, defiance igniting in her chest.

"I know you'd be left penniless if he chose to divorce you. The scandal would ruin your family; I cannot be the cause of that!" he exclaimed, anguish flickering in his eyes.

"He came to see you, didn't he?" Ivy pressed, desperation clawing at her.

"He did, and someone like Marsden would exact revenge on us both if he caught you being unfaithful and had enough evidence to expose our affair! That is what this is, Ivy—an affair! I cannot put our families through the hell he is capable of wreaking," he said, his voice breaking.

"Don't say that! Our love comes at a great cost for us both! I understand this, but why won't you fight for us?" Ivy implored, tears glistening in her eyes.

"Because I deluded myself into thinking he would allow you to seek solace outside the marriage bed. That he would prefer a mistress like so many of his kind, but it's clear he desires you more than ever, and the thought of his hands on you—" He shut his eyes, clenching his jaw as if to contain his fury.

"You must know, I loathe his touch! I shut him out and think of you!" Ivy cried, her voice rising.

"Do not tell me this!" he shouted, his voice grating with emotion.

"I love you, not him! Take me away from here, but please don't abandon our love!" she wept, stepping closer, her heart bare before him.

Tristão remained still, his expression stormy, a whirlpool of emotions darkening his eyes.

"You can't do this!" she cried, desperation threading through her voice as she closed the distance between them.

He extended his arm, a silent command to stop, and when she didn't move, his features hardened, resolve solidifying his expression.

"Go to him, Ivy—now!" he ordered, his voice ringing with an unyielding finality.

Sobbing, Ivy struggled to find words to convey the anguish of her futile marriage, but deep down, she knew Allyn had the power to tear apart everything they held dear. After what seemed an eternity, she turned away, heart shattered, yet unwilling to force her presence on him any longer.

Chapter Twenty

Flávia swept into the room, drawing back the drapes with a flourish that sent morning sunlight spilling across the bed. Ivy blinked against the brightness, still nestled in a hazy comfort as Flávia's familiar voice gently coaxed her awake.

"It's half-past nine o'clock, *minha amor*," she announced, setting a delicate tray beside the bed. "I've brought you a bit of breakfast to start your day."

Ivy sat up, feeling the day had entirely slipped through her fingers. "Oh! I hadn't realized it was so late already. I do hope the servants weren't kept waiting on my account."

"Not to worry," Flávia said, dismissing Ivy's concerns with a graceful wave. "Everyone is well occupied, thanks to my persuasive touch." Her smile exuded a subtle confidence that all was perfectly in order under her watchful eye.

Ivy shifted, intending to slip out of bed, but the moment she moved, a sudden wave of nausea gripped her.

"Perhaps I'll just sit a while," Ivy murmured, her voice faint as the room swayed around her. A wave of nausea tightened her stomach, the sensation pulling her deeper into discomfort.

Flávia's expression shifted to one of concern as she noted Ivy's pallor.

"You don't look like yourself, *minha amor*. Surely, you won't attempt any painting today?"

"No, I think the easel will remain untouched. Perhaps I'll take a small walk in the garden when the evening cools."

Ivy let out a weary sigh, lifting a hand to her stomach as if the mere touch might ease the dull ache settling deep within. The heartache of Tristão's absence twisted inside her, spreading like a sickness through her very core.

Flávia arched an unimpressed brow. "A walk? I'd much rather you eat something first. Now, lie back. I'll place the tray on your lap." Her tone was gentle yet firm, leaving no room for debate, and Ivy relented, easing herself into the cushions.

"My head feels fit to burst," she breathed.

"You're not moving from that bed today, darling," Flávia declared with a tone that allowed no room for debate. "I'll brew you a remedy, one my mother swore by when we were young. It's practically magic."

With a smile of reassurance, she glided from the room, her confidence trailing gracefully behind her.

The moment the door clicked shut, Ivy felt the full weight of her solitude press down upon her. She curled beneath the covers, their embrace providing little solace as memories of her last exchange with Tristão enveloped her like a heavy fog. His words reverberated in her mind, achingly clear.

How could she possibly continue in this farce of a marriage, with Tristão so near yet painfully out of her reach? Or worse—what if he chose to forsake his family's burdens and leave Aramina behind, severing the last fragile thread that tethered him to her? The mere thought of facing each day on this fazenda, stripped of Tristão's love, weighed upon her heart like a stone. It was an ache she feared would unravel her, sinking her into that terrible numbness she'd felt after the ballroom attack, an emptiness she had vowed never to allow again.

She tried to think, to craft some glimmer of a plan that would draw him back to her, yet her mind swirled with only one certainty: she would not let their love slip away without a fight. She *had* to somehow prove that their bond was strong enough to withstand this.

Allyn wouldn't return for another day or so. The realization struck her, sparking a bold idea. She would search his study, perhaps uncover some hint of his dealings with Senhor Gonzaga. Her pulse quickened with a blend of fear and determination. Surely, among Allyn's notes or correspondence, she would find some clue, something to unearth the secrets he held so tightly.

As the sun dipped below the horizon, casting a warm glow over the fazenda, Ivy felt a renewed sense of clarity after taking Flávia's remedy. She sent Izobel to bed early, urging her to rest, and persuaded Flávia to retire before her usual hour. Once she was certain Octávio and the other servants had retreated to their quarters, enveloped in the hush of the night, she felt the weight of resolve settle over her. Wrapping herself in a dark cloak, she slipped a letter opener, a few hairpins, and a matchbox into her pockets.

With a steady hand, she struck a match, lighting a candle whose warm glow flickered softly against the encroaching shadows. Gripping the brass holder tightly, Ivy ventured into the dim corridor, opting for the candle instead of an oil lantern in case she needed to extinguish it quickly. The house loomed ominously in the darkness, but Ivy pressed on until she reached Allyn's study.

As expected, the door was locked. A wry smile played on her lips; picking locks had been a beloved pastime for her and Evelyn in their family estate, where they wandered through vast rooms as regal royalty and whimsical characters from fairy tales. This lock proved more challenging, but a surge of triumph coursed through her as it finally clicked open.

Stepping into the pitch-black study, she raised the candlestick, revealing towering bookshelves that loomed like sentinels. Allyn's massive desk stood at the far end, shrouded in shadows. Closing the door behind her, she dashed to the desk and set the candle down. The middle drawer was unlocked, and her heart raced with anticipation as she rifled through calling cards, a ledger, and a few miniature pots of ink.

The bottom drawers resisted her attempts, their keyholes too small for the letter opener. With a flick of determination, she reached into her pocket and pulled out a hairpin, ready to apply her childhood skills once more.

She manipulated the small piece of metal until her fingers throbbed in protest. After what felt like an eternity, a faint clank rewarded her; the hairpin had snapped, but it had served its purpose.

With a steadying breath, Ivy rifled through the files in the lower left drawer. Each bore the letterhead Marsden & Co. Financial Exchange. Inside, she discovered documents marked with the bold insignias of E.M. Blackburn Banking and Croydon & Co., the names stirring an ominous sense of recognition. Tristão had once mentioned Croydon & Co. as the Marsdens' silent partner. As her eyes darted over the rows of documents, the sheer number of names and properties listed weighed upon her with an inexplicable dread.

She placed the candlestick carefully on the floor beside her, leaning in to study the contents. The papers detailed landowners from across Europe and even India, many of whom had reportedly lost their holdings to the same bank within the past decade. She knew little of Allyn's dealings, only that he and his father, Lord Marsden, had established an investment firm with the solicitor Travers. But why would he need to keep records of so many financial losses—failures that only seemed to affect those outside his inner circle?

The candlelight flickered across the pages, casting fleeting shadows that hinted at something dark concealed within, though Ivy could not quite discern what. After an hour spent poring over endless lists, she moved to the next drawer. Amid the stacks, a single folder caught her attention, its edges frayed and corners slightly bent, as if someone had rifled through it countless times. The label "Great Britain" was scrawled in bold letters that demanded her attention. A ripple of dread crept through her, stealing her breath as her fingers brushed the brittle surface before she opened it. The faint creak of its binding echoed in the stillness, and her mouth grew dry as she read the contents. It read: Earl of Elsmere, Gareth Chandonette—Chetwynd Manor. It was dated December 20th, 1880. The word *paid* was stamped in bold red letters across the top.

A cold sweat beaded on her brow as the realization hit—this was the date her father's estate was spared, but only after she and Allyn wed. The burden of it sank into her, choking and inescapable. She hesitated briefly before reaching for another folder labeled South America, Brazil. She found yet another ominous entry: Roldão Fontes—The Aramina Fazenda. Dated five years prior, it bore a similar stamp across the top, though this one read—*foreclosed.*

Ivy traced the date with a fingertip, recalling the timeframe Tristão had mentioned, when his family had lost their estate to an auction. Her thoughts spiraled as apprehension began to take root. How was it that Allyn had amassed such an extensive collection of records detailing failed enterprises and foreclosed estates when his father's ventures and those of their privileged circle seemed so outwardly prosperous?

Though she lacked a firm grasp of the intricacies of investment dealings, she understood one immutable truth: no venture was ever a guarantee. Even so, the sheer volume of documented failures struck a discordant note that unsettled her deeply. Perhaps the world of investments was far more treacherous than it appeared on the surface.

If only Tristão could see this, she thought, her heart aching with the weight of her suspicions.

Swallowing her unease, Ivy pressed on, finally wrestling open the last drawer. Inside were sheets of blank foreclosure notices, identical to those she had seen on the previous documents. Pushing these aside, she extended her arm deeper into the drawer, her fingers grazing something rigid and smooth. She retrieved a set of seals—stamps that bore the names Croydon & Co. and E.M. Blackburn Banking, just like the records she'd unearthed.

The realization settled cold in her stomach. Could Allyn, his father, and Travers have orchestrated these foreclosures for profit, carefully choosing victims to keep their own investors secure and content?

She slipped the incriminating stamps back into place just as a crack of thunder resonated beyond the window.

Ivy's heart pounded in sync with the urgent rain drumming on the roof, and she grasped the edge of the desk for support. She needed to leave no trace of her intrusion.

Swiftly, she gathered several records related to her father and the Fontes family, along with select papers from Croydon & Co. and E.M. Blackburn Banking, tucking them into a large envelope. The candle guttered, its waning flame casting fleeting shadows that danced against the encroaching dark.

Clutching the envelope tightly, Ivy eased the door open and slipped through, closing it softly behind her. Finding a stray hairpin in her cloak pocket, she locked the door, her heart steadying as she ensured no one would know she had been there.

Once she had retreated safely to her room, Ivy hurried to her hope chest, where she carefully tucked the envelope beneath the delicate linens, silks, and lace that comprised her wedding trousseau. She then collapsed onto her bed, striving to calm her racing heart and steady her breath. Her mind swirled with a tempest of thoughts and unanswered questions, each more insistent than the last. The urge to confide in Tristão gnawed at her, his insight now more crucial than ever.

She pondered her options, her thoughts racing like the wind. Should she pen a letter to her father? How could she ever persuade him that the man he had entrusted her to was entangled in such nefarious schemes? These thoughts haunted her imagination, weaving a tapestry of uncertainty and dread. However, as the gravity of exhaustion pressed upon her, the embrace of sleep eventually overcame her, sweeping her worries into the depths of slumber.

Chapter Twenty-One

*I*n the days that followed, Ivy was consumed by the strange documents she had uncovered in the study. The weight of their contents gnawed at her, the ink on the papers growing bolder with each passing hour. As a young girl, she was taught the delicate arts that would mark her as a refined lady—foreign languages, the piano, embroidery, and all the other exemplary accomplishments expected of a woman of her station. But never had she been schooled in the world of business, nor in the matters that men, with their inscrutable ways, dealt with so efficiently.

Ivy's thoughts raced, attempting to piece together how they were connected—and what dire implications they held for the landowners, particularly the Fontes family. Her mind returned to Allyn's dinners, where he spoke with such practiced ease, praising their neighbors' prosperous ventures and boasting Croydon & Co.'s unparalleled success. What had once seemed like idle chatter now revealed itself as calculated misdirection, designed to veil the elaborate web tying the Marsdens, Travers, and other entities together.

Could it all be true? And if so, how could she possibly prove it? The scattered documents before her—each a fragment of a larger, sinister puzzle—might hold the answers she desperately needed. Could these fragments reclaim the Fontes estate? Could they finally end the cruel system of indentured servitude that had bound the family and their workers for so long? The weight of the possibilities pressed heavily upon her chest, a relentless tide of questions and doubts pulling her deeper into uncertainty.

Tristão would surely have to speak with her if she managed to uncover something important. Yet a sharp thought flared in her mind, cutting through her frustration: 'I may not be a man, but I'm no fool.' Despite her defiance, a lingering shadow of doubt clung to her, its grip as steady as her resolve to uncover the truth.

Unable to bear the mounting tension, Ivy retreated to her desk, her composure faltering. With trembling fingers, she took up her pen. Writing to her father felt like baring a secret, a confession, but there was no other course. Slowly, carefully, she began:

Dearest Father,

I have missed you and Mama more than I can say. I hope this letter finds you both in good health. What I must share is troubling, and I do not wish to alarm you unnecessarily. Yet, I have encountered certain business files belonging to Allyn that raise grave concerns.

Among the papers lie documents listing countless landowners and investors—men stripped of their properties through foreclosure. Others reveal ties to the Croydon & Co. Company, which I cannot fully unravel, but sense holds great significance.

I enclose two of these documents for your review. Please consult with your solicitor to investigate who owns the bank referenced within and how it connects to Allyn and his father's enterprise.

Write to me as soon as you are able.

With deepest affection,
I remain,
Your devoted daughter,
Evangeline

Placing the pen down, Ivy reread the letter, her heart sinking with each word. A knot tightened in her stomach as the enormity of her actions settled over her. She had taken the first step, but it felt like stepping into the unknown. There was no turning back now.

Ivy carefully folded the two sheets of paper along with her letter and sealed the envelope, her movements precise but burdened by a lingering weight. She and Izobel traveled to Senhor Da Silva's merchant shop to post the critical letter.

Senhor Da Silva's familiar face was a welcome sight amidst the turbulence of her life. His smile, warm and genuine, lightened the air between them.

"It is so good to see you, Senhora Ivy," he greeted her, kissing her cheeks and taking her hands. He glanced kindly at her companion before he smiled with approval. "Ah, and who is this lovely young lady?"

"This is Izobel," Ivy introduced, her voice carrying a softness she had not realized was there.

Izobel offered a polite bow, her smile shy but warm.

Senhor Da Silva chuckled, reaching for a jar of brightly colored candies. "Help yourself to any sweets you like, my dear."

As Izobel selected a treat and settled into a seat near the entrance, Ivy turned her attention to Senhor Da Silva. She placed the letter on the counter, her voice steady but laden with quiet urgency. "I have an important letter that must reach my father in England."

"Of course, Senhora," he said with a reassuring nod. "It shall go out by wagon to the coast first thing in the morning." He affixed the postage to the envelope with deliberate care, then glanced up, studying her with concern. "But tell me, what troubles you?"

Ivy hesitated momentarily, then sank onto the stool he had pulled out for her, her breath escaping in a soft exhale as if releasing some of the burden she carried. She leaned closer, her voice dropping lower. "Senhor Da Silva, have you ever heard of the Croydon & Co.?"

He paused, thoughtful, then nodded slowly. "I seem to recall hearing that name around the time of the great famine. They came through, soliciting landowners, but their ventures did not amount to much here. The only exception was Senhor Gonzaga; his land tripled, it seems." He scratched his head in a moment of reflection. "A few others came out better, but many, like Senhor Fontes, faced hardships."

"What about the Fontes family? I believe they also had dealings with Croydon & Co.," Ivy pressed.

He sighed, a deep furrow between his brows. "Ah, yes. They suffered greatly. It all began with the workers from the north bringing disease and destruction to their fazenda. Then, when Senhora Aramina fell ill, Roldão began investing in mines and ventures your father-in-law recommended, but none succeeded. And when Aramina passed, well, God rest her soul, she was a rare beauty, inside and out."

"I can only imagine how much they have endured," Ivy murmured. "And still, they remain strong."

"They have done well, considering all they have lost. They still have their home. It is more than poor Frederico

Dias could claim." Senhor Da Silva's voice softened with pity.

"Who was he?" Ivy asked, intrigued.

"A young attorney and landowner who invested with that company. The mines dried up, and they found him dead, leaving behind a widow and a daughter heartbroken by the loss." He shook his head, his tone heavy with the weight of such misfortune. "It is a tragedy."

"How terrible," Ivy replied, her heart aching for the family.

Senhor Da Silva glanced at the wall of curios hanging in the corner of the shop, a collection of his life's travels. "Yes, it is. I have learned to be wary of businessmen offering promises of prosperity. They rarely deliver."

Ivy looked at him, her brow furrowed with concern. "Senhor Da Silva, you gave up a life of adventure and travel. Are you happy here?"

A smile tugged at the corner of his lips. "I am happy wherever my lovely wife is," he said softly. "This is her home, and so it is mine. I gave up sailing the seven seas long ago. There is nothing more beautiful than waking up to see her smile."

Ivy chuckled, touched by the sincerity in his words. "Well, Senhor Da Silva, I did not know you were such a romantic at heart."

He raised a hand in mock defensiveness, grinning widely. "I am not sure what I said, but seeing your frown transform into a smile is worth more than all the treasures in my collection."

With a final flourish, Senhor Da Silva gifted Ivy a dozen coconut truffles his wife had baked that morning and handed Izobel a few bright ribbons for her hair.

Ivy and Izobel returned home in the pony cart, the sweet scent of the candies filling the air between them.

Chapter Twenty-Two

Upon Allyn's return, his presence loomed over the estate, unsettling Tristão at every turn. He threw himself into work, steering clear of the house and Ivy, yet his focus wavered. No matter how he tried, his thoughts circled back to their last conversation, each memory a distraction he could not shake.

Each time he glimpsed Ivy and Allyn setting off together to call upon neighbors, he forced himself to look away, fighting back the sharp sting that struck whenever he saw her at Allyn's side.

One evening, as he made his way through the grounds, he crossed paths with them as a servant assisted Ivy onto the barouche. Her glance darted his way—a look as swift as it was piercing—before she turned her attention ahead, her expression as unreadable as ever.

Unable to bear it, Tristão stormed back to his workshop, his frustration spilling over as he slammed the door shut behind him. He raked a hand through his dark hair, pacing the floor like a caged animal. The ache of seeing her with Allyn fueled a fire within him, and with a sudden burst of anger, he seized a piece of wood and hurled it to the floor, hoping the force of the throw might release some of the turmoil gnawing at his chest.

As his breathing gradually steadied, his eyes drifted to the workbench—where something peculiar caught his attention. A note lay there, addressed to him. Frowning, he snatched up the envelope, tore it open, and unfolded the letter with tense fingers. The words seemed to leap off the page as he read:

Tristão,

I can no longer ignore the duty I owe my family's honor. I was naive—a girl swept up by your charm, mistaking infatuation for something lasting. However, since I have given myself to Allyn, I see now the depth of his love for me and the loyalty he deserves. My vows bind me, and I must honor them as I pledged on our wedding day.

Allyn Marsden has shown me a steadfast love and devotion that tears at my heart to betray. It would wound him deeply if he ever knew of our dalliance, and I cannot bring myself to break his trust. So, I must say goodbye. I hope you find the happiness I can no longer offer.

Evangeline "Ivy" Marsden

Tristão read the letter repeatedly, each word searing deeper than the last. Finally, his grip tightened, crumpling the paper in his fist before he hurled it across the room. He sank to the floor, his chest heaving as he fought the tears that burned, each breath jagged as if the letter itself had taken aim at his heart.

"Did you leave the letter as I instructed?" Allyn asked, his voice a low murmur that barely pierced the stillness of the midnight hour, as though the night itself held its breath.

"Yes, he is probably reading it right now," Flávia replied, leaning against the veranda's railing. The smoke from her cigarette coiled like ghostly tendrils into the cool air. The house lay enveloped in slumber, its occupants blissfully unaware of the clandestine meeting unfolding just beyond the walls. Among them was Ivy, nestled in her dreams, having sought refuge in her bed hours prior.

Allyn's brow furrowed as he paced the length of the weathered stone floor, moonlight casting sharp shadows across his features and accentuating the tension within him. "I have tried to get close to her, but she is like ice despite all her pretenses," he declared, arching an eyebrow in challenge, fixated on Flávia, daring her to dispute him. His scowl deepened, frustration mingling with a flicker of something darker, something akin to rage simmering just below the surface.

Flávia took a long drag from her cigarette, the ember glowing brightly against the night. Her eyes sparkled with mischief, a playful glint contrasting with the gravity of their conversation. "So, she does not want to warm your bed again, eh?" The words dripped with sarcasm, hanging in the air like the smoke that wafted between them, thickening the tension.

"Not like you, my dear," Allyn replied, brushing a fingertip along her arm—a feigned intimacy that belied his true intentions. "Oh, she comes to me when I ask her, but not willingly. I'm afraid the bastard claimed her in more ways than one before I had the chance," he continued, his expression hardening. "But let us not overlook the fact that you've been out to see him on one or more occasions!"

Flávia's smile faltered, a flicker of unease crossing her features. "No, Senhor!" she exclaimed, desperation sharpening her voice as it rose. "I swear, I—"

"Enough of the lies!" Allyn interjected, his tone as sharp as a dagger, slicing through her feeble defense with ruthless precision. "Let me remind you, Flávia, your eyes aren't the only ones I have enlisted to watch her activities when I am away. I have others—eyes that are far more discerning than yours—and they have reported back to me." His words hung in the air, heavy and charged, sending a shiver through the still night.

Flávia's bravado wavered, leaving her looking vulnerable under his scrutiny.

In a moment of instinctive tenderness, she reached up to caress Allyn's face, a gesture meant to soothe, yet it was met with a forceful response. He seized her wrists, holding them firmly as she flinched at the suddenness of his grip.

"If you value your place in this house and wish to keep our bargain intact, I suggest you remember where your loyalties lie," he warned, his voice dropping to a low growl, the threat clear and undeniable.

"I do! I do, Senhor!" she breathed, her eyes wide with fear, desperation lacing her tone.

A wry smile curled at the corners of his lips, cunning amusement flickering in his eyes as he turned his attention toward the darkened windows of Ivy's room.

"I think it's time for you to demonstrate just how loyal you truly are to me," he continued, allowing the gravity of his words to linger in the air. He paused for a moment, relishing the tension. "By helping me reveal just how devoted her lover is to their little romance."

Flávia knocked softly on Tristão's door, the faint thudding of footsteps resounding from within. A moment later, the latch clattered, and the door creaked open, revealing a pair of sharp, narrowed eyes fixed on her.

"You shouldn't be here" he muttered, his voice low and tense, though his expression faltered when he recognized her beneath the hood.

Flávia lifted the cloak hood with a coy smile, letting it fall back as she tilted her head just so, her eyes glinting with playful mischief.

"Of course, I should be here. Oh—you thought I was her, didn't you?" she teased, a lilting giggle slipping from her lips, even as she took a deliberate step forward.

"I thought you might enjoy a drink," she murmured, her voice softening as she raised a wicker basket to eye level, allowing the neck of a wine bottle to peek over its rim.

Tristão's frown deepened, his tone hardening. "I've warned you not to come back. Now, I want you out of here," he replied curtly, motioning toward the door, his hand rigid and unyielding.

"Oh, surely you cannot mean that." Flávia's smile lingered as she undid the clasp of her cloak, draping it over a chair with elegant indifference. "I am here to make amends," she insisted as she withdrew the wine bottle from the basket. "And look what I discovered in Senhor's prized collection," she announced with a conspiratorial glint, displaying the label as though she had uncovered a rare treasure. "Your favorite, I believe?"

Ignoring his wary stare, Flávia turned and placed two glasses onto a small table, uncorking the wine with practiced ease. As she poured, her hand drifted down to her skirt pocket, fingers deftly retrieving a tiny vial. With a quick, almost imperceptible twist of her wrist, she emptied its contents into the bottle, swirling the mixture seamlessly. She then eased back onto a small sofa, gesturing with one hand toward the seat opposite her.

"Come now, Tristão," she coaxed, her voice a soothing whisper. "Sit with me, as we once did. Let us put the past behind us, a drink, a moment's peace, yes?" Her fingers trailed delicately along the glass's stem, her countenance warm and inviting.

For a moment, he hesitated, his eyes darkening as he turned away. With a sigh, he stepped forward, sinking onto the settee across from her, though his posture remained tense, guarded.

Flávia's smile deepened as she took up her glass, eyes glinting over its rim. "The last time we were together," she began, a wistful sigh escaping her lips, "I was not myself, allowing jealousy to drive me to madness, and it clouded my vision. I had not realized how deeply Senhora Ivy had gotten under your skin." Her eyes lingered on him, softened by a calculated tenderness.

"Whatever we had," he replied tersely, lifting his glass to his lips, "it's over now." With a single gulp, he drained his glass, his expression unmoved by her confession.

Without missing a beat, Flávia leaned forward, refilling his glass with smooth, unhurried grace. She watched him lift it to his mouth again, his movements quicker and less restrained. A faint flush crept into his cheeks, and his breathing grew heavier. Moments later, his hand rose instinctively to his face, fingers pressing over his temples.

Flávia slid onto the seat beside him in one fluid motion, her hand drifting to his arm, rubbing gently. "You and I," she murmured, her voice low, almost tender, "we have shared more than most. Despite everything, we understand each other, don't we? I am here, always, as your friend, your confidante." Her touch lingered, tracing soothing circles over his shoulder as he let his head fall back against the seat, tension slowly melting from his frame.

She poured him another drink, pressing the glass gently into his hand, her eyes glimmering with a silent satisfaction as he accepted it, his defenses slipping further with each sip. Leaning closer, she watched his features soften, his eyelids drooping as the drink began to weave its effect. Flávia's smile was subtle yet infused with quiet triumph, as though she were savoring a long-awaited victory in the stillness of their shared moment.

Allyn beckoned Ivy to join him in the tub. The air was thick with the steamy aroma of herbs and oils, a scent that did little to soothe her nerves as she breathed it in. She disrobed slowly, trying to steady her breath, and stepped carefully into the water opposite him. Dried and delicate petals floated on the surface as she hugged her knees, trying to conceal her unease.

"Come here," he urged. "I'll rub your shoulders."

Reluctantly, she allowed him to approach, feeling the coldness of his hands as they began their slow, insistent massage. Then came the wet heat of his kisses against her neck, the press of his lips like a weight she couldn't shrug off. A surge of revulsion coursed through her, urging her to flee, but she swallowed it. She could not afford to show even the slightest hint of resistance.

Just as her breath quickened, he abruptly stopped and drew back. For a long moment, there was only silence between them. When she dared to turn, her heart leapt into her throat.

"So, you're still not over him, are you?" His words cut through the air, a sneer in his voice.

"I—I don't know what you mean," Ivy stammered, though the color drained from her face.

"The manservant," Allyn said with a mocking edge. "You lust for him, don't you?" He hissed the words.

"No—no! I was foolish and confused before," she cried, desperation coating her voice. "I do not want him!"

Allyn's eyes darkened, and a sinister smile played at the corners of his mouth. "If you honestly believe he loves you, then come with me and see what your so-called true love does when you're not watching. Come." His tone left no room for argument, and before she could protest, he seized her arm and yanked her to her feet.

Once dressed, they walked together, the cold air biting at Ivy's skin as her damp hair left a trail of water behind them. The night seemed to engulf them as they made their way down to the tenants' village, the darkness pressing in like a heavy cloak, its silence broken only by the faint rustling of leaves in the cool breeze. They stopped outside of Tristão's cottage, where Ivy stood trembling. Allyn held a finger to his lips and peered into the window with a predatory gleam in his eyes.

"Look there, see what your true love does in his spare time," he whispered.

Ivy's heart thundered in her chest, but she did not want to look. Nevertheless, Allyn's hands were relentless on her shoulders, forcing her to peer into the room.

Her breath caught in her throat. Flávia, her maid, was locked in a passionate embrace with none other than Tristão. He was half-dressed, and Flávia, her hands desperate and insistent, pulled at his shirt, kissing his chest with a hunger that left Ivy numb.

Ivy recoiled, her stomach churning, and turned away from the window. She could feel the sting of tears welling in her eyes, but she refused to let Allyn see. She pressed her palm to her face, hiding the torrent of emotion threatening to spill.

"Your face betrays you, Ivy," Allyn said, his voice a low murmur, rich with triumph. "Come, my dear," he continued, his tone darkly possessive as he motioned for her to follow. His grip tightened in an unspoken command that left no room for refusal.

"I can't do this—not with you," Tristão muttered, pushing Flávia away.

"You cannot mean that." Flávia purred, slipping off her white ruffled blouse with provocative grace.

Tristão's voice was low and strained as he pressed his fingers to his temples, struggling to clear the fog clouding his thoughts.

"I'm sorry, but this was a mistake," he said. Rising slowly, he moved toward the door, his steps heavy. "You must go," he added, holding the door open.

Flávia shook her head, frustration and disbelief flickering across her face. She swiftly drew the blouse over her arms and head.

"I suppose your unwavering loyalty will lead to years of yearning for that woman," she said, gesturing toward the main house. "She'll never be more than a fantasy to you."

"Goodbye, Flávia," Tristão replied.

Flávia looked at him for a moment, her expression softening, then turned and walked through the open door, leaving his cottage behind.

Allyn stood beside Ivy, who sat on his bed, the heat from the crackling fire contrasting sharply with the cold emptiness settling within her. The room was bathed in a soft, golden light, but Ivy felt no comfort.

"Forgive me for showing you that scene," Allyn said, his voice tight with regret. "But you had to know the truth about him."

Ivy's eyes met the floor, and she blinked back the sting of the images still fresh in her mind. "How long have you known about them?" she asked, her voice barely above a whisper.

"From the beginning," Allyn replied, his tone darkening as if the memory soured him. "I spotted him with his hands all over Flávia the first month we arrived. My valet—who happens to be his relation—warned me that it wouldn't be wise to let them work together." He paused, his eyes narrowing, the words slipping out with a sharp edge. "But you see, he womanizes every pretty thing he comes across. Don't you see? He is a liar."

Ivy shut her eyes, the weight of his words pressing down on her chest. She remained silent, unable to speak, as the room seemed to shrink around her.

Allyn stepped closer, his voice softening. "My dear, you may hate me for what I've done, but it would never have worked. He is not in your class. He would have abandoned you the moment you came out with child," he said, his words tender but laced with something deeper—something more unsettling.

Kneeling before her, he reached for her hand, his fingers warm against her chilled skin. "Please, my dear," he pleaded, his voice thick with emotion. "Give me the chance to make you happy. I've been wild with jealousy, but it's all misguided love. Love for you." His breath caught, and the words faltered as he fought back tears. "I have only ever wanted to please you. Please, say you'll give me that chance."

Allyn's tears fell onto her lap, and Ivy, still numb, gently placed a hand on his head. His sobs filled the room, raw and unrestrained. She didn't know if she could feel sympathy, only an empty hollow where her emotions used to be.

He looked up at her, his face wet but brightening as if a flicker of hope had returned. He smiled, but it was a smile she could not return. Then, before she could even pull back, he kissed her—his lips urgently claiming.

Ivy didn't resist. There was no warmth in Allyn's kiss, no spark in his touch—only emptiness. Her mind churned with the tormenting image of Tristão in Flávia's embrace, the bitter sting of betrayal cutting deeper with each thought. Had he truly turned his back on her? The ache threatened to consume her, but she buried it beneath a cold, suffocating numbness. What was the point in fighting when he had already let her go? Her body stiffened under Allyn's grasp, yet she did nothing, allowing him to claim what could never truly be his.

Chapter Twenty-Three

Flávia's deft hands worked with quiet precision as she helped Ivy into the pink taffeta gown, the delicate fabric shimmering under the room's soft light. The village would host its charity auction that day, a much-anticipated event where a few of Ivy's paintings would be sold to benefit the local orphanage. The thought of displaying her work stirred a mixture of pride and unease in her.

Ivy sat before the mirror, her face a perfect mask of indifference, while Flávia carefully arranged ribbons in her hair. She wound several ringlets around her finger, shaping them into an elegant bouffant atop Ivy's head. Once the style was set and the pins secure, Flávia paused, her eyes catching the melancholy reflected in Ivy's expression.

"You are quiet today, Senhora," Flávia remarked, her voice laced with a hint of concern. "You haven't seemed like yourself for days," Flávia said, pausing as she straightened a loose strand of Ivy's hair, her fingers brushing gently against her scalp. She tilted her head slightly, observing Ivy with a soft frown. "Is something troubling you, or are you feeling unwell?" She placed a hand on Ivy's shoulder, her touch light yet insistent, as though urging her to speak.

Ivy shook her head briefly. "Oh, no, I'm perfectly fine. Just haven't been sleeping well," she replied, her voice devoid of emotion.

Flávia's eyes softened as she gave Ivy a gentle smile. "You still look beautiful for your husband, Senhora. He adores you."

The words echoed in Ivy's mind as a faint, almost imperceptible smile tugged at her lips. Her thoughts involuntarily drifted to Tristão—the warmth of his touch, the taste of his lips lingering in her memory. Then, as if intruding upon her mind, came the image of Flávia's lips on his, his arms around her. A fleeting surge of envy rose within her, unwelcome and irrational. She tried to push it away as though it were a shadow she had no right to entertain. Yet, its weight settled heavily in her chest as she forced herself to face Flávia, careful not to reveal the ache simmering just beneath the surface.

Ivy couldn't help but notice the extra cheer in Flávia that morning, a joy that seemed almost exaggerated as she proudly displayed the red marks on her breasts, the evidence of an intimate encounter in the form of a daring low-cut dress. It starkly contrasted Ivy's quiet turmoil, and she felt relief as she prepared to spend some time away from the house and in the company of others. The two people she had considered dear, the ones she'd trusted in this new life, had betrayed her, and she needed to escape, even if only for a little while.

Sitting in the barouche, Ivy wiped away a small tear that had escaped before she could blink it away. Her regard drifted toward Tristão, who was carrying firewood into the house, his movements strong and deliberate. But the moment was fleeting, and as she turned her attention back to the present, she found Allyn climbing into the carriage beside her. Without a word, he wrapped his arm around her, pulling her close as the horses descended the path.

The following day at breakfast, Ivy stared at the spread before her—bacon, sausage, and grits—yet nothing seemed to sit well in her stomach, no matter how tempting the aroma. She could not bring herself to eat. Excusing herself from the table, Ivy rose and hurried to her old bedroom, her hand pressed tightly to her mouth. Once inside, she knelt by the chamber pot, heaving violently.

As the tremors subsided, a soft tap on her shoulder startled her. She turned to find Flávia standing there, her face a picture of quiet concern.

"Here you go, Senhora," Flávia said gently, offering a glass of water. She brushed a few strands of Ivy's damp hair back from her forehead with a tenderness that felt almost motherly.

"Thank you, Flávia," Ivy murmured, taking the glass. She sipped slowly, the coolness soothing her parched throat. "I don't know what's come over me. I don't feel hungry. I could not even look at the food." She shook her head in disbelief, her voice distant.

Flávia's eyes softened with understanding. "I have seen this before, *minha amor*," she said quietly, her tone shifting. "When my sister was with child, she had this morning sickness often. Could it be that you and the senhor are expecting a child?" A smile tugged at the corners of her lips, almost teasing but gentle.

Ivy's heart lurched at the thought. Her eyes widened, and the room seemed to close in on her. Pregnant? With Allyn's child? The idea sent a wave of nausea rising once more.

'*No, it couldn't be his,*' she thought desperately, and a small gasp escaped her lips as she felt a cold chill run through her.

Sensing her distress, Flávia gently guided her to settle into the plush chair by the window; the cushions' softness offered a small comfort.

"No," Ivy said, her voice quivering slightly. "We are not expecting a child."

"Expecting has little to do with it, *minha amor,*" she said, a glimmer of amusement dancing in her eyes. Her tone was light, but the words carried the weight of knowing. "Sometimes, it simply happens."

Seeing the bewilderment on Ivy's face, Flávia's expression softened with understanding. "Let me inform the senhor that you are not feeling well," she said gently. "I shall also ask the cook to prepare a comforting bone broth. It always helped restore my sister's appetite when she was expecting."

Ivy looked up at her, gratitude flooding through her. "Oh, thank you, Flávia," she said, squeezing her hand in earnest, then suddenly feeling vulnerable. She quickly withdrew her hand and rested her head against the chair, a slight flush creeping to her cheeks.

Flávia blinked, her focus settling to her own hand for a fleeting moment, as if she were acutely aware of the stain of betrayal it carried—and of the cause behind Ivy's subtle recoil. A flicker of something unspoken passed between them, but then, with a soft sigh, a warm smile returned to her lips as if she were willing to let the moment pass unnoticed.

"You will be ready to eat in no time," Flávia said, her tone light, though the warmth seemed forced as if trying to dispel the tension between them.

Ivy lay in bed beside Allyn that night, the weight of surrender pressing upon her like an unyielding shroud. The delicate hopes she had once harbored—of fleeing with Tristão and escaping the confines of this life—had slipped away, piece by fragile piece, until nothing was left to hold. She pushed them aside, just as she had pushed away every tender feeling that had once blossomed within her. Even the paralyzing fear that rose at the thought of Allyn's touch—his claim upon her—seemed to dull, swallowed by a resignation so deep it all but numbed her.

Each time he reached for her, she gave in. It was a truth she could no longer deny: she was his. That bitter reality lodged itself in her chest, cruel and unwavering. Ivy recoiled, though only within herself, at the thought of his lips moving over her, his hands possessive in ways she had never desired. His low and insistent moans lingered in her mind like a dreadful melody she could never entirely banish. The heat of his sweat still clung to her skin, an indelible mark she could never seem to wash away.

She had become, in his eyes, little more than an instrument of his will, and though her body responded—as if it were not entirely her own—it was as if her soul had withdrawn entirely, retreating to a place where his touch could not reach.

Yet what truly wounded her was the thought of her beloved Tristão making love to her trusted maid—the two people she had allowed herself to trust, the only ones who offered her comfort, companionship, and the semblance of love. Now, those who had once been her pillars of solace were the very cause of her torment.

Had she only imagined the bond between herself and Tristão? Had she deluded herself into believing that joy, in any form, was within her grasp once more?

She sat up in the dimness, clutching the covers to her chest as if they could shield her from the overwhelming wave of betrayal that threatened to engulf her. Her eyes drifted reluctantly to Allyn, lying beside her, his presence a reminder of yet another layer of complication she had not wished for. A new, unsettling thought crept into her mind. Perhaps she could learn to care for him. Despite the shadowy nature of his dealings, he had saved her family's estate. It should have meant something, perhaps.

Her gaze lingered on his face, trying, desperately, to force the notion that he loved her as he had promised. Maybe, just maybe, he would do his best to make her happy, even if it came at the expense of her heart's true desires. But no matter how she attempted to convince herself, a profound, visceral truth settled within her: it would not work. The mounting resentment she felt for Allyn was a festering wound, one she feared might consume her entirely.

Yet, there was one more thought that troubled her. What if Flávia was right, and she was with child? It didn't matter what she felt for Allyn—she now had a duty to provide a home for this child and give it love, no matter the complexities of her heart.

She rubbed her temples, trying to clear the fog that clouded her mind. Yet something else lingered, something more subtle, a quiet unease in the depths of her thoughts. What if this child wasn't Allyn's?

Would she be complicit in robbing Tristão of his rightful claim, aware that Allyn had already taken so much from him?

A faint rustle pulled Ivy from her thoughts, the soft sound of Allyn shifting beside her, breaking the oppressive silence. The pale moonlight spilled across his face, its cold glow emphasizing the refined lines of his features and catching the silver sheen at his hairline. But then her attention fixed on something else—a faint, jagged scar stretching from just above his left temple to the curve of his ear. She hadn't noticed it before, as he seemed to have taken great care to conceal it beneath the sweep of his hair or the shadow of a hat. Yet the scar betrayed him—a flesh-colored line where hair refused to grow. It lingered there, a silent witness to some past ordeal.

Her hand moved instinctively, her fingers trembling as they traced the scar, the sight of it tugging at something deep within her. She pulled her hand back as Allyn stirred again, his breath a soft murmur in the stillness.

She tried to convince herself that anything could have caused that scar—a misstep, a clash, a fall from a horse, perhaps, or something far more deliberate. Yet the words felt hollow in her mind, offering little comfort. Then, an intrusive thought struck: Anything, she thought, like the teeth of a hair comb.

The next day, Ivy fumbled with the paintbrush, her hand trembling with thoughts from the night before. The paint on her canvas blended into a blur, refusing to follow the rhythm of her mind. She hoped her usual creative outlet would offer solace, but it only amplified the tension in her chest.

Her thoughts kept circling back to Allyn's scar. The revelation, sharp and jarring, gnawed at her. Had he been the one? The very man who had haunted her memories for years. If so, the knowledge gnawed at her more than she cared to admit—he was the specter that had torn apart the peace she had built, the cause of the turmoil she still couldn't escape. She let the brush slip from her fingers, the sound of it hitting the canvas a dull echo in the silence that followed. And then, as if her body could no longer hold it together, she gave way to the sobs she'd been trying so desperately to suppress.

The raw grief felt like a weight crushing her chest. She missed Tristão—his steady presence, the solace of his trust. The bond they had shared was something she hadn't realized how much she needed until now. She wiped her eyes, her heart clenching as she wondered what her next step should be. Should she reach out to him again?

She recalled Tristão asking her to keep her eyes and ears open for anything involving Senhor Gonzaga. As it happened, Allyn would host a business dinner with his associates that evening. Perhaps it would offer her something of value to share with Tristão—something he could not ignore—until she could unravel the meaning behind the documents she had found. But if Tristão refused her, she wasn't sure she could bear it. The thought of facing that rejection twisted inside her like a blade, but what other choice did she have?

That evening, Ivy carefully avoided the dinner table, excusing herself under the pretense of a headache. She asked one of the servants to bring her two small desserts to her room. Alone, she waited for the signal. Her heart drummed in her chest as she thought of the meeting downstairs—Allyn, his associates, and most crucially, Senhor Gonzaga.

The dinner seemed to last hours. Then, the door to her room opened with a quiet creak. Izobel entered, her face holding the glimmer of triumph.

"They are going in now, Senhora."

Ivy nodded, her breath steadying as she handed the girl a napkin with one of the desserts. "Thank you, darling. You can eat this here, in my room. I won't be long."

Izobel's smile was bright, her gratitude silent as she settled onto the bed, placing the napkin on her lap. Ivy gave her a final glance before leaving, her mind focused on the task at hand.

The staircase creaked beneath her feet as she descended, careful to avoid any sound that might give her away. The voices of men drifted up the hallway, their words muffled but distinct enough to recognize—Allyn's, unmistakable in its smooth cadence, followed by the deep tones of his associate Travers. Then, a third voice, gruff and commanding—Senhor Gonzaga.

Inside the drawing-room, laughter bubbled faintly, the clinking of glasses mingling with the murmur of conversation. Ivy's pulse quickened. She leaned closer to the door, careful not to make a sound—the scent of cigar smoke in the air. The door cracked open just enough for her to see them—men gathered around a table.

"Now, Senhor Gonzaga," Travers said, gesturing toward the papers, "sign here. Once the land is transferred, Aramina will be yours outright."

Gonzaga leaned forward, the glint of triumph in his eyes as he picked up the fountain pen. "Ah, how I've waited for this day. Roldão Fontes has been a thorn in my side for far too long! Finally, the best land in the Paraíba Valley will be mine." He paused, the pen hovering above the page.

"You are certain this will hold? I can expect no interference from the bank, yes?"

"My good man," Travers replied, a rare and unsettling giddiness in his tone, "we own the bank. With Blackburn's backing, this is as ironclad as they come."

"And our associate here," Allyn added smoothly, gesturing to the fourth man, "has ensured every legal nuance has been accounted for."

The fourth man, small and middle-aged, cleared his throat, his solemn expression betraying nothing. "As an official in the property department in São Paulo, I shall see to it that this contract is filed and notarized first thing upon my return," he said, his accent thick but his English precise. "Once it is registered, the transfer will be official. No one will question its validity."

Gonzaga grinned, his earlier hesitation vanishing. "Excellent. I trust there will be no resistance from that infernal family when my men move in and seize control of the coffee harvest?"

"They'll receive the formal eviction notice in a fortnight," Travers said, his expression cold and calculating. "We have the records to prove the Fontes family failed to honor their agreement. Any legal resistance by them will be futile. You should prepare to take full ownership in less than a month," he said, his voice smooth with cold certainty.

Ivy's breath caught, a flash of disbelief cutting through her. She stood rigid, her mind racing to process his words. How could he speak of their destruction with such casual confidence? His eyes gleamed with an unsettling satisfaction, the flicker of triumph lighting his features as if he had already claimed victory.

He leaned back in his chair, the air thick with his self-assuredness. "By then, I will return to England, where my family home and reputation will be restored among our peers. This," he tapped the table sharply, "is justice, gentlemen!"

Gonzaga laughed, raising his glass. "To justice, then!"

"To justice," Travers echoed, though the gleam in his eye suggested his version of justice was less about fairness and more about profit.

The official gave a curt nod before lifting his glass, his face betraying no emotion, marking their dark transaction's quiet, grim conclusion.

Ivy backed away from the door, her steps deliberate and soundless, retreating to sit on the stairs where the men's voices carried faintly in the distance, their raucous tones softened by the walls between them.

She drew a steadying breath, her thoughts churning with urgency. They were mistaken if they thought they could bar her from the tenant village. She would find a way in, no matter the obstacle. A plan began to take shape as she sat there, plotting the most discreet route to reach Tristão without detection.

Minutes slipped by, Ivy's thoughts swirling until they were interrupted by the faint chime of a servant bell emanating from deeper within the house. The delicate sound barely reached her ears, but it was enough to stir her from her musings. Moments later, she caught sight of Octávio, the elderly butler, shuffling toward the summons with his usual measured pace.

The creak of the drawing-room door pulled Ivy's focus back to the corridor. She froze, her breath catching as laughter spilled out, voices thick with the unmistakable slur of too much drink. Polite farewells followed, spoken with exaggerated camaraderie toward the departing official. His footsteps echoed down the hallway, deliberate and fading.

Octávio, ever precise, escorted the man to the door with practiced dignity. The faint click of the latch closing marked the man's exit while the butler's stooped figure briefly lingered in the warm glow of his lantern. Then, with a quiet efficiency that matched the rhythm of the household, Octávio turned back inside, disappearing toward the servants' quarters. Ivy knew she would not see him again that night.

Ivy stayed still as she heard Allyn and Travers moving out of the drawing room.

"It looks like you will be staying here tonight, old chap," Allyn said, a smirk curling at the corner of his lips. "I'll not have you taking the fruit of our Brazilian conquest out there while you can barely stand straight."

Travers, swaying slightly on his feet, grinned back, his words slurred but amused. "It has been lovely here, but I have had enough with this damned sub-tropic weather. I yearn to return to jolly old England!" He paused, squinting slightly. "Ah, but for now, I must visit your privy."

"Steady, old boy. Can't handle Brazilian spirits, eh?" Allyn teased, guiding Travers toward the privy.

Ivy descended the staircase, watching them stumble down the hall.

Travers paused and gestured toward the small stack of papers in his hand. "Better put these in the safe," he said.

"Blast, that old thing," Allyn muttered, shaking his head. "Practically takes years to open. No matter, I'll go up and set this in my desk, under lock and key."

Ivy tiptoed back up to her room before Allyn could make his way upstairs.

She reached the door, and though it was dark inside, she saw that Izobel had fallen asleep on the bed. It was just as well. Ivy needed the solitude to stay hidden until Allyn was out of sight. The sound of his boots ascending the staircase caused Ivy to lock her door. She listened as he moved down the hall to the left of her room, then waited for the sound of him returning to his own.

She heard Allyn lock his study door and head toward the stairs when a sudden rustle from further down the hall caught her attention—a soft, practiced whisper followed by bare feet against the floor.

"Are you ready, Senhor? I have all of the oils ready for you," came Flávia's voice, low and expectant.

"Flávia, for once, you're right on time," Allyn's voice replied, laced with cold, mocking amusement.

Ivy's breath caught. She cracked the door just enough to see them. Flávia leaned up to kiss Allyn fiercely, pressing her body into his as they moved toward the alcove in the wall. Their movements were desperate and urgent, and Ivy flinched slightly, her stomach turning at the sight. They disappeared, their whispered laughter and footsteps echoing down the hallway.

When they were gone, Ivy reached into her dressing table drawer for hairpins to act as makeshift keys for the study door. Then, she slipped from her hiding spot, moving like a shadow. She passed the alcove silently, her heart pounding, and something caught her eye. Allyn's jacket was carelessly draped over the small table in the hallway as though forgotten.

Ivy's breath hitched. The urge to investigate overwhelmed any hesitation. She crossed to the table, brushing her fingers over the jacket's fabric. She swiftly rifled through the pockets, feeling the familiar shape of something cold and metallic—a set of keys.

Her pulse quickened. These keys could unlock secrets she was not meant to uncover.

She glanced down the hall, ensuring no one was near, then slid the keys into her pocket. A rush of adrenaline coursed through her veins. With a small but victorious smile, she turned back toward her room, her feet barely making a sound on the wooden floor. Tonight was not yet over.

The house was eerily still as Ivy hurried toward the study. Allyn and Flávia had retired hours ago, leaving only the faint, distant sound of Travers' snores echoing up through the rafters, a reminder of his drunken stupor somewhere below.

She held her breath as she slipped the key into the lock, turning the knob with measured care, careful not to make a sound. The door creaked open, and the dim light from two hanging oil lamps cast a flickering glow across the room, illuminating the desk just enough for her to find her way.

Her fingers trembled as she reached for the lower left drawer, pulling it open. It yielded nothing of interest. She tried the right drawer next and felt a surge of triumph when she saw the document atop the others. The date, that very day, scrawled across the top sent a chill through her.

Her breath caught in her throat when she noticed two identical copies. She seized one quickly, thinking they might mistake one for being misplaced amid the drinking and debauchery.

Ivy closed the drawer with a soft click, locking it once more. She eased the door open, straining her ears for any sign of movement in the hall. Only the steady snores from downstairs reassured her that the house remained undisturbed. With the key back in Allyn's jacket pocket, Ivy stepped into the cool night air, her thoughts fixed on finding Tristão.

The guards were nowhere to be seen, likely asleep or drunk in their quarters. Her feet flew across the darkened grounds, the vast valley swallowed by night, the towering mountains looming like titans in the distance. The only light in the world seemed to come from the lanterns that dotted the tenant village, their pale glow offering little comfort.

When she finally reached the workshop, breathless and pulse quickening, she saw Tristão through the window, bent over his sketches near a lantern.

She knocked briskly on the door.

Tristão opened it with a frown, his stern eyes locking onto her.

"You shouldn't be here," he said, his voice clipped.

"You must listen!" she urged, her voice tight with urgency. "It's Senhor Gonzaga. He and Allyn plan to evict your family!"

Tristão stiffened, disbelief flashing across his face. "That is impossible. Our attorney assured us they must fulfill their side of the agreement. My family has honored it for nearly five years." He turned away, avoiding her scrutiny.

"They have corrupt allies," Ivy shot back, her voice rising. "You said you didn't trust them to keep their word.

And now this—" She slammed the contract onto the workbench with a sharp snap. "This confirms everything, Tristão. Look! Gonzaga's name is right here on this new agreement. He's poised to take ownership of Aramina."

Tristão's eyes darkened, a storm brewing behind them.

"And what does any of this have to do with you?" His voice cracked like a whip as he stormed toward her. "Why does it matter to a well-bred British lady who married one of her own? Why should the fate of a poor, disgraced family concern you?" His words cut through the air, each one a blow. He stopped just inches from her, his glare searing.

Ivy's heart hammered, but she steadied her breath and locked eyes with him.

"You asked me to be your eyes and ears," she said, her voice low but firm.

Tristão's anger faltered momentarily, his eyes dropping to the floor. "I shouldn't have asked that of you," he muttered.

He snatched the contract from the workbench, his hand unsteady as he unfolded it.

"Very well, I'll show my father," he said, his voice rough with emotion. "Now, you must go."

Ivy crossed her arms tightly, struggling to hold back the tears that burned at the corners of her eyes. "I won't leave," she said, her voice trembling. "Not when there's still so much left unsaid between us."

"There's nothing more to say!" Tristão's voice erupted, raw with frustration, sending a shiver through her.

"Did you enjoy using me?" Ivy's words exploded from her, bitter and raw. "All I've ever been is an object for a man's lust. You are no better than he is!" Her chest heaved with each breath, her heart pounding. "I put myself in danger coming here. So, you're right. Why should I care about any of this? About any of you?" she cried, her voice breaking.

Ivy wiped the tears that had streaked her cheeks. With one last glance at Tristão, she turned and fled into the night, her heart a tangle of emotions, her body moving on instinct as the darkness swallowed her whole.

Chapter Twenty-Four

ristão's grip tightened on the papers, his pulse quickening as Roldão Fontes spoke. "What is this you are showing me?" Though his father's voice was steady, a faint tremor of unease betrayed the weight he already sensed.

"Father, I knew the Marsdens were nothing but wolves masquerading as friends the moment you invited them into our home," Tristão replied, his voice thick with frustration. His words came sharper than he intended, but he refused to temper them. They had all been blind for too long. "They never intended to honor their agreement. This—" he extended the contract with a pointed motion— "is their betrayal laid bare."

Roldão's brows furrowed as he scanned the document, disbelief deepening the lines on his face. Tristão watched him flip the paper, vainly searching for some hidden clause or error to soften the blow. However, Tristão had pored over it already. The words seared into his mind, a testament to the Marsdens' treachery.

"This cannot be," Roldão muttered, shaking his head. Tristão caught the subtle slump of his father's shoulders, and his frustration hardened further.

"They have been playing us for fools from the start," Tristão said, his tone bitter. The disillusionment sat heavy in his chest, but he forced his voice to remain even. "Now their deceit is exposed for all to see."

When Roldão finally met his gaze, the weight of his father's unspoken question hit Tristão like a physical blow. There was no blame, only a shared weariness, but it stung all the same.

"How did you come by this?" asked Roldão, his eyes narrowing.

Tristão's eyes shifted downward, his hands instinctively flexing at his sides. The shame of withholding the truth gnawed at him, but he could not allow it to show. Admitting Ivy's role was a risk he could not take. He took a breath, forcing his voice to remain composed despite the turmoil stirring within him. "I would rather not say," he said.

"But there's no time to lose. We must act swiftly before the Marsdens tighten their grip further."

Roldão nodded slowly, the wheels of his mind already turning. "We will take this to Don Miguel Velázquez," he said with quiet authority. "He is the only one who can unravel their web of deceit."

Across the room, Joaquim paced with restless energy, his movements grating on Tristão's nerves. His brother stopped abruptly and turned toward their father. "It will take at least two days to get to Valença by train," Joaquim said, his determination in his voice. "I will go myself if need be."

"No," Roldão said, his tone brooking no argument. "Your brother and I will handle this. You must stay here and ensure nothing falters. The estate cannot afford any disruptions now."

Tristão shot Joaquim another glance, catching the flash of frustration in his brother's features before he nodded. Though the decision made sense, Tristão couldn't shake the sense of responsibility that settled squarely on his shoulders. The room fell silent, each absorbing the magnitude of the Marsdens' betrayal.

For Tristão, the sting of their deceit seared deeper, igniting a fire within him that refused to be extinguished. The Marsdens had underestimated him—he would show them just what he was capable of before this was over.

Two days had passed before Don Miguel, accompanied by Tristão and Roldão Fontes, returned. The lawyer had agreed to stay until the matter was thoroughly investigated and resolved. Once settled, the three men gathered around the table, coffee cups in hand, as Don Miguel began recounting the events that had led to his brother-in-law's untimely demise.

"About fifteen years ago, a few of his colleagues had become very wealthy—almost overnight. He begged to know how. That is when they introduced him to a man named Travers. Frederico was young and just out of law school. Others in his circle had already seen large returns on their investments. By then, he had become convinced that he, too, would become wealthy," Don Miguel relayed.

He fell silent momentarily as if the memory itself had stilled him. After a long pause, he continued, his voice thickening with emotions that had long remained unspoken. "Despite my fervent objections, Frederico invested with their firm in every venture they recommended. At that time, I lacked sufficient evidence to contest Travers' actions, but what truly haunted me was the profound melancholy that overtook Frederico after he received one of those cursed letters—the one that informed him it was all gone. Every last bit of it," Don Miguel continued, his voice growing heavy. "Then so was he. My sister was devastated by his loss."

He removed his spectacles and wiped them with a handkerchief, quickly dabbing at a tear that had escaped his eye. Tristão watched closely, noting the visible grief that seemed to have remained within Don Miguel for all these years.

"I cannot help but wonder," Don Miguel added, his voice barely above a whisper, "had I fought harder, perhaps I could have spared us all this grief."

Tristão's throat tightened, but he forced his hand to rest briefly on Don Miguel's shoulder. "We are truly sorry for your loss," he said quietly, unable to find words more fitting. Don Miguel nodded, his eyes lowering to his coffee cup, unwilling to meet the others' eyes.

Silence descended like a suffocating fog. After a moment, Tristão rose from the table, his legs stiff, and moved toward the window. His thoughts churned— memories and regrets colliding within him. His hand clenched by his side as he gazed out, sorting through the tangled threads of the past. Slowly, he turned back toward Don Miguel.

"I must admit," Tristão began, his voice even though the turmoil inside him was far from calm. "At the time, I did not understand why you did not intervene to help my father keep Aramina. Now, I see it clearly. The Marsdens built an entire operation based on deceit and layering lies so thickly that no one could prove they were nothing more than swindlers."

Roldão's voice cut through the tension, soft but resolute. "Don Miguel did what he could to warn me, but I was too consumed by your mother's death, Tristão, to see the truth. I could not fathom that Lord Marsden would betray us."

"Yes, Father, I understand that now," Tristão replied, nodding, though a deep sense of frustration still lingered. His mind raced, calculating what more could have been done. A few moments passed the weight of their conversation settling on him like a stone in his chest.

"I've written to Uncle Estevo," he said, his eyes unwavering. "As you know, he is a prominent businessman and diplomat in Lisbon. He has connections all over Brazil, and he may be able to uncover more about Croydon & Co."

Roldão's expression darkened, his eyes hardening as he met Tristão's gaze. "You know Estevo has never forgiven me for your mother's death. Do you truly believe he will put himself at risk for us?"

Tristão's jaw tightened, but he held his ground. "I do," he said firmly, his voice steady. "He expressed his regrets while I was in Lisbon. For her sake—our mother's sake— he's the one who urged me to return and fight for what is ours," he added, sweeping his hand out to encompass the land that was their legacy.

Roldão turned to Don Miguel. "What say you, old friend? Do we have a case?"

Don Miguel, silent for a long moment, looked up with newfound resolve. "If we can prove that the Marsdens misused investor funds in Brazil, we have a solid case for fraud and embezzlement. I will send word to the best legal firms I know here and abroad. We shall begin by gathering affidavits, signatures, whatever it takes."

Tristão moved behind his father's chair and touched his shoulder, his voice unwavering. "We will do everything in our power to fight this, Father—for those we lost."

Don Miguel nodded solemnly, and the men shared a look of quiet determination. They locked arms in agreement, one by one. The battle was far from over—but now, they would fight it together.

Chapter Twenty-Five

Weeks stretched on, each one heavier than the last, and Ivy found herself trapped in a relentless cycle of fear and yearning. Her thoughts blurred together in a haze of dread and fragile hope, each more suffocating than the last. The weight of secrecy pressed on her chest like an iron shackle, unbearable and constant. The missing contract, with its fragile folds, gnawed at her—the document that could either save or damn the Fontes family. She could not help but wonder, with a sickening twist of unease, if Tristão had entrusted it to his father. Or worse—if the winds of fate had already turned, condemning them to a future they could not escape. Yet, despite her mounting anxiety, no word came. There were no whispers of their eviction or rumors of their lands being transferred to Senhor Gonzaga. It was as though the storm had not yet made landfall but was still gathering, unseen, unfelt, yet inevitably approaching.

Until one fateful day, Allyn casually announced they would soon return to England, to Marsden Hall. The news struck Ivy like a cold gust of wind. She felt her heart sink, the finality of it hanging in the air between them. The estate, his inheritance—it would all be waiting for him there, but Ivy knew that once they left, she would never see Tristão again. That chapter would close, and all that remained was the life she was being dragged toward, whether she wanted it or not.

Blissfully unaware of the turmoil within her, Allyn seemed consumed by the revelation that Ivy was carrying his child—the heir he had longed for, the symbol of his legacy. He glowed with pride at the news, but Ivy felt nothing but the cold weight of a future she never asked for. His attention was a fleeting thing, a dutiful acknowledgment in the daylight hours, but when night fell, he retreated into his own world, where she was no longer needed or wanted. The separation did not trouble her; his nocturnal habits were his alone, and she had long grown accustomed to the silence he left behind.

Ivy's nights were a far darker affair, her dreams haunted by the horrors of the past. Each night, she relived the attack, her body paralyzed by an unseen figure, a presence that loomed over her in the darkness. Slowly, the shadowy form began to take shape, its features growing more apparent with every restless hour. And then, one fateful night, it became undeniable—the face of her assailant was none other than Allyn's.

Had her mind betrayed her, distorting fragments of truth into a nightmare?

The truth had become a ghost, lingering in the shadows of her thoughts, elusive yet ever-present. More urgently, she had to confront the harsh reality of what she would do with it should she uncover it. She would have to find a way—not merely to endure but to safeguard herself and the child she carried. Hope, fragile as it was, flickered within her heart, a steady beacon she refused to let fade. That night, as the rain beat relentlessly against the clay roof, Ivy decided to search for the answers she desperately longed for.

As she moved cautiously toward Allyn's room, the rain masked her every step. There was no time for hesitation.

Her hands, quivering with a mixture of fear and resolve, turned the handle to his chamber. Inside, she was greeted by heavy silence and shadows, stretching across the room like an extension of him, lingering in the corners as if they were watching her.

The wardrobe loomed at the far end of the room, its dark wood towering like a silent sentinel, mirroring the man who owned it. Inside, the neatly arranged garments—gray waistcoats, lustrous shoes, trousers so crisp they seemed to hold their breath—spoke of his unyielding control, his obsession with perfection. Beneath, a row of boots stood in solemn order, their quiet presence almost mocking her desperate search. She turned to the chest of drawers, her hands moving swiftly through his nightclothes and undergarments, but the contents revealed nothing more than a dull sense of disappointment.

Her fingers brushed along the top shelf, and she stopped, her breath catching as she encountered a small frame. Gently, she wiped the dust away, revealing Allyn as a child, his innocent face frozen in time beside a woman whose features had been intentionally obscured. She set the photo down with a heavy exhale, frustration tightening its grip around her chest. Yet, just as quickly, her gaze swept across the room once more—and this time, something caught her eye. A flicker of hope, small but potent, ignited within her. Beneath the bed, almost hidden in the shadows near the headboard, sat a small wooden box, its subtle presence undeniable, as though it beckoned her closer.

Kneeling, she reached for it, her fingers brushing against the dust before carefully wiping it with a handkerchief. The box was engraved with Allyn's initials, and though the lock was a modest one, it posed a brief obstacle. Ivy pulled out a letter opener from her pocket and pried it open, the clasp snapping with a decisive click as the tiny screw flew across the room. She had no time to worry about the broken lock. Her breath quickened as she lifted the lid.

Inside was something eerily familiar—her comb. The pearl-encrusted accessory she had worn the night of her attack. Ivy's heart lurched in her chest, and her hands quivered as she held it to the lamp's light, examining it with a dread that seemed to root her to the spot. Her pulse pounded in her ears as images of that night flooded her mind—of a dark figure, a brutal grasp—and her hands trembled so violently that the comb slipped from her fingers. Pearls scattered across the floor, and Ivy's breath caught in her throat. The realization, stark and unbearable, sank in: Allyn had been the monster all along.

She was trapped here, as his wife. She shuddered as the weight of her situation pressed upon her, and a cold sweat broke out across her brow. The sudden fear that Allyn might return at any moment sent her into a frenzy. But no—he was not due back until the following day. She fought to steady her breath, to quell the panic rising in her chest, and began searching for the missing pearls. Two larger ones she found under the bed, but the smaller ones eluded her. When at last she forced the comb back together, she closed the box, making everything appear as it had been—save for the broken lock.

Perhaps he would believe the box and its contents had become damaged during transport back to England. As Ivy settled back into bed, a chill gripped her. Drawing the sheets close, she silently prayed the damage story would suffice—that he would never learn the truth of what she had uncovered.

The following day, sunlight streamed through the tall windows of the parlor, casting golden patterns across the floor. Ivy sat with her embroidery in hand, her fingers moving mechanically over the delicate fabric. Each stitch was painstakingly precise as if the act alone could still the tempest churning in her mind. She could hear the muffled chaos of departure unfolding around her as servants bustled about. Their voices mingled with the muffled sound of packing crates and footsteps echoed down the halls. It was truly happening. Soon, she would bid farewell to this paradise—a place that had both sheltered and unsettled her.

Ivy glanced at her brushes and palette, left forgotten in the corner of the room. She had poured the last of her creative spark into three paintings for the Ladies of Lisbon charity auction—a work born of both pride and desperation to distract herself. But now, the very thought of painting was unbearable. Picking up those brushes again meant confronting emotions she was unprepared to face. Raw and aching, the memories attached to her artistry in this place threatened to break through her fragile calm. However, soon they too would be left behind. All she would carry back of this place would be a collection of wistful memories and a few painted canvases to mark its beauty.

Setting aside her embroidery, she surveyed the parlor, now nearly empty. The rich floral motifs lingered in the stillness like dear old friends murmuring their soft farewells. Ivy was reluctant to leave them behind, just as she mourned the loss of her desire to paint. A painful constriction formed in her throat, and for a fleeting moment, she fought the urge to cry. Quickly, she moved her hands along the velvet arms of her chair, grounding herself in the soothing texture of the fabric as she sought to steady her breathing.

The sudden sound of footsteps drew her from her thoughts. Izobel entered, her expression brimming with excitement. "Senhora, I found this on the kitchen steps," she said, her voice alight with intrigue.

"What could it be?" Ivy asked, her voice carrying a hint of interest.

"He has returned," said Izobel as she handed Ivy a folded handkerchief embroidered with the initials TF. Ivy's breath caught as she unwrapped it, revealing Tristão's precious pendant necklace. Her heart swelled as she held it up to the light, her eyes fixed on the dark lock of hair enclosed within.

The pendant felt both heavy and fragile in her hands, its presence evoking a frenzy of emotions—joy, sorrow, and longing, all tangled together. Could Tristão have heard of her impending departure and left this as a parting token?

She clasped the necklace around her neck, tucking it beneath her collar like a sacred relic. Having something of his, however small, brought a sliver of solace amidst the heartache. It served as a reminder that, even in parting, their connection would remain unbroken.

When Allyn returned home, Ivy greeted him with a measured smile as he entered the library.

"You seem in remarkably good spirits. I trust the arrangements have gone smoothly."

Allyn's face broke into a wide grin, a rare sight. He leaned back in his chair, a glint of satisfaction in his eyes. "Indeed, they have my dear. I've secured passage to

Southampton," he announced, his voice brimming with a sense of accomplishment. "We depart in ten days."

"Ten Days," Ivy echoed, the words lingering on her lips though a whirlwind of thoughts stirred beneath her composed exterior. "How... splendid," she added, the word carefully chosen to mask the churn of her emotions.

"Splendid?" Allyn chuckled, his voice rich and self-assured. His eyes flickered with a faint, almost imperceptible glint of amusement. "I would call it positively marvelous, my dear. In but a month's time, we shall be ensconced in the restored family home, preparing for its new heir." His smile deepened, a quiet satisfaction in his eyes.

"More importantly, my father will be most pleased with how I've managed the family's affairs. While we may be parting ways with Aramina, my time here has afforded me invaluable experience in running an estate. Now, the Marsden legacy will thrive back home, where it rightfully belongs," he said, his voice steady, a trace of pride beneath his words.

Ivy's smile wavered briefly, but she quickly masked the shift, her voice smooth yet carrying a subtle weight. "Yes, how wonderful it shall be to return home. I'm sure your father will be pleased," she murmured, sounding more distant than she intended.

As the night deepened, she retired to her room, once again leaving Allyn to his cigar and scotch on the veranda.

The house descended into silence, broken only by the relentless ticking of the clock. Lying awake, Ivy pressed the pendant close to her heart, drawing comfort from the thought that their love still lingered—a quiet flame, faint yet enduring. It was enough to sustain her, even as she accepted the painful truth that he must let her go.

Exhaustion finally claimed her in the hours before dawn. However, just as sleep began to take hold, a chill swept through the room, more biting than the early morning air. Her eyes snapped open, her breath catching in her throat. A shadow loomed beside her bed. The figure stood still, its presence oppressive.

"Allyn? What are you doing here?" Ivy asked, her voice barely above a murmur.

Allyn's eyes gleamed with malice, his voice low and cruel. "I know what you have been doing, my dearest," he said, the words slipping out like poison.

A chill ran down Ivy's spine, but she forced herself upright, her back straight despite the fear coiling inside.

"I don't know what you mean," she muttered, her voice trembling.

The oval pendant dangled from Allyn's grasp, its familiar gleam twisting like a knife in her chest. Her fingers instinctively brushed the hollow space at her throat where it should have rested.

Her heart pounded in frantic desperation as his hand clamped around her wrists, pulling her from the bed with a force that stole her breath. He hauled her into the dimly lit hallway, each of his heavy steps reverberating through the suffocating stillness of the house, the sound closing in on her like a vice tightening around her chest.

Her focus, wild and unsteady, settled on a small, dark object in the center of the hall—the wooden box with her pearl-encrusted comb, discarded on the floor. Its delicate sheen gleamed with a harsh, mocking clarity, an undeniable revelation to him that she had uncovered his secret.

Ivy's breath quickened as Allyn's voice pierced the heavy silence.

"Ah, this feels all too familiar, doesn't it, my dear?" His words dripped with condescension, his weight pressing down on her, suffocating the space between them. "Did you truly believe you could escape me? You were always meant to be mine, Ivy. No amount of resistance will change that."

"Allyn, stop this!" she cried, writhing beneath his grip, her body straining against his hold as fury and desperation propelled her. "I won't let you hurt my baby!"

Allyn's smile widened, his eyes gleaming with a dark, twisted satisfaction. He leaned in closer, his breath cold against her ear. "Sweet child," he murmured, a mocking lilt in his tone. "Tell me, Ivy... am I the real father of your child? Or is it that wretched manservant you've chosen to love in my place, like some common whore?"

Ivy struggled beneath him, her pulse pounding in her ears, but his grip on her arms remained unyielding, his strength a constant force holding her in place.

"You can't have me, Allyn," Ivy said, her voice low but unwavering. "I love him too much."

His lips curled into a cruel snarl. "You're mine, Ivy. By law. By name. Resistance is useless."

Her heart thundered as she strained against his hold. With a sharp jerk, she freed one arm and felt for anything within reach. Her fingers closed around the discarded comb. She struck without hesitation, dragging the jagged edge across his cheek.

He bellowed in pain, jerking back as blood streaked his face. "You bitch!" he snarled, his hand lashing out to slap her hard enough to sting.

Ivy's cheek throbbed, but she glared at him, her breaths ragged. He towered over her, seething, but she refused to look away.

'*I am not defeated. Not yet.*'

Flávia's heart hammered in her chest as Ivy's whimpers echoed down the hall, each sound a cry filled with urgency, hanging heavy in the air. Panic surged as she hurried from her room, Izobel close behind. She caught the girl by the shoulders with a firm grip, stopping her in her tracks.

"Stay in your room, child! I'll be back," Flávia commanded, her voice thin with urgency, breathless from fear. Without waiting for a reply, she turned and fled, her footsteps loud and frantic as she approached the door.

The first light of dawn cast a pale glow over the mountains, the sky bleeding gold as Flávia raced through the village. Time seemed to slip away with each stride, every second carrying Ivy closer to danger. Flávia's breath came in ragged gasps as she reached Tristão's cottage. She pounded her fists against the door, her voice rising in frantic desperation.

"Please, come out! Senhora Ivy needs help—Senhor Marsden has gone mad! He's showing her the monster he truly is!"

When there was no response, she slammed her fists against the door again, the sound echoing through the narrow avenue of cottages.

The door creaked open, revealing Tristão's face, clouded with suspicion.

"Why should I trust a word you say?" he demanded.

Flávia's words faltered, lost in the wake of her desperate cries.

"Because I have no reason to lie," she replied, breathless, her voice trembling. Tears welled in her eyes as she collapsed to her knees, clutching his sleeve with frantic urgency.

"I was wrong. Please, Tristão! I'm afraid he'll kill her!" Each word spilled out, more pleading than the last. "She may be carrying your child!"

Time seemed to stand still for Tristão. His eyes fixed on her, narrowing as though he were searching for a lie within her words but finding none—only the raw truth in Flávia's tear-streaked face.

"Please, he may hurt your child—you must go!" Flávia's voice quivered as she wiped her eyes with the hem of her skirt, trying to steady herself.

The words hit Tristão like a blow to the chest. His jaw tightened, the weight of the revelation settling over him like a heavy cloak. In that instant, something inside him shifted—his heart, once steeled against the weight of duty and the demands of his family's reputation, softened with the sting of truth. He had long been unable to face the things beyond his control, retreating into a fortress built from pride and the need to shield his family from disgrace. However, now, in an urgent call to action, the reality of Ivy's suffering broke through his defenses, leaving him exposed to the full extent of his failure to act when it mattered most.

Without a word, he turned. His feet hit the earth, and with swift, purposeful strides, vengeance drove him forward.

He would not merely save her but protect his one true love—a vow etched deep within his soul. He would destroy the monster who dared threaten her and bring her back to him, no matter the cost.

Tristão rushed into the house, his heart pounding as he heard Ivy's murmurs echoing from upstairs. Her voice spurred him forward, her words broken and faint.

"He won't touch me again!" she whimpered.

Tristão reached the bedroom door, but it was locked. Slamming his fist against the wood, he called for her, the desperation in his voice matching the urgency in his heart. Still, the door remained firm, offering no mercy.

With no time to spare, he surveyed the corridor until he found a solid wooden bench. Lifting it high, he drove it into the door with force, the wood splintering and the lock giving way with a resounding snap.

As the door flew open, Tristão's eyes landed on Ivy, bound to the bedpost. Her face was drawn, drained of color, but her resolve remained unbroken.

"*Meu Deus*—no!" Tristão muttered, his voice rough with emotion as he rushed to her side.

"I won't let him touch me again. I won't!" Her breathless, defiant voice struck him like a spark to dry tinder. The words reverberated in his chest, igniting a fierce, unrelenting resolve. Though the fire in her eyes had dimmed, it was not extinguished; he could still see it flickering, a fragile ember beneath the weight of exhaustion.

She wasn't broken. Not truly. Shaken, yes. Hurt. But the unyielding spark of her spirit, however faint, demanded his protection—his very life, if necessary.

"I'm taking you out of here," he said, his voice steady despite the trembling in his hands. He moved swiftly, his fingers working the bindings with a precision born of desperation. Each motion carried a singular, driving purpose: to free her from the nightmare that had ensnared her.

At first, she flinched, pulling back with a gasp. "No—don't," she cried, twisting against him, her resistance instinctive—the reflex of someone who had fought too long and too hard. Her struggle stung, a vivid reminder of what she had endured. Yet even now, as her strength waned, the fight in her had not fully dimmed.

Then her eyes found his. Confusion clouded her gaze for an instant before recognition dawned, softening the tension in her body. Her trembling fingers reached for him, and without a word, she collapsed into his arms. She clung to him, her grip fierce despite her weariness, as though he were the only solid thing in a world that had crumbled around her.

The feel of her against him—raw, vulnerable, and still so resolutely alive—shook him to his core. His arms tightened around her, his hold imbued with a protectiveness he hadn't known he possessed. Whatever horrors had preceded this moment, they would not touch her again. Not if he could help it.

"You're safe now, my love," he murmured, the words rough in his throat as though pulled from the very depths of him. His thumb brushed a tear from her cheek, the tenderness of the gesture incongruous with the storm of emotions raging within him. "I swear, no one will harm you again. Not while I still breathe."

It wasn't just a promise. It was an oath forged in the depths of his soul, a vow as unyielding as the steel of a blade. While he could not undo the past, he would be her shield from this moment forward, her sanctuary against whatever darkness remained.

Tristão kept Ivy close, his arm steady around her as they approached the door. Each step forward seemed to draw the air tighter, the tension around them palpable.

Just as they reached the doorway, the sound of heavy footsteps echoed, halting their progress.

"Well, well—it's the footman who fancies himself some great Lothario. Or perhaps the knight in this little fairytale?" Allyn's sneering voice sliced through the air, his tone dripping with venom. He stood in the dim corridor, a handkerchief pressed to the scratches running from his cheek to his chin—stark reminders of Ivy's defiance. He dabbed at the marks with exaggerated care, his lip curling in disdain.

Tristão's jaw tightened, fury simmering just beneath the surface as he anchored Ivy against him, feeling the tremor in her form. A sharp cry pierced the charged air— "Senhora!" Izobel's voice rang out, edged with panic. She emerged from the shadows of the corridor, moving swiftly toward Ivy. She guided her away with urgency, their retreat fading into the periphery.

With Ivy out of harm's immediate reach, Tristão stepped forward, focusing now on Allyn. His eyes burned with a fire that dared the other man to move. Without hesitation, he lunged, slamming into Allyn with the force of all his pent-up rage. They hit the ground in a violent tangle of fists and fury.

"You'll never lay a hand on her again, you bastard!" Tristão growled, his grip tightening around Allyn's throat. Every movement, every ounce of strength he possessed, was driven by the singular need to end this nightmare.

Allyn's fingers clawed at Tristão's hands in a futile struggle, but Tristão's grip held firm. Only when he sensed Allyn's fight draining did he ease his hold. In that instant, a glint of defiance flashed in Allyn's eyes. He lunged forward, his fist swinging wide, desperately trying to strike. Tristão moved instinctively, sidestepping the attack, allowing Allyn's momentum to carry him forward.

Allyn's feet slipped at the edge of the step, and Tristão could only watch as he lost his balance. The cry that escaped Allyn was quickly drowned out by the heavy thuds of his body crashing down the stairs, limbs flailing with each jarring impact.

Tristão rushed to the railing, his heart pounding in his chest. Below, Allyn lay crumpled at the bottom of the stairs, barely moving. Tristão darted into the bedroom without hesitation and gathered the rope behind Ivy's bed. With a dash down the hallway, his bare feet pounded against the wooden floor, each step echoing in the silence.

But when he reached the staircase, Allyn was nowhere to be seen.

The house grew eerily quiet as if holding its breath. Tristão slowly descended the stairs, his muscles taut with tension—still silence. Then a rustling sound came from the parlor. Allyn reappeared, sword in hand, its cold steel gleaming in the faint light. Tristão recognized the weapon at once—one of the pair displayed on the hallway wall. With a fluid motion, he pulled the other sword from its mount, his fingers tightening around the hilt as his instincts took over.

Allyn raised the sword with trembling hands, swinging it erratically. Each arc was driven by desperation rather than skill. His breath came in jagged bursts, and his body swayed with each uncoordinated movement.

At the top of the stairs, Ivy and Izobel stood closely together, watching the scene unfold below.

"Drop it," Tristão commanded, his voice low and firm. "My years of mastering the blade in Lisbon make this a fight you cannot win. You are finished here, Marsden."

Tristão advanced, his movements deliberate and composed, and with a single, fluid motion, he swiped at Allyn's sword, sending it flying from his grasp.

Allyn's eyes widened in panic. "No!" he shouted, his voice shaking as he stumbled backwards, his hand reaching in vain for the weapon now out of his reach.

"She is mine. I won't let you have her!" Allyn's breath came in ragged bursts as he scanned the room for another weapon. His gaze landed on the butler standing near the entrance.

"Octávio!" he barked. "Get my guards in here—now!"

The elderly butler glanced briefly from Allyn to Tristão, exchanging a silent look—an understanding forged through years of service and loyalty to the Fontes family.

Octávio turned away and stepped toward the kitchen.

"You useless old fool!" Allyn's voice cracked with frustration. In a rage, he grabbed a glass from a nearby tray and hurled it at the retreating figure. The glass missed its mark, striking the door's ornate molding and scattering shards across the floor.

At that moment, Tristão seized the opportunity. With a flash of instinct, he dropped his sword—already knowing

Allyn was no longer a threat in that regard—and lunged forward.

With a swift and calculated move, Tristão forced Allyn onto his stomach.

"Get off me!" Allyn bellowed, thrashing wildly.

Tristão ignored him, his hand darting into his pocket to retrieve the length of rope Allyn had intended for Ivy. "How fitting," he muttered, quickly binding Allyn's wrists.

"You won't get away with this!" Allyn spat, thrashing in a hopeless attempt to free himself.

With a forceful jerk, Tristão pulled the rope taut, the knot locking in place. "Struggle all you want," he said, his voice firm. "It only tightens the rope. Much like your web of lies, Allyn—the more you fight, the stronger they will bind you."

Allyn's face contorted in fury, but his efforts waned as the rope bit into his skin.

Tristão leaned closer. "First, you shall answer to my father, and then the law will have its say on what becomes of you."

Before he could lift Allyn to his feet, a heavy thud echoed through the hallway as the front door slammed open. Two uniformed officers stormed in, followed closely by Roldão Fontes and Don Miguel.

"Officers! I demand you arrest him immediately. He broke in and attacked me!" Allyn cried, his voice sharp with desperation.

The officers moved swiftly, pulling Tristão away from Allyn and undoing the ropes he had secured. Allyn stumbled to his feet, his face flushing crimson, his anger bubbling over. "He came here to assault my wife! He is trespassing! Remove him from my house!"

"Liar!" Tristão bellowed, his voice thundering as he struggled against the officers' hold. His chest heaved with righteous fury. "I was summoned to rescue her from this abusive man!"

Roldão Fontes stepped forward, his piercing gaze fixed on Allyn with glacial intensity. "Enough of this!" Roldão declared, his voice steady yet seething with restrained wrath. "You dare speak of justice while you, a thief, stand here unrepentant for all you have stolen from us! Release my son—now."

Without hesitation, Don Miguel pressed his hand firmly against Roldão's chest, halting him with quiet authority. "He is right, officers. Allyn Marsden is the one you seek!" he declared, cutting through the rising tension. He turned, pointing directly at Allyn. "He is the man named on the arrest warrant. Along with his partner, he deceived countless investors both here and abroad in numerous fraudulent schemes. He is the trespasser— release Tristão at once!"

The officers complied, freeing Tristão and restraining Allyn in his place.

"Release me at once, you imbeciles!" Allyn barked, straining against their hold. "I shall have my guards here this instant!"

"Your guards have been relieved of their posts and their weapons confiscated. They are no longer under your command," Don Miguel stated matter-of-factly.

"My father will hear of this!" Allyn sputtered.

"I'm afraid he cannot assist you either," Don Miguel replied, his voice firm. "Your father, Lord Marsden, has been taken into custody by the English authorities in London."

Tristão's eyes narrowed as the realization slowly set in. "So, we finally have the evidence to prove the Marsdens and Mr. Travers deceived investors all along?"

"Indeed," Don Miguel affirmed. "Over a dozen lawsuits were filed against their companies, starting with Croydon & Co. for fraud and misuse of funds." He handed a stack of papers to Tristão. "We have several plaintiffs prepared to provide testimony, which will strengthen our case against his son, Allyn Marsden, and Mr. Travers, who was arrested just this morning en route to the coast."

His tone softened as he turned slightly to acknowledge Ivy, then motioned for her to approach. "Senhora Ivy, you may come down."

Ivy's fingers gripped the handrail, the cool wood offering a brief sense of stability, though her pulse quickened with each step. She moved deliberately, concealing the turmoil that churned inside her. With every motion, the moment seemed to stretch, the weight of the impending confrontation with Allyn hanging in the air. However, as she reached the bottom, she knew—this was it. She was finally free of him.

Don Miguel's hand was warm as it took hers, his tone soft and genuine.

"My dear, your correspondence with your father to question the Marsdens has resulted in a solid case against them. Given your circumstances, that must have been a difficult thing to do."

Ivy felt the gravity of his words, their meaning settling over her like a comforting cloak.

He paused, gesturing to Tristão and his father. "This family owes you a debt of gratitude. Without your actions, they would still be trapped in deceit. Your courage has brought us to this moment, where justice can finally be served."

As the officers began to escort Allyn to a police wagon, Ivy could feel his eyes on her, his presence still thick with hostility. She braced herself, waiting for the words she knew would come.

"You ungrateful bitch! You are still my wife!"

Ivy met his eyes, feeling the strength in her voice as it carried the weight of her defiance. "I was never yours, Allyn. You only sought to possess me, as you've done with everything else. But not anymore."

The officers hauled Allyn into the back of the police wagon, the clang of iron bars echoing behind him. Next to him, Travers stood motionless, shock evident on his face.

I hope to be rid of him once and for all," Ivy murmured, the weight of every heartache and betrayal bearing down. A fragile cry stirred, but it vanished as Tristão's arms enveloped her, his embrace a silent shield.

"You shall be, *minha querida,*" Tristão assured her. "I will make certain he never dares to touch you again. You have my word."

As if to seal his promise, Tristão placed his hand gently on her belly, the gesture tender yet profoundly reassuring. Ivy's heart fluttered, a rush of emotion welling inside her. She looked up at him, her eyes searching his for solace, and found it there. He smiled softly, his gaze filled with quiet certainty, before leaning down and kissing her—a kiss that conveyed all the promises they had yet to voice and the end of their shared suffering.

In the stillness that followed, they stood together, watching as the police wagon grew fainter, taking the last remnants of the turmoil that had plagued their lives, the sound of its wheels fading into the distance.

As they walked toward the house, Ivy and Tristão spotted several figures near the entryway. It was the Fontes family, standing in reverence to them. Tristão nodded as he passed. Izobel and Flávia stood in the doorway, their faces bathed in relief, tears shimmering in their eyes.

Izobel stepped forward, extending her hand to Ivy. "For you, Senhora," she said, her voice heavy with meaning.

It was Tristão's pendant necklace—still gleaming with its pristine luster. The sight of it, unscathed amid the chaos, brought a rush of emotion. Ivy reached out, her fingers trembling slightly as she accepted it, pressing it to her chest.

Tristão swept Ivy into his arms, and she felt herself nestled close to him, her heart quickening in response. The sounds of collective awe filled the air, a murmur of admiration from those gathered around them. His family moved closer, their presence solid and comforting, forming a protective circle around them. He faced them, his eyes lingering on each familiar face before announcing, "Everyone, I present my future wife, the Lady of Aramina," his voice brimming with pride, a clear note of triumph and joy threading through every word he spoke.

Epilogue

In the following weeks, Don Miguel worked tirelessly with his colleagues to expose the Marsdens' fraudulent schemes and their involvement in Croydon & Co. and E.M. Blackburn Banking. Tristão's uncle, Estevo Vieira, a respected Portuguese diplomat stationed in Rio de Janeiro, used his influence to rally key government officials and ensure the prosecution of the Marsdens and Mr. Travers for their crimes against their citizens.

Estates and investments seized by the Marsdens were rightfully returned to those they had defrauded. At the Aramina Fazenda, the Fontes family liberated the enslaved workers, granting them their freedom and the dignity of fair wages and honorable employment.

Finally, with the law moving in Ivy's favor, she and the Fontes family worked with the church to annul her marriage to Allyn, allowing Ivy and Tristão to marry at last, their love finally unshackled and free.

The sun rose majestically above the village church, casting a golden glow over the scene as the pews filled with elegantly dressed guests. Tristão stood at the altar, resplendent in his dark gray morning suit, a regal purple ascot at his throat. Ivy, radiant in a cream-colored, silk gown trimmed with delicate lace and adorned with violet accents, stepped forward. Her auburn ringlets cascaded beneath a beaded veil that shimmered in the soft morning light.

Their flower girl, Izobel, gracefully scattered petals from her basket as she made her way down the aisle. The sound of the organ swelled, its powerful notes echoing through the vaulted rafters, as Lord Elsmere led his daughter down the aisle, his expression one of pride and joy. Ivy's hand rested gently on his arm, her heart fluttering beneath her bodice as she neared the altar.

Tristão's eyes locked with hers, filled with a tenderness that transcended words, as Ivy stepped beside him. With solemn grace, he slipped a gleaming gold band onto her finger and recited his vows in Portuguese, his voice deep and steady. He then repeated the pledge in English, each word wrapping around Ivy's heart.

When her turn came, Ivy placed a matching band on Tristão's finger, her voice soft but firm as she spoke her vows in both languages, their unity sealed in two worlds.

At the pronouncement of their marriage, the church erupted in joyous cheers, the blessing to kiss solidifying their bond. As they embraced, the church bells rang triumphantly, their sound carrying through the valley, mingling with the jubilant cries of the gathered crowd. Senhor Da Silva, his wife, and their sons smiled warmly among the onlookers, their approval evident.

Lord and Lady Elsmere hugged their daughter, their faces glowing with pride, while offering heartfelt congratulations to their new son-in-law, Tristão. Senhor Fontes and his family followed suit, bestowing their blessings with warm smiles.

Outside, the newlyweds reached their open white carriage that was festooned with ribbons. Ivy, brimming with joy, turned to toss her bouquet of freshly picked orchids and purple hydrangeas. It soared through the air before landing squarely in her sister Evelyn's hands. Evelyn beamed, holding the bouquet aloft to show her sister.

Flávia approached, carrying a baby girl dressed in a white lace gown, her dark curls peeking from beneath a dainty bonnet. Tristão's expression softened as Flávia placed the child in his arms. He nodded, a silent agreement passing between them. Ivy, overcome with love, took their daughter into her arms, pressing a gentle kiss to her cheek.

"This is what my heart asked for," Ivy whispered, her eyes glistening as she waved to the crowd.

Tristão squeezed her hand, his smile filled with quiet contentment. "As did mine," he replied softly.

The couple climbed into the carriage, and with their little family complete, they rode back to the Aramina Fazenda for their wedding reception. As they approached the grand gates, Ivy admired the restored Fontes family emblem, the symbol of their legacy gleaming proudly under the afternoon sun. Awaiting them on the grounds was a banquet brimming with flowers, where family and friends gathered in celebration.

Senhor Veiga and his wife, Gertrudes, joined the festivities, adding to the laughter and merriment that filled the valley. The day passed in a blur of music, dancing, and revelry, with joy ringing from every corner of the estate. As the day wore on, a deep sense of peace settled over Ivy, accompanied by a contentment she had long thought lost.

As nightfall descended, fireworks burst above the mountaintops, their brilliant colors painting the sky. Beneath this dazzling display, Tristão and Ivy shared a lingering kiss, the moment seared into their hearts.

Now, as Tristão's wife, as the mother to their daughter, Aramina, and as the Lady of the Fazenda, Ivy knew she could finally embrace the fullness of her womanhood. She had found her place, her heart filled with love and a life she could truly cherish.

Glossary

Belas Águas–Beautiful waters
Don–Spanish title of respect meaning "Sir."
Eu presume–I presume
Fazenda–plantation
Fazendeiros–fazenda owners
Meu amor–my love, masculine
Minha amor–my love, feminine
Meu Deus–my *God*
Minha querida–my darling
Senhor–sir
Senhora–ma'am
Patrão–employer
Perdoe-me, não te vi aí–Pardon me, I did not see you there.
Pão de queijo– A traditional Brazilian cheese bread.

Acknowledgments

To Joe, Joseph, and Joven—Your unwavering love and support are the bedrock of everything I do. Thank you for indulging my flights of fancy to distant times and places—and for grounding me when I need it most.

To Katelyn Silva—Your guidance has been my north star, and your encouragement the wind in my sails. I'll always be grateful for your wisdom and belief in me.

A heartfelt thank you to those who rallied around my first edition and helped bring this book to life: Andrea Black, Andrea Barringer, Carol Moore, Casie L. Williams, Cynthia Billotte, the late Mari Stein, Jake Waller, Ginine Hanco, Christina Marie Shadowyn—your unwavering support and kindness mean the world to me.

To Heather—for being my cheerleader, confidante, and the kind of friend who finds just the right words (and the perfect moments) to lift me up. Your belief in me is a gift I'll treasure always.

To the readers of this second edition—thank you for embracing this story and venturing into its world. Your willingness to meet these characters and share in their journey makes every moment of dedication and effort truly rewarding.

Thank You For Reading!

Dear Reader,

Thank you from the bottom of my heart for reading *Forbidden at the Fazenda*! I hope you found as much joy in the journey as I did in bringing it to life. If you have a moment, I'd be truly grateful if you could share your thoughts in an honest review on Goodreads or your favorite platform. Your feedback is appreciated and helps fellow readers discover the story.

I can't wait to welcome you back for more captivating tales.

With gratitude,

MJ. Marleigh

About the Author

M.J. Marleigh writes steamy historical romance, blending intrigue and passion into captivating stories. Her debut novel, *Forbidden at the Fazenda*, weaves a thrilling tale of forbidden love set against a rich historical backdrop. M.J. also writes poetry, adding a lyrical touch to her creative work.

Outside of writing, she's a wife and mom to two energetic boys. She loves exploring historical sites, diving into creative crafting, and watching period dramas, all of which inspire her storytelling. Her fascination with the Victorian and Edwardian eras brings depth and historical richness to every page she writes.

Stay Connected!

Scan the QR code to follow me for bookish fun and a peek into what fuels my creativity. Let's share our love for romance!

Facebook
facebook.com/MJMarleighAuthor

Instagram
instagram.com/mjmarleighauthor

TikTok
tiktok.com/@mjmarleigh

Thank You

Thank you for joining my reader community!

9 798985 489620